THEY MADE THE WEST WILD

EARL "CACTUS" CORRIGAN—The old frontiersman-turned-impresario had a score to settle—if outlaws or old age didn't finish him first.

JOHN "THE YAKIMA KID" TRAVERS—Only one thing meant more than winning the race against Corrigan. Corrigan's blond-haired, blue-eyed daughter.

JASPER MORTON PRESCOTT—In his wager with William Randolph Hearst, the respectable publisher was ready to step outside the law . . . and would.

WES BALLARD—Only fate could have brought him to Corrigan's Wild West. Only a quick hand with a gun could get them all out alive.

The Stagecoach Series
Ask your bookseller for the books you have missed

STAGECOACH STATION 51:

WILD WEST

Hank Mitchum

Created by the producers of
The Holts: An American Dynasty,
The Badge, and **White Indian.**

Book Creations Inc., Canaan, NY • Lyle Kenyon Engel, Founder

BANTAM BOOKS
NEW YORK • TORONTO • LONDON • SYDNEY • AUCKLAND

WILD WEST
A Bantam Book / Book Creations, Inc.
Bantam edition / January 1991

Produced by Book Creations, Inc.
Lyle Kenyon Engel, Founder

ISBN 0-553-28826-1

Published simultaneously in the United States and Canada

Bantam Books are published by Bantam Books, a division of Bantam
Doubleday Dell Publishing Group, Inc. Its trademark, consisting of
the words "Bantam Books" and the portrayal of a rooster, is
Registered in U.S. Patent and Trademark Office and in other
countries. Marca Registrada. Bantam Books, 666 Fifth Avenue,
New York, New York 10103.

PRINTED IN THE UNITED STATES OF AMERICA

RAD   0 9 8 7 6 5 4 3 2 1

STAGECOACH STATION 51:

WILD
WEST

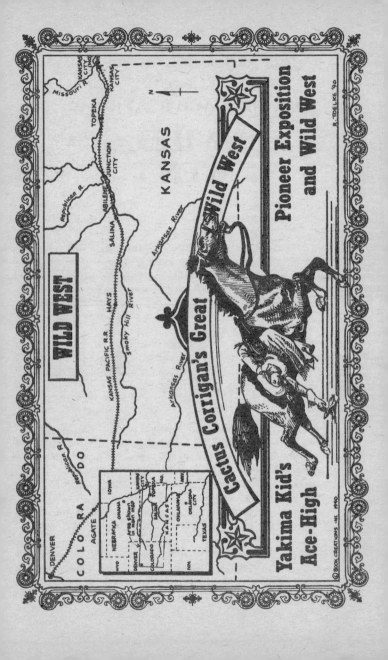

Chapter One

Earl Corrigan hauled back on the reins clasped in his big work-roughened hands, bringing to a stop the team of mules pulling the garish wagon that served as his home and office. The legend CACTUS CORRIGAN'S GREAT WILD WEST was painted in bright red letters on both sides, surrounded by drawings of cowboys on horseback and Indians wearing feather headdresses. Behind the rugged old scout's wagon, the other vehicles in the procession also came to a halt. Corrigan leaned forward on the hard wooden seat, studying the scene before him.

It was a warm early-June evening, and spread out before the leader of the traveling troupe was the booming city of Kansas City, Missouri, its lights sparkling in the twilight. Compared to some of the metropolises back East that Corrigan had seen, Kansas City did not look like much, but after the crossroads settlements and tank towns in which the show had spent most of its time in recent months, this sprawling community on the banks of the great Missouri River represented a big step up.

"Look at all the lights, Father," breathed the attractive young woman seated beside Corrigan. "Kansas City has really grown since we were here last."

"Yep," he grunted in agreement. "There're lots of people here now, Lucy. I just hope some of them want to see a Wild West show."

Father and daughter made a striking pair. In his early sixties, Corrigan had led a rugged life, which had left him in excellent shape for a man his age. His clean-shaven, rough-hewn face could not be called handsome, but it had

1

strength and character. More than a few threads of gray touched his thatch of dark hair, and he was starting to thicken around the middle a bit; nevertheless, the barrel-chested showman still possessed plenty of vigor.

Corrigan always said that Lucy had inherited her good looks from her mother, and it was true that she had the same long blond hair, fair skin, and trim figure as his late wife. But Lucy's eyes were those of her father—dark blue, alert, and intelligent. A trick rider in the show, she wore corduroy pants, a fringed buckskin jacket, boots, and a broad-brimmed white hat studded with silver conchas.

An old Concord stagecoach, painted the traditional red with yellow trim, followed closely behind Corrigan's wagon, and handling its six-horse team was a bearded old man perched on the seat of the driver's box. One of the highlights of the Wild West show was a mock stage holdup, complete with a chase around the arena by gun-toting desperadoes, followed by a shoot-out between the outlaws and a group of valiant lawmen who arrived just in the nick of time to save the passengers. Such an exhibition required an experienced hand on the reins, and Jackrabbit Dawkins, an old friend and colleague of Corrigan's who had been riding with him for years, was as skillful a jehu as anyone was likely to find in this modern day and age.

A dozen other enclosed wagons, all of them painted with the name of the show, made up the rest of the procession, and bringing up the rear was a herd of several dozen horses and a few steers being driven by a handful of bored-looking cowboys.

From Corrigan's viewpoint on the bluff overlooking the town, he could see Kansas City spreading out along the eastern bank of the broad, sluggish Missouri. On the far side of the river, the lights of the smaller Kansas City, the one in Kansas, were visible in the gathering darkness under a wide band of reddish-gold, marking the spot in the western horizon where the sun had set not long before.

Corrigan shoved back the battered black Stetson on his head. So far, this year of 1899 had been a difficult one for the show, but he hoped Kansas City would prove to be the turning point. All they needed was a successful run here to recoup some of the losses they had suffered over the last few months. Recalling the days when he had helped to bring civilization to this part of the country as a U.S. Army scout, a wagon-train guide, and a frontiersman, he knew he had never dreamed he would wind up as the owner and operator of the most ragtag Wild West outfit in creation.

An elbow dug into his ribs. "You're being gloomy again, aren't you, Father?" his daughter asked wryly.

Corrigan turned and grinned at Lucy. "Just taking a breather before we go down and get set up. It's been a long haul."

"That's right," Lucy agreed. "So the sooner we get finished and can rest, the better."

Corrigan knew better than to argue with her. Leaning out from his seat, he waved for the other vehicles to fall in behind him. The grizzled old-timer on the stagecoach box waved back in acknowledgment, and the stage and the other wagons lurched into motion, following Corrigan's lead.

As Corrigan's wagon rolled along the gentle slope of the road that led down from the bluff, the door behind the seat opened, and a man stuck his head out. A mild-looking, balding individual in his late forties, with wire-rimmed spectacles perched on the bridge of his nose, he said, "Ah, I see we've almost arrived. I was wondering why we had stopped, but I didn't want to break off my calculations until I was finished."

"Got some good news for us, do you, Nathan?" Corrigan asked hopefully.

Nathan Sanford had been the bookkeeper for the Wild West show ever since it had begun, and Corrigan could remember only a few times when he had seen the little man smile. This moment was not added to that list. With his usual dour expression, Sanford answered, "I think I should wait until we've reached our destination and have gotten settled down for the night to explain the situation properly. Finances are a complicated matter, Mr. Corrigan."

The showman sighed. "Reckon I know that all too well," he said, as much to himself as to Sanford. The bookkeeper had been going over the accounts during this trip to Kansas City and probably had some grim results. It was likely that without a profitable run here, Cactus Corrigan's Great Wild West would be forced to close down for good.

If that happened, a lot of people would be out of work, from the lowliest roustabout to Jackrabbit Dawkins. Some of them would be able to find jobs with other Wild West shows or carnivals or circuses, but for old-timers like Jackrabbit, and even Corrigan himself . . .

He clenched his jaw, deciding there was no point in worrying about that now. He had never been one to give up until the last card in a hand was played.

As the wagons wound their way through Kansas City toward the area near the river where the show was supposed to set up, Lucy commented to her father, "I wonder when Mr. Ballard is going to get here with those new horses."

Corrigan tried not to grimace at the reminder of yet another debt. Six months earlier he had contracted with a rancher in Texas to provide fresh horses for the show, but at the time he had not known that revenues were going to fall off as much as they had. In the meantime the rancher, Wes Ballard, was supposed to drive the horses up from Texas to Kansas City and deliver the animals.

"Could be he's here already," Corrigan stated. "He knew when we were supposed to arrive, and we're on schedule, so it's just a matter of whether or not he ran into any trouble on the way up here."

Thinking of that brought back memories for Corrigan. He had ramrodded a couple of cattle drives up the trail from Texas himself, and he knew there was plenty of trouble for a man to run into along the way. Indians, rustlers, floods, stampedes . . . He shook his head, chiding himself for living in the past again. There had not been any Indian trouble in this part of the country for twenty years or more. Sure, rustlers were still a faint possibility, but it was unlikely that anyone would try to steal the horses from Ballard. Floods and stampedes could always cause problems, of course, but it had been a dry summer, so creeks and rivers would be low, and a few dozen horses running wild was a lot different from several thousand crazed cattle running over everything in their path.

Ballard's biggest problem with those horses, Corrigan reflected, was going to be getting paid for them.

Maybe the Texan would not mind waiting. Corrigan had never met him, but he had known his father fairly well, and Gene Ballard had always been willing to give a man the benefit of the doubt. Could be his son was the same way.

Putting his worries aside, the showman concentrated on finding their destination. Even though it was dinnertime, plenty of people were on the streets of Kansas City, and the troupe drew a great deal of attention as it passed through the town. Corrigan took the stares as a good sign: If folks were curious, they would come out to see what the show was all about.

As the procession moved on, Corrigan caught sight of a railroad bridge spanning the Missouri. The first one had been completed thirty years earlier, in 1869, and he remembered how people had said at the time that the frontier was about to open up. Well, it had. Civilization had come to the prairies and the mountains, bringing with it a flood of settlers that had forever changed the face of the land. And Corrigan was not always sure that it was a good thing.

He flicked the reins and clucked to his team, urging the animals to pick up the pace. Lucy had been saying for a long time that he brooded too much about the past, about the way things had been when he was young. The girl was right, Corrigan thought. A man had to live in the present.

He briskly drove the wagon past the stockyards, the meat-packing plants, and the flour mills. It was still not completely dark when the troupe reached the large open field where they would be camping and putting on their performances.

Abruptly Corrigan jerked back on the reins and pulled the team to a stop again, but this time he stared wide-eyed in surprise and anger at what he saw. What should have been a grassy, vacant field was full of wagons and horses and people milling around. Dozens of lanterns and torches lit up the area as bright as day, and the sound of hammering filled the air as workmen put together grand-stands surrounding the area that would serve as an arena.

Lucy gripped Corrigan's arm and asked anxiously, "Father, what is this? Who are all those people?"

Corrigan felt his face flushing and his pulse starting to beat harder. The intrusive wagons were even more color-fully decorated than were his, and they were familiar—all too familiar. "It's that damned Travers!" he barked, glaring at the interlopers.

He heard shouting up ahead and knew that word of their arrival was being passed to the headquarters wagon, and it took him but a moment to spot that vehicle near the center of the encampment. It was hard to miss, since it was painted a brilliant yellow that would almost put the sun to shame. John Travers always had thrived on folks' paying attention to him, Corrigan thought disgustedly.

"Hey, Cactus!" Jackrabbit Dawkins shouted from the stagecoach. "That's the Kid's outfit, ain't it?"

Corrigan turned around, calling back, "It's him, all right."

"What are we going to do now?" Lucy asked.

Corrigan muttered, "Wait and see if the scoundrel has an explanation for this, I reckon. Don't know what else we can do. But I'd be willing to bet I won't like what he's got to say."

Several men were now walking toward Corrigan's wagon. In the lead was a man wearing boots, jeans, a work shirt, and a black hat. A little below medium height, he had a compact, muscular build that would be well suited for riding, and when he came closer, Corrigan recognized the beard-stubbled face as belonging to Quint Fowler, the head wrangler for the rival Wild West show.

"That you, Corrigan?" Fowler called as he neared the wagon. "If it is, I reckon you must've got lost."

The mocking tone of the wrangler's voice made the old scout stiffen. There had been a time when he would have climbed down from the wagon and made Fowler eat those words.

Lucy's fingers tightened on her father's arm, as if she had read his mind. "We came here to put on some shows, not to start trouble," she quietly reminded him. "Let's wait and see what Mr. Travers has to say."

Corrigan nodded curtly. "Don't worry about me, gal." He lifted his voice and told Fowler, "If I've got business with anybody here, mister, it's your boss, not you. Why don't you go fetch him?"

"I don't fetch anybody, Corrigan." Fowler hooked his thumbs in his belt and stood insolently regarding the newcomers. "The Kid'll be out here to talk to you in a minute or two, I expect."

Lucy scooted closer to her father as the wrangler's eyes rested on her. The other men standing behind Fowler were staring at her as well, and Corrigan's anger boiled up even more. When the young woman was trick riding, she wore a short split skirt and was the object of plenty of attention—but this was different. The leer on Fowler's face was nothing less than an insult.

Suddenly the group standing in front of the wagon parted, and a tall, lean figure in a buckskin jacket strolled through the gap. He had a shock of silver hair and a mustache and goatee the same color. A handsome, dashing figure about the same age as Corrigan, John Travers had for years also been known as the Yakima Kid.

Corrigan had known him even longer than that.

Travers stepped beside the wagon and smiled. "Hello, Lucy," he drawled politely, then extended a tanned, long-fingered hand to Corrigan. "Howdy, Cactus. What brings you here?"

"You know damned well what brings us here," Corrigan snapped, disregarding the offered hand. "We've come to put on our show."

Travers shook his head, finally lowering his arm. "Not here, you won't. We were booked into Kansas City months ago. This is *our* spot."

"You're making a mistake," Corrigan warned, his eyes narrowing. "You'd best get out while you still can." He felt Lucy's fingers dig into his arm again, but he ignored her. There were some things a man could not back down from.

Travers took a deep breath. "Look, Cactus, we're old friends, and there's no need for old friends to fight—"

"Maybe we rode together once," Corrigan cut in, "but that doesn't make us friends now. Simple fact of the matter is, the Kansas City *Clarion* made arrangements with me for my show to perform here. *Right* here. In this field!" Corrigan thought he was being as reasonable as anybody could expect, even Lucy. But if that did not work, there was going to be trouble.

Travers lifted his bushy eyebrows in surprise. "*My* arrangement was with the *Clarion*. The paper's sponsoring all the performances of the Yakima Kid's Ace-High Pioneer Exposition and Wild West."

Corrigan winced, as he did every time he heard the grandiose full name of Travers's show—especially when it dripped mellifluously off his rival's tongue. "Reckon you'll have to settle that with the paper," he said. "Right now I'll thank you to pack up your people and your wagons and get the hell out of here."

Travers's smile disappeared, and he began to look as angry as Corrigan. More members of the Kid's troupe had crowded up behind him, some of them carrying torches, and the burning brands revealed their hostile expressions.

Corrigan glanced over his shoulder. Most of his wranglers had ridden up alongside the stagecoach, leaving a skeleton crew to watch the livestock, while the drivers, more cowboys, and Indians wearing trail clothes had jumped down from the wagons and were drifting forward. All of them looked tense and watchful, ready for trouble to break out. Corrigan felt a surge of pride, knowing his people were just as quick to back him up as Travers's were.

Suddenly there was a lot more in the warm air of the summer night than the chirp of crickets, the buzzing of mosquitoes, and the rich smells of dirt and wildflowers and the nearby river. There was a sense that violence could explode at any minute.

Jackrabbit set the brake on the stagecoach, dropped nimbly from the driver's box, and hurried forward in his usual bowlegged gait. "Howdy, Kid," he said, his voice friendly.

Travers summoned up another smile and turned it

briefly on the newcomer. "Hello, you old reprobate," he greeted the wiry jehu. "Stolen any horses lately?"

Jackrabbit cackled and slapped his thigh. "Stolen any horses, the man says! That's a good 'un, Kid. When're you goin' to start believin' that I just borrowed that paint pony of yours? I never stole it."

"You never brought it back, did you?" Travers quipped.

"Well . . . no, I reckon I didn't. That feller sort of took me by surprise. To this day, I still ain't got no idea where that fourth ace come from—but I'd lay odds he was bottom-dealin'."

Travers shrugged. "You should have called him on it."

"Figured he was too slick with a gun for me to do somethin' like that. 'Sides, it was *your* horse I was bettin', not mine."

"At least you've finally admitted—"

Corrigan broke into the conversation, saying, "This is all as funny as hell, Travers, but you're still in our spot. Now, are you getting out or not?"

He saw Jackrabbit grimace and knew that the old jehu had been trying to forestall the trouble that seemed bound to happen. Jackrabbit well remembered the times when the three of them were saddle partners, and he did not want to admit that Travers had turned into a low-down skunk.

Quite a bit of muttering was going on among Travers's men now, and one of them questioned arrogantly, "How much longer are you going to put up with that broken-down old man's mouth, boss?"

Travers sent a sharp, angry glance toward the man who had spoken, but murmurs of agreement came from the others—or from most of them.

Corrigan spotted one man in the crowd who was watching the confrontation with only an interested expression on his face rather than an angry or mocking one. This man was young, not much over twenty, with a tall, strong build and blond hair that fell in waves to his shoulders. He was hatless, wearing a buckskin shirt and pants and calf-high moccasins.

Corrigan looked back at his rival when Travers began, "Look, Cactus, I'm sure we can work this out—"

Dropping the reins, Corrigan lithely hopped down from the wagon seat, landing just a couple of feet in front of Travers. Although the Kid was a few inches taller than he, Corrigan's anger made him seem just as tall at the moment. Putting his fists on his hips, he glared at the ex-frontiersman.

Lucy leaned down anxiously from the seat. "Please, Father!" she begged.

Ignoring his daughter's entreaty, Corrigan told Travers coldly, "If you're not moving, I'll put you off, damn you."

Their men all crowded around. Corrigan saw a glitter in Travers's eyes that said very plainly his former friend was not going to back down. Not like this, not in front of everyone.

"I guess you can try, Cactus," Travers said softly.

Corrigan did not wait any longer, deciding bitterly that he had waited too long already. He should have done this years ago, he told himself—and threw a punch at Travers's head.

The hard right failed to connect. Travers darted aside and snapped out a blow of his own, his fist thudding into Corrigan's midsection. The old scout grunted from the impact, which was the effect he had hoped *his* blow would have had on his adversary. But in throwing the punch, Travers had left himself wide open for the left hook that Corrigan now slammed into his jaw, and the Yakima Kid staggered backward into the arms of his men.

Howls of anger went up, and curses sizzled in the night air as the two groups of men surged together. Fists flew all around Corrigan, some of them grazing him as he pushed forward, trying to locate Travers again in the me-lee. Over the grunts and yells and thuds of fists against flesh and bone, Corrigan heard Lucy vehemently shouting for the men to stop fighting. He glanced up toward her in time to see her roll her eyes in disgusted surrender and lean over from the seat to clout one of Travers's men on top of the head.

That was the Lucy he knew, Corrigan thought with a grin, and then somebody's hand came down hard on his shoulder and spun him around. Catching his balance, he saw Travers standing before him, and in the next split second a hard, knobby fist caught Corrigan flush on the nose. He felt blood spurt as pain shot through his head.

The scuffle was now a full-fledged brawl. As the battle ebbed and flowed around them, Corrigan and Travers stood toe to toe, trading punches. Travers's nose began to bleed, too, and bruises appeared on the faces of both men. One of the Kid's employees staggered by with Jackrabbit Dawkins clinging to his back. The old-timer had his skinny legs wrapped around his opponent's middle and was flailing away at him with little effect.

Suddenly the shrill sound of whistles penetrated the night air, and both Corrigan and Travers abruptly stepped back, pausing in their conflict to see what was happening. All around them members of their troupes stopped fighting and began to look about.

Burly men in blue uniforms and black caps were pushing their way through the mob, some holding pistols and others carrying wicked-looking billy clubs. "Break it up! Break it up, dammit!" one of them shouted in a voice that boomed through the field.

With a sigh, Corrigan recognized them as Kansas City police officers. Using the back of his hand to wipe off the blood that was beginning to dry beneath his nose, he faced the officer who had been calling for order. "Are you in charge of these cops, mister?" he asked.

The large blue-suited man glowered at Corrigan and snapped, "Who the blazes wants to know?"

"I'm Cactus Corrigan." He waved a hand at the wagons behind him. "I own this show, and these other fellows are trying to steal our place."

"That's a blasted lie!" Travers exclaimed. "I'm the Yakima Kid, Officer—maybe you've heard of me—and *my* troupe is supposed to be here, not his."

Several men on both sides of the battle started to call out denials of what had been said, but they fell silent as the policemen glared at them. The big officer said harshly, "Well, I'm Sergeant Fergus O'Shaughnessy, and I want ye both to shut up! I suppose ye got papers to prove who ye are and where yer supposed to be, so let's be havin' a look at 'em." He glanced at Travers and stated sarcastically, "And by the way, mister, I don't know ye from Adam!"

Travers flushed, but he said, "If you'll come with me back to my wagon, Sergeant, I'll be glad to show you all the documents necessary to prove I'm in the right."

"Well, let me get my papers, too," Corrigan snapped. Turning toward his wagon, he bellowed, "Nathan! Get out here, and bring that contract with you!"

The door behind the seat opened tentatively, and Nathan Sanford cautiously stuck out his head. "Is the fight over?" he asked.

"For now," Corrigan growled. "Come on."

Sanford climbed awkwardly through the doorway, Lucy shifting aside on the seat to give him room. He stepped down. "Is this what you need?" he asked his employer, handing over a sheaf of papers.

Corrigan took the papers and glanced at them, then nodded. Turning to Travers, he insisted, "Come on, let's get this settled."

While the rest of the patrolmen stayed where they were to keep the fight from breaking out again, Corrigan, Travers, and O'Shaughnessy walked over to Travers's bright yellow wagon. The sergeant cast a dubious eye at the gaudy vehicle but went inside without making any comment.

Inside the wagon was an old rolltop desk, and Travers took only a moment to locate several sheets of paper in one of the drawers. He handed them to O'Shaughnessy, and Corrigan did likewise with his contract. The Irishman scowled as he began reading, looking back and forth between the documents. Corrigan waited nervously, unable to tell anything from O'Shaughnessy's expression.

Finally the sergeant returned both sets of papers. "As far as I can tell," he grunted, "ye both have valid contracts to put on Wild West shows here in this location." He looked over at Travers. "But yer contract is dated a couple o' months earlier than this other feller's. So that means ye've got first call on the place."

"But that's impossible!" Corrigan exclaimed. "Maybe Travers got his dates mixed up."

O'Shaughnessy shook his head solemnly. "Both contracts have the same dates for the performances. Sorry, bucko, ye'll have to find someplace else to put on your show."

Corrigan's jaw tightened. "What about *my* contract?"

"Ye'll have to take that up with the newspaper folks, I imagine. It's none of the police's business." O'Shaughnessy lifted his billy club and tapped Corrigan's broad chest with its tip. "But keepin' the peace is, and I won't have any more riots down here. Ye and yer people clear out now without any more fuss."

Corrigan was seething with anger, but he was still a law-abiding man. He gave O'Shaughnessy a curt nod and said, "We'll leave. Do you have any idea where we might be able to camp for the night?"

The sergeant shrugged. "Head north on the river road another couple of miles. There's some vacant land up there, just past a bunch o' warehouses. The property belongs to the same company that owns the buildings, so ye'll have to talk to the owner about rentin' the place. I'll give ye the address of his office."

Corrigan sighed and nodded, grateful for that much help. He made a mental note of the address O'Shaughnessy told him, then asked, "Will the owner be there at this time of night?"

"Should be. He works late nearly every night, from what I hear." O'Shaughnessy grinned. "Likes his money, he does."

That was not a good omen, Corrigan thought. Renting the other property might prove to be an expensive proposition. But there was nothing else they could do.

He tried not to let his shoulders slump as he left Travers's trailer, for he would be damned if he would let his rival see his despair. Striding back to his own wagons, Corrigan called out to the members of the troupe, "All right, everybody get back to your places and start turning the wagons around. We're leaving."

There were a few exclamations of anger and protest, but Corrigan's people did as they were told. The old showman avoided looking at Travers's men, knowing that they would be wearing smirks of victory. Lucy gave her father a sad smile and then tried to look encouraging.

"I'm sorry about this, Cactus," Travers said, coming

up behind Corrigan. "But business is business, after all."

Corrigan turned to stare coldly at his rival. "First thing in the morning," he stated, "I'm going to pay a visit to that newspaper publisher, and then we'll see who's got to clear out. But I'll tell you one thing for sure right now. Kansas City isn't big enough for the both of us."

Chapter Two

When a still-furious Earl Corrigan rode into downtown Kansas City the next morning with Jackrabbit Dawkins, in search of the building that housed the *Clarion,* he discovered it was unusual to see riders on horseback in the middle of the city. Anyone who had business there came in a carriage or rode the electric streetcars, and the two men drew plenty of stares as they clopped along the streets—the attention not improving Corrigan's mood.

It had been quite late the night before when the Wild West show and all its members had finally gotten settled down. After Corrigan had located the owner of the property along the river, the negotiations had taken a while and had not gone to Corrigan's satisfaction. He had had enough money to meet the man's price, but the transaction had drained most of the troupe's available cash—and that was just for one night's rental.

No mistake about it, Cactus Corrigan's Great Wild West was in deep trouble, and unless he could straighten out this mess with Jasper Morton Prescott, the publisher of the *Clarion,* the situation was going to be even worse.

The wiry Jackrabbit leaned over to Corrigan as they rode and said in a loud whisper, "Folks're sure gawkin' at us. Ain't they never seen a couple of cowboys afore?"

The showman looked over at his friend, who despite the warmth of the day was wearing a woolen shirt with the sleeves rolled up a couple of turns to reveal the sleeves of a pair of long underwear, as well as a stained leather vest and his ever-present battered Confederate campaign hat with the bill pushed up. Smiling to himself as he looked

15

fondly at the old jehu's bushy white hair and scruffy beard, Corrigan thought that these folks had probably *never* seen the likes of Jackrabbit Dawkins.

"Probably not in a long time," Corrigan finally replied. "Kansas City's not the jumping-off place it used to be, my friend. But there's no point wasting time mourning that change."

Spotting the newspaper office—a sturdy-looking red brick building with a sign over the doorway in fancy gold script reading THE KANSAS CITY CLARION—EST. 1888—the old scout indicated it to his companion. As Corrigan headed toward it, he looked for a hitch rail to tie their horses to but found none. Grimacing, he tied his reins to a wrought-iron lamppost and motioned for Jackrabbit to do the same. Then the showman led the way up the short flight of stairs to the entrance.

On one side of the lobby was a long wooden counter, and a young man with slicked-down hair and a bow tie stood behind it. As Corrigan and Jackrabbit stepped up to it, the young man gave them a puzzled frown and asked, "Can I help you, ah, gentlemen?"

"We're here to see your publisher," Corrigan replied, taking the folded contract from the rear pocket of his Levi's. "Mr. Prescott, it says here."

"Yes, indeed, Mr. Prescott is, ah, the publisher of the *Clarion,* but I don't know if—"

Corrigan's callused palm slammed down on the counter, making the young man jump. "I'm in no mood for a bunch of folderol about how Prescott can't see me, boy," he snapped. "Now, is Prescott here or not?"

The young man ran a nervous finger around the inside of his stiff celluloid collar. "Why, yes, he *is* here—"

"Then point me to his office."

Glancing around as if looking for help, the young man hesitated. There were quite a few people coming and going in the large lobby of the building, but the few who were paying any attention to the confrontation did not seem inclined to come rushing to the young man's assistance. Corrigan could see the growing fear in the youth's eyes. The boy thought he was crazy. Well, let him think that, Corrigan decided, if it accomplished his purpose.

"Of course, sir," the young man finally said. "You just go up those stairs on the other side of the lobby to the hallway on the second floor. Mr. Prescott's office will be the third door on your right."

"Much obliged," Corrigan stated, then started across the lobby. Jackrabbit hurried after him, occasionally giving one of the little hops that had been responsible for his name as he tried to keep up with Corrigan's longer-legged strides.

The door of the office to which they had been directed bore Prescott's name and title. Opening the door, Corrigan found himself facing another startled little man in a suit and tie.

"I'm here to see Prescott," Corrigan announced curtly, his eyes taking in the details of the small room. It was functionally furnished, with a desk, a chair, and a cabinet. On the desk sat a telephone, the kind that you did not even have to crank. All you did was pick up the receiver, jiggle the little hook on which it sat, and wait for an operator to answer and then connect you with your party.

When the man merely looked goggle-eyed at him and Jackrabbit and made no reply, Corrigan went on, "Jasper Morton Prescott, like it says on the door. You him?"

The man managed to shake his head, mumbling almost inaudibly that he was Prescott's secretary.

Noticing a door on the opposite side of the room, Corrigan knew Prescott had to be on the other side of it. He strode forward. For a second he thought the small man was going to try to get in his way, but if that was what the secretary had been considering, he gave up the idea in a hurry. No one tried to stop the showman as he grasped the doorknob, opened the door, and stepped into the inner office.

That room was larger and more opulently furnished, with a rug on the floor, pictures on the walls, and a handsome maple desk. A man looked up from the chair behind the desk and asked Corrigan with a frown, "Who the devil are you, sir, and what are you doing here?"

As the man rose to his feet and leaned forward, resting his palms on the desk, he cut an impressive figure. Tall and powerfully built, he had a broad, florid face and penetrating eyes. He was clean-shaven, with silver hair and long iron-gray sideburns, and although Corrigan was no judge of clothes, he figured the man's suit was expensive.

"Are you Jasper Morton Prescott?" the showman asked.

"I am. Now I'll thank you for an answer to *my* questions, sir."

"Earl Corrigan. Some folks call me Cactus. I own the Wild West show you just brought into town."

Prescott's frown deepened. "Corrigan, Corrigan . . ." he mused, obviously rolling the name over in his mind. Suddenly he lifted his thick eyebrows. "Ah, yes, Cactus Corrigan's Great Wild West! But— My God, man, what are you doing in Kansas City now? You're not supposed to be here for another four months!"

Corrigan shook his head and tossed the folded contract onto Prescott's desk. "Don't know how you figure that," he said. "According to that paper, my show is scheduled to put on its first performance four days from now."

Prescott snatched up the document, spread it open, and studied it intently. As he did, he murmured, "I just don't understand. Mr. Travers's troupe is in town at the moment."

"You admit you hired Travers, too?" Corrigan asked sharply.

"Of course. Or rather, the *Clarion* made arrangements with him to sponsor his show. The paper gets the publicity and a percentage of the ticket revenues, just as it specifies here in your contract, as well." Prescott looked up at Corrigan. "But there's been some mistake made. Your group was not supposed to be here until the fall."

Corrigan held up a pair of fingers. "Let me get this straight. You brought *two* Wild West shows into town at the same time?"

"That was never intended!" Prescott exclaimed. He took a deep breath and put a courteous smile on his face. "Please, Mr. Corrigan, why don't you and your . . . companion . . . sit down? I'm sure we can work this out. There's been an honest mistake made somewhere."

Corrigan shrugged and pulled up one of the chairs in front of the desk; then he jerked a thumb at another one and nodded to Jackrabbit. Introducing the old-timer, he explained to Prescott, "This is my friend and assistant, Jackrabbit Dawkins."

"Pleased to meet you, Mr. Dawkins," Prescott said as he settled once more into his own chair, which was luxuriously padded and covered with leather.

"Likewise," Jackrabbit muttered, shoving his chaw of tobacco into a corner of his cheek.

"Could I offer you gentlemen a drink?"

Jackrabbit's eyes lit up, but Corrigan shook his head firmly. "Too early in the morning," he stated.

"So it is. Besides, we'll need clear heads to sort this out, won't we?"

The publisher was smiling and being polite, but Corrigan still felt nervous. A man like Prescott moved in circles far removed from an old scout like Cactus Corrigan, and it was impossible for him to predict how the publisher might want to handle the mess.

Prescott studied the contract for what seemed to Corrigan like many long minutes, then finally pushed it to one side and nodded decisively. "I see what must have happened," he said. "The *Clarion* frequently sponsors events of interest to the city, ranging from cultural affairs such as the visit of a touring opera company, to appearances of shows like yours, intended for more simple entertainment. Somehow, when the contracts for your visit were being drawn up, Mr. Corrigan, the wrong dates for the performances were placed on your copy of the document. No doubt one of my clerks used Mr. Travers's contract as a model for this one and inadvertently copied the incorrect dates."

"You're saying it was just a mistake?"

Prescott nodded again. "An unfortunate but honest mistake."

"What are you going to do about it?"

Spreading his carefully manicured hands, Prescott said solemnly, "There's nothing I *can* do about it, sir. John Travers has a valid contract that predates and therefore supersedes yours. Now, if you and your troupe would care to come back this fall, on the dates you were supposed to be here, we'd certainly be glad to have you and would honor our commitment. But other than that . . ."

As the publisher's voice trailed off, Corrigan heard a roaring in his ears like a raging river, but he knew it was just his blood boiling up. "Goddamm it!" he railed, standing abruptly. "You're saying somebody made a mistake, so we're just out of luck? Travers gets to put on his show, and we don't?"

"I've explained it to you, Mr. Corrigan," Prescott replied, his voice tightening with anger. "There's nothing I can do unless you want to come back—"

"And what are we supposed to do for money between now and then?" the showman roared.

As soon as the question was out of his mouth, Corrigan knew he had made a mistake by admitting what desperate financial straits his show was in. Prescott's mouth pulled into the beginnings of a smile, implying that since he knew his interrogator had money trouble, he himself could safely feel superior.

"I'm afraid that's not my problem," the publisher said smoothly, pushing himself to his feet again. "I'll check our copy of this contract to make sure the correct dates are on it, but I'm certain they are." He shrugged, adding, "I suppose you could take legal action against the paper, but frankly, I don't think it would do you any good. Lawyers cost a great deal of money, you know."

Prescott was smirking at him, Corrigan thought, just as Travers and all those other people had. The publisher obviously figured he had the power of civilization and law on his side in this dispute—but in the old days, a man settled his problems himself. . . .

Corrigan started to lunge across the desk, his hands balling into fists. As Prescott's eyes widened in fear and surprise and he flinched backward, Jackrabbit grabbed desperately at his friend. The old-timer's bony fingers closed on Corrigan's arm and hung on for dear life. "Hold it, Cactus!" he cried. "Hold on for a minute, pard!"

"Let me go, blast it!" Corrigan barked, pulling against Jackrabbit's grip. He could have broken loose, he knew, but there was a part of his brain that was still calm enough to realize the old jehu was trying to help him.

"Thrashin' this feller ain't goin' to accomplish nothin',"

boss," Jackrabbit advised. Casting a glare at Prescott, he went on, "Appealin' as the prospect is, it'll just cause more of a ruckus."

"But what he's doing isn't right!" Corrigan protested.

"I know it, but we'll figure out a way to fix things. Come on," Jackrabbit urged, distaste evident in his voice. "Let's get out of this here *office*."

Corrigan let himself be tugged toward the door, but as he went, he glared hotly at Prescott. "This isn't over," he promised the publisher.

Prescott drew himself up and curled his lip in a sneer as he said, "I assure you, Mr. Corrigan, it is."

Jackrabbit gave another tug and got Corrigan out of the room before he could say anything else. The secretary must have heard the argument, because he was careful to stay out of their way as they left the office. Corrigan shook his colleague's hand off his arm and stalked into the hallway, not looking back as he marched down the stairs and through the lobby.

As he roughly pushed open the front door of the building and stormed outside, he was oblivious of the pleasant summer morning and of the man alighting from a carriage at the curb. The well-dressed, obviously wealthy individual was going up the steps to the entrance as Corrigan was going down, trailed by Jackrabbit, and he gave the furious old scout a curious glance as he passed him.

All Corrigan saw at the moment were the faces of his enemies—John Travers and Jasper Morton Prescott. When he reached his horse and jerked the reins free, he forced himself to stop and take a deep breath. Losing his temper was not going to help solve the problem, and that was all that mattered now, because if he didn't find some way to salvage this situation, Cactus Corrigan's Great Wild West was about to come to an ignominious end.

Returning to the campsite, Corrigan held a council of war in his wagon. Seated around his small dining table with him were Lucy, Jackrabbit, and Nathan Sanford, all of them appearing as glum as the slight bookkeeper.

"Well, let's figure something out," Corrigan declared, looking around at his companions. "Anybody got any ideas?"

Sanford cleared his throat nervously, then said, "I'm afraid I don't have any suggestions, Mr. Corrigan, but I do know there are some inescapable conclusions." He held up a finger. "One, we can't stay here. The rent is exorbitant, and we simply can't afford it." Another finger joined the first. "And two, we don't have enough money to travel to another town and put on any shows."

"So you're saying we can't stay, and we can't go."

Sanford nodded grimly. "That is correct, yes, sir."

"So what are we going to do?"

No one responded to Corrigan's question. He waited a moment, and when it became clear that there was not going to be an answer, he leaned forward. "I'll tell you what we're going to do," he said. "We're going to find another spot here in Kansas City where we can put on our shows, and we're going to raise enough money to head to the next stop on the tour. That's our only hope."

"Where're we goin' to find a place for the performances?" Jackrabbit asked.

"That'll be your job," Corrigan told him impulsively. "Scout us out a location that we can rent cheap."

Jackrabbit pulled on his beard in thought. "Might work," he mused. "Like you said, Cactus, there ain't much else we can do."

Lucy reached over and rested a slender hand on her father's callused one. "I'm sure it'll work out," she offered. "It has to. We can't lose the show."

Corrigan, trying to look encouraging, forced himself to grin at her. Lucy's mother had died when the girl was just a child, and she had grown up in the rough-and-tumble atmosphere of the Wild West show. The troupe was her whole world, and Corrigan had no idea how losing that world would affect her. He never wanted it to come to that.

"We'll be all right, Lucy," he said. "Just don't you worry—"

A knock sounded on the rear door of the wagon, interrupting Corrigan's reassurances. He looked up impatiently and called, "What is it?"

The door opened, and one of the troupe's cowboys

stuck his head in. "Fella from Texas is here with those fresh horses, boss," he said.

Corrigan tried not to grimace at the news that Wes Ballard had arrived with his stock. Standing, he stated, "I'd better go talk to the boy. Jackrabbit, come with me for now, then get busy on that other chore."

"Darn tootin'," the old-timer agreed, shoving his chair back. "I want to take a gander at this new horseflesh."

"I'm going, too," Lucy announced, getting to her feet. "After all, I'll be riding them."

Corrigan nodded and let Lucy and Jackrabbit precede him out of the wagon. He glanced back, saw the bleak look on Sanford's face, and shook his head, trying to force those particular worries out of his thoughts for the moment. Right now he had to find some way of telling Ballard that he might have come all that way for nothing.

Lounging easily in his saddle, Wes Ballard had one leg hooked around the saddle horn while he listened to the rowdy byplay of the cowboys who had accompanied him on the journey. This had to be a little like it was in the old cattle-drive days, he thought, his wide mouth curving slightly in a smile that was partly obscured by his drooping black mustache. The young wranglers were eager to blow off steam after the trip, and some of them were seeing a big town like Kansas City for the first time.

Not that his men were so much younger than he, since he was only thirty years old, after all. But he had worked as far back as he could remember, and for the last ten years he had been on his own, taking on the responsibility of running the ranch his late father had passed on to him.

A tall, lithe man with thick black hair, Ballard had the deep tan of someone who spent most of his time outdoors. He wore an old white Stetson, a khaki work shirt, denim pants, and comfortable old boots. A Colt .45 rode in a holster strapped around his trim hips, and a Winchester '94 was in the saddle boot. Ballard was no gunman, but he could use both weapons fairly well, for out on the range a man had to be able to deal with all kinds of varmints.

As he waited for the showman, he idly wondered

what was going on. On arrival in Kansas City, he and the men and the horses had gone directly to the spot where Cactus Corrigan was supposed to meet them, but instead of finding Corrigan's show camped there, a troupe belonging to the Yakima Kid was in its place. The Kid's name was familiar to Ballard—his late father had been acquainted with both Cactus Corrigan and John Travers—but he had never met either of them. When a roustabout at Travers's camp had directed him up here, several miles north along the riverbank, Ballard knew something strange was going on, but his opinion was that it was none of his business. All he wanted to do was get paid for his horses and head back to Texas.

Two older men and a young woman emerged from one of the wagons and walked quickly toward him, and Ballard figured he was about to meet Cactus Corrigan. The man leading the small group was wearing range clothes and did not look much like a showman, but he carried himself with an air of command. The other man was smaller, a short, wiry, bowlegged oldster who as he walked scratched repeatedly at the faded red underwear poking out of the sleeves of his shirt.

The young woman, with her long honey-blond hair, man's shirt, and tight jeans, drew most of Ballard's attention. She was just about the prettiest thing he had ever seen, and as she approached, he could see that she was studying the animals in the herd with an intelligent gaze. He sensed right away that she knew more than a little about horses.

The man in the lead stopped next to Ballard's horse and extended a hand up to him. "I'm Earl Corrigan," he said in a firm voice. "You must be Wes Ballard."

"I am," he acknowledged, leaning over to shake hands. "Pleased to meet you, sir." He inclined his head toward the herd. "Feel free to take a look. That's the best horseflesh you're going to find anywhere."

"They do look wonderful, Father," the girl said excitedly.

Ballard permitted himself another slight smile. The horses were in fine shape, not gaunt at all from the drive. He had pushed them at an easy pace to achieve just that result. They were a little nervous, stamping and snorting and occasionally letting out a whinny or two, but that just showed they had spirit. Ballard was proud of them.

"Mighty fine animals, son," Corrigan commented. "I appreciate you bringing them up here from Texas"—he hesitated—"but I'm afraid I've got some bad news for you."

Ballard frowned. "Bad news?" he repeated. "Don't reckon I much like the sound of that."

"I don't much like having to tell you. But I can't pay you for those horses, son. At least not right now."

His stomach tensing into a knot, Ballard said coolly, "Our deal was payment on delivery of the herd, Mr. Corrigan. You know that."

"I know. But we've run into some trouble." He sighed, murmuring, "There's just no money to pay you."

Ballard bit back the angry response that came to mind. Corrigan was an old-timer, a product of the same frontier existence as the rancher's father, and Ballard realized how much it must have hurt the man's pride to make such an admission. But that realization did not solve the problem. Grimly he asked, "What am I supposed to do with these horses? Drive them back to Texas?"

"I was hoping you'd agree to wait here in Kansas City until I can come up with the cash," Corrigan replied. "We're going to be putting on our show as soon as we can find another site for it."

Ballard waved a hand at the field where the troupe was camped. "What's wrong with right here?"

The girl spoke up, answering him by saying, "That's a long story, Mr. Ballard. What's important is that you'd be doing us a great favor if you'd let us go ahead and use the horses." She smiled up at him. "They're lovely animals. I can't wait to ride them."

Ballard was well aware that she was trying to use her charm on him. "Horseback rider, are you?"

"Lucy was ridin' before she could walk," the bearded old man said. "Best darn trick rider you'll ever see."

The girl blushed prettily at the praise, then asked, "What about it, Mr. Ballard? Will you give us a chance to make good on our debt?"

Ballard rubbed his jaw as he thought it over. He was not at all interested in turning around and driving the herd back to Texas, for that would mean the whole trip had been for nothing. It might also be hard to get his drovers to agree to such a thing, especially since he did not have enough cash to pay them for a return drive. Many of the boys, he knew, would take the pay he already owed them and head for other places, drifting along as cowboys often did.

His ranch northwest of Fort Worth was in good hands at the moment. He had left his foreman in charge, and he anticipated that everything would run smoothly until his return, so there was no logical reason he could not remain in Kansas City for a while. And it was possible that was the only way he would ever get paid. . . .

He nodded abruptly. "All right. I'll stay for a while, and you can have the use of the horses for the time being. But if I run into somebody else who wants to take them off my hands, I can't guarantee that I won't accept the offer."

"Fair enough," Corrigan responded briskly. "Thanks, Ballard. You won't regret it."

The rancher made no reply. He just hoped that Corrigan was right.

Chapter Three

Earl Corrigan was taking a turn around the camp that afternoon, assuring the members of the troupe that everything would work out, when someone called his name. Recognizing the raspy voice of Jackrabbit Dawkins, he frowned. More bad news, Corrigan thought.

But there was a big grin on the old man's face as he came hurrying up. "Quit your worryin', Cactus!" Jackrabbit exclaimed. "I done solved all our problems!"

Jackrabbit had disappeared right after lunch, heading into Kansas City to try to locate another site for the show to use. Corrigan had not held out a great deal of hope that his friend would be able to accomplish that goal, but obviously the old-timer had come up with something.

"Well, stop crowing and spit it out," Corrigan insisted. "Did you find us a place?"

Jackrabbit hopped up and down in excitement, and a crowd was gathering around them, drawn by the commotion. "I looked for a while, just like you told me to, Cactus, but then I got a mite thirsty," the old jehu explained.

Corrigan suppressed a groan of frustration. "So I reckon you stopped at a saloon and got something to drink," he muttered.

"Seemed like the thing to do at the time," Jackrabbit agreed with a grin. "Anyway, who should I run into inside that tavern but Edgar Swope."

Corrigan waited, but nothing else was forthcoming. Fighting the urge to grab Jackrabbit's scrawny neck and start squeezing, he asked, "Who the hell is Edgar Swope?"

27

"I didn't know him neither, till I started drinkin' with him. Then, come to find out he's a sodbuster who's got a farm on the other side of the river. There's a big field on it that ain't bein' used right now, and ol' Edgar's willin' to rent it to us." Slapping his thigh and cackling, the oldster added, "The best part is, Edgar only wants twenty-five bucks, and he said we could wait till we was ready to leave to pay him."

Corrigan's eyes widened. That *was* good news, if it was true. Twenty-five dollars was a very reasonable price, and if this farmer was willing to wait for his money, that made the deal all the more attractive. "You think Swope can be trusted?" he asked suspiciously.

The old jehu nodded. "I reckon so. He didn't strike me as a bad sort . . . for a sodbuster."

Corrigan frowned again. "You say this land is on the other side of the river?"

"Don't worry 'bout that," Jackrabbit replied with a wave of his grimy hand. "Swope says there's a ferry that runs just about half a mile from his place. We'll just tote ever'thing across on it—wagons, horses, and all."

Somehow, through sheer blind luck, Jackrabbit might have solved one of their major problems, Corrigan thought. It would not be the first time. The old man might be a rather comical figure, but he had a knack for being in the right place at the right time. That ability had kept him alive through some mighty wild times.

"All right, where can I find this Swope?" Corrigan asked. "I want to get the deal wrapped up before he can change his mind."

"I brung him with me," Jackrabbit announced. "Left him over at the Injuns' wagon so's he could take a look at Chief Fightin' Eagle and the braves. Edgar said he'd never seen no real heathen savages before."

Corrigan nodded and strode toward the Indians' wagon, motioning for Jackrabbit to follow him.

Edgar Swope proved to be a plump, red-faced man of about forty who wore overalls, a wide-brimmed hat, and work shoes. He was grinning broadly as Chief Fighting Eagle—an Omaha Indian whose real name now was Fred Smith—spun a fanciful yarn about battling Custer's Seventh Cavalry. The chief was too young to have ever met Custer, let alone fought him, and the rest of his story was equally ridiculous, but Swope seemed to be thoroughly entertained. When Jackrabbit introduced Corrigan to him, the farmer shook his hand eagerly and said, "It's sure an honor to meet such a famous pioneer, Mr. Corrigan. It sure is."

Jackrabbit had been right. Swope was more than happy to rent his empty field to the Wild West show, and he insisted that Corrigan pay him whenever he was good and ready. "If you can't trust somebody like Cactus Corrigan, then who can you trust?" Swope asked sincerely.

"Well, I thank you for that compliment, son, and I appreciate you giving us a hand like this," the showman said. "You'll be welcome at any and all of our performances, free of charge."

"I'll be there," Swope promised. "Wouldn't miss it for the world. This is the most exciting thing that's happened around here in a long time."

If that was true, Corrigan thought wryly, then this part of the country really had gotten too civilized.

Everything went fairly quickly after that. Corrigan had previously made sure that all the members of the troupe knew their present camp was only temporary, so packing did not take long. Teams were hitched to the wagons and the old stagecoach, and the procession was on its way by late afternoon. Jackrabbit took the lead with the Concord this time, with Edgar Swope riding proudly beside him as he directed them toward the ferry.

Wes Ballard and his cowboys handled the chore of moving the herd of horses, but once they reached their destination, the regular members of the troupe would have to start taking care of the animals. When Ballard had explained the situation to his men, none of them had opted to remain in Kansas City. Some of them were heading back to Texas, and the rest were planning to draw their pay and ride on.

"You have enough money to pay them off?" Corrigan had asked Ballard, still feeling more than a little embarrassed by the matter.

Ballard had nodded. "They got half their wages before we started, and I brought enough cash with me to make up the other half when we got here."

"I was afraid you wouldn't be able to pay them until I paid you."

"Don't worry about them," the Texan had told him. "*I'm* the one you owe your debt."

The boy was angry about not getting his money, Corrigan knew, and he could not blame him. He was just glad the rancher was a gentleman and was willing to give him some extra time. Still, owing the money galled Corrigan. When the day came that Cactus Corrigan could not pay his way . . .

Corrigan cast that thought aside and concentrated on driving the wagon as he followed Jackrabbit along the river road. The show would be back on its feet soon, and then he would never let anything like this happen again.

By nightfall, Cactus Corrigan's Great Wild West was across the river in Kansas, setting up camp on Edgar Swope's farm. Paying the ferry operator used up the last of Corrigan's funds, and until they started selling tickets for the shows, they would have to make do with what they had on hand.

Corrigan called a meeting of the troupe after supper, and as he looked out at the faces watching him and waiting to hear what he had to say, he felt a surge of pride. All these people had given him their loyalty, and he had to give them something in return.

"You all know things haven't turned out here in Kansas City like we expected," Corrigan began, lifting his voice so that he could be heard over the crickets and the birds singing their evening songs in the trees at the edge of the field. "We've got a rough chore ahead of us. Travers and his bunch have been here a couple of days already, and they're probably just about set up and ready to go. If we're going to compete with their outfit, we can't afford to take the usual amount of time getting ready." He paused to take a deep breath, then went on, "I know it's asking a lot, but I want us to put on our first show two nights from now!"

There were murmurs of surprise from the crowd. The portable grandstands that the troupe carried had to be erected, and that in itself took an entire day, sometimes longer. Although the performers knew all their routines by heart, they still had to rehearse, because the ground in each arena was slightly different. A performer racing his horse and putting it through tight maneuvers in a small area had to know every inch of the ground to prevent accidents.

But no one wanted to let Corrigan down, and Jackrabbit Dawkins was the first to call out, "Sure, Cactus, we'll be ready!" Instantly, all the other members of the troupe were nodding and shouting their agreement.

Corrigan nodded curtly, not wanting them to see the depth of emotion that their display aroused within him. "Thanks," he said simply. "I knew I could count on you."

While the group broke up, many of them to start on their appointed tasks, Corrigan returned to his wagon. On the way he spotted Lucy talking to Wes Ballard beside the rope corral holding the horses, and Corrigan grinned. Lucy loved horses and was always eager to be around them. And while Ballard was too rugged-looking to be called handsome, Lucy might be taking an interest in him, too. She could do worse, the showman thought. At least he was not some fancy-pants Easterner.

That thought crossed his mind as Corrigan stepped into his wagon through the rear door. He reached for the door to pull it closed behind him, then suddenly stiffened as pain coursed through him. Sweat popped out on his forehead that had nothing to do with the still-hot air of the summer evening, and he fumbled with the door, managing to pull it shut. Staggering over to his bunk, he collapsed onto it, crossing his arms across his middle and hugging himself against the pain in his belly.

Not now! he thought bitterly. It had been months since he had had one of these spells, and this was not a good time for them to start again—not with everything he had to take care of. But for the moment, all he could do was lie there and wait for the pain to end . . . and pray that it would not come again anytime soon.

Nobody had asked Ballard to help out with the preparations for the Wild West show, but he had never been one just to sit around and take life easy, so he pitched in, giving the wranglers a hand with the horses, hammering together grandstands with the carpenters, and setting up tents with the roustabouts. He learned that few people with the show had just one job. Indians and phony cavalrymen who would be engaging in fierce battle once a performance got under way worked side by side building the seats. A roustabout who pounded tent stakes into the ground might put on a high-crowned hat and some fancy duds and become a trick roper. The troupe was like a family, Ballard discovered, with everybody working together to get ready in time.

After the grandstand was completed early on the morning of the second day, Ballard climbed into the seats to watch Lucy Corrigan practicing her act. She could do some amazing things on the back of a horse, from mounting and dismounting at a full gallop to riding underneath the animal's belly to balancing with her feet on the backs of two galloping ponies, Roman style. Ballard shook his head in admiration as he watched her going through her paces. He could believe what Jackrabbit Dawkins had said about Lucy's being able to ride before she could walk. It was not often you ran across a young lady who could ride like that—especially not one as pretty as Lucy Corrigan.

The rancher smiled at that thought. He wondered just how much Lucy's presence had influenced him into waiting around for the money that was owed him.

Later that afternoon, he strolled into the arena just as Jackrabbit was bringing the stagecoach through the big entrance on the far side. Several men were riding behind the coach, and Ballard assumed they were about to practice the mock holdup and chase that he had heard about from some of the wranglers. That was their big moment in the show; they got to play desperadoes, yelling and shooting off blanks as they pursued the stagecoach.

Ballard walked over to the railing that divided the arena from the first row of the stands and leaned against it. He wanted to see this.

After talking briefly to his companions and pointing out where all the turns would take place, Jackrabbit flicked the reins and started his team in motion. The group ran through the performance at a fairly slow speed, with the phony outlaws cantering along behind the stagecoach instead of galloping. The "lawmen" did not fire their guns during this rehearsal, either; blank black-powder cartridges cost money.

Once the routine was established, Jackrabbit led the men through it again, a little faster this time. Finally he paused and called out, "We'll do 'er one more time, fellers, and this time really let 'er rip!"

Rebel yells from several of the wranglers answered the old jehu, who was grinning as he sat down on the box and picked up a long whip from the seat beside him. Grasping the reins firmly, he used the other hand to pop the whip over the backs of the six-horse team. The animals plunged ahead, immediately breaking into a gallop.

Ballard pulled himself up and sat on top of the railing, well out of the way of the riders and the stagecoach as they circled the arena. Jackrabbit yelled and cracked the whip as he urged his team on to greater and greater speed, and the "outlaws" chasing him got into the spirit of the thing, whooping and shouting as they rode. Ballard found his own pulse beginning to pound, and he imagined the spectacle was even more exciting in front of a grandstand full of cheering people. He could almost hear the bang of the guns and smell the gun smoke.

Suddenly, as Jackrabbit reached the far end of the oval arena and jerked the stagecoach into the tight turn, something went wrong. Even as far away as he was, Ballard could hear the sharp cracking sound over the pounding of hooves. The coach began to tip over, and the oldster flew crazily through the air as he was flung from his perch on the box. Ballard lost sight of him in the cloud of dust that had been raised by the practice runs.

Pushing himself off the railing, the rancher landed running just as the stagecoach rolled over. He suspected an axle had snapped, breaking the tongue as well and freeing the horses from the careening vehicle. That was a stroke of luck, and so was the fact that no one had been riding inside the stagecoach. If the accident had happened during a regular performance instead of a rehearsal, the coach would have been full of phony passengers. As it was, Jackrabbit was the only one who might have been hurt in this incident.

Still Ballard was worried as he ran toward the scene of the wreck. He had not known Jackrabbit for long, but already he was fond of the colorful old man. The wranglers were shouting for help as they swung down from their saddles and raced toward where Jackrabbit lay sprawled in the dirt. To Ballard's relief, the jehu was sitting up by the time the rancher reached him. His Confederate cap was gone and his hair was sticking up wildly, but he did not seem to be seriously hurt. As the cowboys gathered around him, he snapped, "Back off, the lot of ya! Give a feller a chance to breathe!"

With Lucy behind him, Corrigan came running into the arena and rushed over to kneel beside his longtime friend. Lucy dropped to one knee on Jackrabbit's other side, an anxious look on her pretty face.

"What happened, Jackrabbit?" Corrigan asked. "Are you all right?"

"I'm fine, goldarnit! An axle snapped and tipped her over, is all. Busted the tongue when she went. She'll need some fresh paint here and there, and we'll have to replace that axle and the tongue, of course, but there ain't no reason she can't be ready to go tonight. Now, just let me get up on my feet."

Corrigan and Lucy stepped back as a couple of the wranglers grasped Jackrabbit's arms and lifted him to his feet as he had requested. He balanced there precariously on his high-heeled boots while he smacked his palms against his vest and shirt, raising small clouds of dust. Glancing around, he muttered, "Where's my cap?" then spotted it lying several feet away. He took a step toward it . . . and promptly folded up again as his right leg gave out.

"Dammit, Jackrabbit, you're hurt!" Corrigan cried as he leapt to catch the old man and lower him gently to the ground.

"Aw, shoot, it's just this here leg," the oldster protested, slapping his thigh and wincing. "It's a mite twisted, but it ain't nothin' a little rest won't fix."

"We'd better have a doctor look at it anyway," Corrigan stated.

"A sawbones won't tell you nothin' different."

"Maybe not, but there's no point in taking chances," Corrigan countered. "No matter what the doc says, one thing's sure already: You're not going to drive that stagecoach in the show tonight. We can patch *it* up in time, but not you."

"Blast it, Cactus, I said—"

"I know what you said," Corrigan cut in. "But I saw how that leg gave out on you." He shook his head. "I can't take a chance on you hurting yourself or somebody else even worse, Jackrabbit."

"But who's goin' to drive the stage?"

Corrigan looked up, his gaze darting around the circle of worried bystanders. His eyes reached Wes Ballard and stayed there. After a moment of intensely studying the young Texas rancher, Corrigan said, "I'm playing a hunch here, son, but can you handle a six-horse team?"

Ballard hesitated. He knew what Corrigan was about to ask him, and it already seemed as if he was more involved with this Wild West show than he had ever intended to be. But he finally nodded and said, "I reckon I can."

"Then how about taking Jackrabbit's place in the show?"

The jehu nodded enthusiastically. "I seen him watchin' us practice, Cactus, and I figure the boy can handle it."

When Ballard still did not answer, Corrigan asked, "Well, how about it?"

The more successful the show's run in the Kansas City area, Ballard realized, the sooner he would stand a chance of getting paid. Besides, he could see the same question in Lucy's eyes, and since he was already going to be waiting around for the next few days . . .

"All right," he said, hoping he was not making a terrible mistake. "I reckon you've got yourself another stagecoach driver."

Chapter Four

Wes Ballard had never seen so many people packed together in one place. Looking out at the hundreds of spectators in the arena as he stood next to the old stage-coach parked just outside the main entrance, he felt nervousness nibbling around at his insides. In a few minutes he would be driving the coach in there to begin his part in the performance.

Jackrabbit Dawkins limped up to him, using a cane to take most of the weight off his hurt leg. A doctor brought across the river from the Missouri side had diagnosed the injury as a severe sprain and advised that Jackrabbit stay off the leg for a few days. But since it was impossible to keep the old man in his bunk, Jackrabbit had compromised and promised to use the walking stick. Leaning on the cane, he used his free hand to slap Ballard on the arm. " 'Bout ready to go, are you?" he asked.

"I'm not sure," Ballard replied slowly. "There's a heap of folks out there."

A smile wreathed the old man's bearded face. "You're gettin' what they call stage fright, boy. Ain't nothin' to worry about. Ever'body gets it now and then, even folks what've been doin' this sort of thing for years."

Ballard shot him a glance. "Even Corrigan?"

"Even ol' Cactus hisself," Jackrabbit chortled.

That was hard to believe, Ballard thought. He had been watching the show since it had begun earlier, and Corrigan had seemed to be in complete control. The old scout had led the parade that opened the performance, resplendent in a big cream-colored hat, fringed buckskin jacket, tight brown pants, high black boots, and a hand-tooled leather cartridge belt that supported a brace of ivory-handled pistols in well-oiled holsters. Riding at the head of the procession of cowboys and Indians, Corrigan had waved his hat and smiled at the crowd, playing them like the expert showman he was. Watching him go through his paces, Ballard would have thought the man had ice water in his veins.

"He looks right at home out there," Ballard murmured as Corrigan introduced a team of trick ropers to the crowd.

"Maybe so, but I know for a fact that Cactus don't like all that fancy, flashy, phony cowboy stuff." Jackrabbit shrugged. "But he always says you got to give the audience what it wants, and folks want flash and glitter."

Ballard nodded. This Wild West show was a totally different world from the one he was accustomed to, and he could not expect to understand everything about it, at least not right away. Not that it mattered whether he understood or not. In what he hoped was just a few days, he would have the money that was owed him and would be on his way back to Texas.

"You'll be on soon as the trick ropin's over," Jackrabbit reminded him, breaking into his reverie. "Just remember not to try to take the turns too fast." He patted the wood of the coach's door. "This ol' gal's mighty dependable, if you don't ask her to do too much."

Once again Ballard nodded. He had watched as the broken axle and tongue were replaced on the stagecoach, and he was sure that everything was back in good working order. However, with his inexperience, he would take the routine a bit easier than the old driver normally did. The spectators would never know the difference.

Four men and two women, all dressed in the frontier fashions of thirty years earlier, stepped to the coach. One of the men asked Ballard, "Are we about ready to go?"

"Just a few more minutes," the Texan replied. "You folks can go ahead and get on board."

The passengers nodded and climbed into the coach, taking their usual places. All six of them were actors, and in addition the women were seamstresses and the men performed various other chores, doubling up on their jobs like practically every other member of the troupe. Now, for a brief time, they were performers, enjoying the attention and the applause of the crowd.

The spectators were now clapping heartily following the conclusion of the trick-roping act. The two cowboys who made their lassos dance came running out of the arena, waving to the crowd as they departed. After they were out, Corrigan rode the big palomino he used as his personal mount to the center of the arena. Lifting his voice, he announced, "And now, ladies and gentlemen, Cactus Corrigan's Great Wild West brings you the vehicle that really won the West, the magic carpet, if you will, that provided transportation all across this great land—the stagecoach!"

"You're on, boy!" Jackrabbit said urgently, and Ballard cursed himself for letting his attention get caught up in what Corrigan was saying. He had almost missed his cue. Vaulting onto the box, he settled down on the driver's seat and snatched up the lines with one hand while releasing the brake with the other. The well-trained team responded instantly when he flicked the reins, and the coach rolled through the entrance into the arena.

The arena had been cleared and leveled with sand, and then the sand had been packed down as much as possible. That made for a fairly smooth surface, and Ballard had no trouble controlling the coach. Swinging to the right, he followed the perimeter of the oval, keeping close to the grandstand so that the audience could get a good look at the coach. The passengers grinned and waved at the spectators, who responded with cheers and applause.

These were people eager for entertainment, Ballard realized. Even with a rival Wild West show in the area, they had packed the stands, and it was likely that many of them would come back to watch more than one performance. Opportunities for entertainment and diversion were more plentiful than they had been in the days when Kansas City was on the edge of the frontier, but shows like this were still not so common that one could be ignored. Using a term that Ballard had heard some members of the troupe bandying about, the show was a "hit."

He had completed one circuit of the arena when Corrigan, his voice carrying with practiced ease to every corner of the grandstand, went on, "A trip by stagecoach was not always such a serene journey, however. Sometimes there was danger! A coach might be attacked by road agents!"

Ballard had just passed the entrance when over the sound of the coach's wheels he heard hoofbeats, yells, and then the explosions of blank cartridges. The "desperadoes" had appeared for the mock holdup. Acting as he thought a real stage driver would, he cast a fearful look over his shoulder at the charging riders and then frantically whipped the team into a run. The coach began to bounce and sway more as it picked up speed. The phony outlaws, wearing long dusters and colorful bandannas tied over the lower halves of their faces, closed in, yelling and shooting.

The chase led twice around the arena, and with each circuit the cheering from the audience got louder. Ballard risked a glance at the grandstand and saw that many of the crowd were on their feet, caught up in the make-believe drama and exhorting the stage to get away. Close behind him, he heard the cracks of pistol shots from the passengers inside the vehicle as they tried to fight off the robbers.

He tried not to grin as he felt the excitement of the moment gripping him as well. Maybe this was not the real thing, but that just made it better. The performance made people *feel* as though it were real, without the actual danger that would have existed in such a situation.

Ballard took the coach through a series of sharp turns, trying to throw off the pursuit. The curves were not as sharp nor taken as fast as the ones Jackrabbit had been practicing that afternoon, but they were thrilling enough for the spectators—and for Ballard, too. His pulse was pounding from more than the exertion required to control the team.

Another group of riders suddenly galloped into the arena, and Cactus Corrigan shouted, "But then the lawmen arrived, bringing six-gun justice to no-good owlhoots!"

Ballard slowed the coach slightly and looked back to watch the running gunfight. More shots blared as the posse closed in on the outlaws, "shooting" several of them out of their saddles. The supposedly wounded bandits took some spectacular falls as they left their horses, and the Texan knew they had to practice for long hours to be able to do such things without killing themselves or, at the very least, breaking every bone in their bodies.

It did not take long for the posse to take care of the outlaws, and when the shooting was over, Corrigan called out, "And so the stagecoach went on its way in peace, bringing progress to the West!" That was Ballard's cue to head for the entrance again, and as he drove out he plucked his hat from his head and waved it at the crowd. The action was impulsive, and the audience seemed to like it.

He piloted the coach out of the arena and turned left toward the group of parked wagons. Spotting Jackrabbit waiting up ahead, Ballard brought the stagecoach to a halt and dropped down off the box.

"How was it?" he asked as his feet hit the ground.

Jackrabbit grinned at him. "Looks like the performin' bug done bit you, son. You did good, mighty good."

"Don't get the wrong idea," Ballard said with a shake of his head. "I wouldn't want to do this all the time. I'm just interested in getting paid for those horses I brought up here to Corrigan. But"—he grinned back—"I reckon it *was* a little more enjoyable than I expected."

From behind him a female voice asked, "Would you care to elaborate on that, Mr. Ballard?"

Ballard stiffened in surprise. He turned around slowly and found an attractive young woman watching him with an intent gaze. She was wearing a stylish dark blue dress, and a neat hat of the same shade was perched atop a mass of upswept raven hair. Her dark eyes regarded him intelligently, and her beauty would have been striking had she not been wearing such a solemn expression on her face.

Frowning, Ballard asked, "What did you say, miss?"

"I asked if you'd care to elaborate on your feelings, now that you've become a part of this Wild West show. I know that you're not the regular stagecoach driver, so I asked around and found out some information about you." She took a small notebook from her purse and glanced at it. "Your name is Wes Ballard, you're from Texas, and you're normally a horse rancher. You were pressed into service when Mr. Dawkins here was injured this afternoon. How do you like it? Are you going to continue with the show?"

Ballard's frown deepened. "Pardon me, ma'am," he said slowly. "But just who are you, and why are you asking all these questions?"

She snapped her notebook closed and held out a hand to him. "Morgan Dixon," she introduced herself. "I'm a journalist. I write for the Kansas City *Clarion*."

"Newspaper reporter, huh?" Ballard grunted, shaking her hand. Her grip was firm and cool, as he would have expected from looking at her.

"I prefer to call myself a journalist," she responded, her tone a little sharper now. "I'm doing a series of stories on Mr. Corrigan's Wild West show, and I'd like to begin my accounts with you."

Ballard shook his head. "You already know I'm not one of the regular members of the troupe, so there's no point in writing about me, since I'll only be here a day or two. Maybe you'd better just go talk to Corrigan when the show's over. I expect he can tell you anything you want to know."

"But it would be much more interesting to get your point of view, Mr. Ballard," the journalist insisted. "You're an outsider, and I'd like to know what the world of a Wild West show looks like to such a man."

"Not interested," Ballard said, his tone short. It was bad enough his plans had been delayed without making things worse by adding a lot of publicity about him. Being a part of the show had turned out to be more enjoyable than he had expected, but that was none of Morgan Dixon's business.

"I'd be right happy to talk to you, ma'am," Jackrabbit spoke up, hurriedly tugging the Confederate cap off his unruly mop of white hair. "I'm Jackrabbit Dawkins, the rootin'est, tootin'est hombre you'd ever want to meet, and I can tell you some stories that'll curl your hair—not that it ain't mighty purty the way it is right now, ma'am."

"Thank you, Mr. Dawkins, but I'm really more interested—" Morgan broke off as she turned to look for Ballard again.

But Ballard was striding away into the night.

Drifting into the grandstand late in the performance, the tall buckskin-clad young man with wavy long blond hair drew a few curious stares as he and several companions made their way to some vacant seats, but the attention did not bother him. Brian Nichols was used to drawing a lot of attention as a featured attraction in the Yakima Kid's Ace-High Pioneer Exposition and Wild West. A trick-shot and fast-draw artist par excellence, Brian regularly drew the cheers and applause of audiences with his talents. At the moment, though, his guns were back at the Kid's camp, and Brian was not interested in anything except watching what remained of Cactus Corrigan's show.

The evening's performance of Travers's troupe was already over, and Brian had been more than willing to go along when somebody suggested that they check out the rival show. Half a dozen members of the Kid's outfit, including Brian and the head wrangler, Quint Fowler, had come, and they settled down in the seats they had found just as the stagecoach was rolling out of the arena. A moment later, Corrigan introduced his daughter, who he claimed would startle and amaze the audience with her trick riding.

Brian pushed back his wide-brimmed brown hat, letting it fall so that it was held behind his head by the leather thong around his throat. He watched as Lucy rode out into the arena on a magnificent black horse and cantered around next to the grandstand before starting her act.

"My God, she's lovely," Brian breathed as the young woman passed closely beneath his position. In her short skirt, beaded and fringed jacket, and snowy hat, she was a vision.

"Damn right," Quint Fowler agreed from his seat beside Brian. "One thing you can say for Corrigan—he's got a mighty pretty daughter."

Brian watched raptly as the surprisingly agile and athletic Lucy began performing some stunts on horseback that Nichols would have thought impossible even for seasoned cowboys. With his attention centered on Lucy Corrigan, he was not aware at first that one of his companions had pulled out a flask and was passing it around. But gradually the wranglers became so raucous that even he noticed.

Frowning, the blond young man said to Fowler, "I don't know if that's a good idea, Quint. We didn't come over here to get liquored up."

"Maybe you didn't, kid," Fowler replied, tipping the flask to his lips and taking a swig of whiskey, "but the rest of us came to have a good time." Grimacing, he replaced the cork in the flask. "Reckon you're right, though. We don't want to get booted out of here."

The other cowboys protested loudly, but Fowler shook his head and tucked the liquor away inside his shirt. "Just settle down and watch the show," he told them sharply.

Denied the whiskey, the group calmed down somewhat, although several of them were still muttering complaints when the performance ended a short while later. Brian stood as the audience got to its feet to leave, and turning to Fowler, he asked, "What did you think?"

The wrangler shrugged. "We didn't see enough of the show to tell, but it looks like Corrigan's bunch does a pretty good job—and that trick-ridin' gal's mighty fine."

"She sure is," Brian agreed. "I'm going to see if I can find her and tell her how much I enjoyed her act."

Fowler's heavy brows pulled together in surprise and bafflement. "Don't know if I'd do that, boy," he advised. "Corrigan's not very fond of anybody who works for Travers."

"I don't care," the sharpshooter replied with a shake of his head. "It's none of Corrigan's business if I want to pay a compliment to his daughter."

Fowler looked dubious but did not say anything else.

Instead of turning to the right with the rest of the crowd leaving the grandstand, Brian headed left, toward the area where the troupe's wagons were located. Spotting Corrigan's wagon in the light from the torches and lanterns scattered through the vicinity, he strode up to the vehicle and knocked boldly on the rear door.

It opened after a moment, and Lucy Corrigan peeked out, still wearing the outfit she had worn during her act. She had removed her hat, which was the only difference, but it was an important one, because it allowed her lustrous blond hair to fall freely around her shoulders.

"Yes?" she asked when Brian did not say anything.

He realized he was standing there and staring dumbly at her beauty. Licking his lips nervously, he managed to say, "I'm sorry, ma'am. Didn't mean to disturb you, but I wanted to tell you I thought your riding was fine, just fine."

He was babbling like a fool, he thought, but Lucy did not seem to mind. She smiled and said, "Why, thank you. I'm always glad to know that the audience enjoys my work."

"Yes, ma'am, all of us surely did."

Surprisingly, she came down the two steps from the door of the wagon to the ground and looked up at him. She was fairly tall for a woman, but he still towered over her. Assessing him, she told him, "You look like a horseman. I especially appreciate compliments from someone who knows what he's talking about."

"Well, I can ride all right, I suppose, but nothing like you. I never saw anybody who can do the things that you did tonight."

She studied him, frowning slightly in thought. "You look familiar, Mr. . . ."

"Nichols, ma'am, Brian Nichols."

"Have we met before?"

Brian shook his head and felt himself growing more nervous. Although he had not taken part in the brawl between Corrigan's men and several members of the Kid's troupe a few nights earlier, he had been there when the fight started, and Lucy might remember him from that. He wondered if she would still be so nice to him if she knew he worked for John Travers.

She gave a tiny shake of her head and smiled at him. "I don't suppose it matters. Thank you for coming back here to tell me you enjoyed the show, Mr. Nichols. That means a great deal to me. And would you do something else for me?"

"Anything, ma'am," he said sincerely.

"Well, first of all, you can stop calling me ma'am and start calling me Lucy." Her smile was dazzling now, and he could see definite sparks of interest and attraction in her eyes. "The second thing is to promise me that you'll tell all your friends about the show. To be honest, we need the business."

She was unwittingly putting him in a bad position. But he was so overwhelmed by the power of her smile that he said, "Sure, ma'am—I mean, Lucy. I'll do that."

Jackrabbit Dawkins found Wes Ballard checking on the horses, and the young rancher dryly asked, "Did you fill that reporter's head full of stories?"

"Naw, she weren't that interested. But if'n you ask me, she was a mite taken with you, son."

"Nobody asked you," Ballard grunted. He turned away from the corral and strolled toward the wagons, Jackrabbit falling in step alongside him. Slowing his pace to allow the old man to keep up on his bad leg, the Texan stopped abruptly after a few moments and asked, "Who's that talking to Miss Corrigan?"

"Great jumpin' Jehosaphat!" Jackrabbit exclaimed. "I seen that feller the other night. He's part of the Yakima Kid's outfit!"

Ballard felt unaccountably angry. Lucy seemed to be chatting pleasantly with the long-haired stranger, so she must not have been aware that he was from the enemy camp. Over the last couple of days Ballard had heard a great deal about the rivalry between Corrigan and Travers, and he could not imagine Lucy being so nice to the buckskin-clad man unless she was ignorant of his identity.

"Come on," he told the old man tightly. "We'd better go put a stop to this." Ballard walked briskly to where Lucy and the man stood, this time not waiting for Jackrabbit to keep up. "Pardon me, Miss Corrigan," Ballard said as he stepped behind the stranger.

The blond-haired man turned around and nervously looked at Ballard.

"What is it, Mr. Ballard?" Lucy asked.

Jackrabbit was moving up beside Ballard as he jerked

his head toward the stranger and remarked, "Jackrabbit and I were just wondering, Miss Corrigan, if you knew you were being so friendly to somebody who works for the Yakima Kid?"

After putting the question to Lucy, Ballard wondered fleetingly why he was getting himself involved in this. It was none of his business whom Lucy Corrigan talked to . . . was it?

But he felt good when her expression turned cold and angry and she demanded of the man, "Is what Mr. Ballard says true, Mr. Nichols?"

The blond man shot a furious glance toward Ballard, then turned back to the woman and told her, "I meant what I said, Lucy. I think you were wonderful—"

"It's Miss Corrigan," Lucy shot back. "And you didn't answer my question."

The man called Nichols flushed. "Yes, I work for John Travers. But that doesn't mean—"

"It means you don't have any business around here," Ballard stated coldly. "You'd better get moving, mister."

"Who's going to make him?" another man asked roughly as he emerged from the shadows nearby. Several other men were with him, and all of them wore cowboy garb.

"Stay out of this, Luke," Nichols snapped. To one of the other men he added, "Quint, you and the boys don't have to get mixed up in this."

The one called Quint said, "If this yahoo is givin' you trouble, Brian, then we're already mixed up in it. We're your pards, and we're not goin' to let Corrigan's flunkies shove you around."

Ballard's hands balled into fists as he glared at Quint. The odds were six to one against him—Jackrabbit could not be counted on for any help in the shape he was in—but the Texan had never been one for backing down. "If you're looking for a fight, mister, you've come to the right place."

"Nobody's looking for a fight—" Brian began.

"Maybe *you* ain't, Nichols," Quint countered, his stance challenging, "but it'd please me just fine to take this guy down a peg or two."

"Please, all of you!" Lucy interrupted hurriedly. "There's no need for violence!"

Nonetheless, violence seemed about to happen, for the air was charged with it. Then, suddenly, Earl Corrigan's voice crackled in the night as he demanded, "What's going on here?"

Corrigan strode out of the shadows, several of his men with him. *This evens the odds,* Ballard thought grimly.

But Lucy stepped forward, putting herself squarely between the two groups. "It's nothing important, Father," she said firmly. "Just a slight disagreement, and it's all over now." She looked meaningfully at Brian. "Isn't it?"

The tall young man in buckskins heaved a sigh. "Yes, I think it is." Turning to his cohort, he barked in a commanding tone, "Come on, Quint. Let's get out of here."

"You sure that's what you want, kid?" Quint asked.

"I'm sure," Brian asserted, nodding. He cast one more look at Lucy, then turned and strode away. Grudgingly his companions followed.

Corrigan turned to Lucy. "That was some of Travers's bunch, wasn't it?" His tone was vaguely accusatory.

Lucy obviously heard the censure and bristled. "What if it was? Mr. Nichols was just being polite and telling me that he enjoyed my riding."

"You can't trust any of those snakes who work for Travers, gal. You ought to know that by now."

"I know that Mr. Ballard here had no business sticking his nose into things," Lucy replied, swinging her angry gaze toward the rancher.

Ballard was taken aback by her response. "I was just trying to help!" he protested.

"By starting a fight?" Lucy countered. "Thank you for your concern, Mr. Ballard, but I can take care of myself. I've been doing just that for a long time!"

The Texan's mouth tightened into a taut line, and he shrugged. "If that's the way you want it, Miss Corrigan. . . . Sorry I offended you. That wasn't my intention."

Lucy's expression softened a little. She started to reach out toward him, then stopped. "I . . . I didn't mean to sound so harsh. . . ."

"No problem, ma'am," Ballard told her. He nodded to her, then to Corrigan. "Looks like the show's over in more ways than one, so I'll say good night, folks."

He turned and walked away before either of them could stop him. A jumble of thoughts crowded his mind. Obviously Lucy had resented his meddling in what she considered her business—and he wondered if, despite her anger, she was still interested in the blond man.

Brian Nichols and his friends did not have too big a head start, Ballard thought. Maybe what he needed to do was catch up to them and make sure the young man understood he was not to bother Lucy again.

Striding toward the corral, the Texan mused that it might be a mistake, but he was going after Brian Nichols to continue the discussion that had been interrupted. And if it *was* a mistake, it would surely not be the first one he had ever made.

Chapter Five

Brian Nichols tossed back the drink, then set the empty glass on the scarred table in front of him. Wiping the back of his hand across his mouth, he shook his head. "I guess it was a mistake to go see her in the first place."

Quint Fowler tipped the bottle of amber liquid, splashing more of the whiskey into Brian's glass. "She's a mighty pretty girl. Nobody could blame you, kid. It's just a damned shame she's Corrigan's daughter."

Nodding, Brian picked up the refilled drink. "Yeah," he agreed. "A damn shame."

He and Fowler were sitting in a saloon called Red Mike's, a tough waterfront tavern near the Missouri River. The bar was nothing but a broad plank laid across several whiskey barrels, the floor was thickly covered with sawdust, and the smoky air was dimly lit by a couple of lanterns. Brian, Fowler, and the other men had gone back across the river on the ferry, which ran night and day. Fowler had suggested stopping for one last drink, and while the others had begged off, saying they wanted to return to Travers's camp, Brian had taken him up on it, since he was still smarting from the angry words that Lucy had lashed him with.

"Uh-oh," Fowler suddenly cautioned in a low voice.

Brian glanced up, a bit light-headed from the whiskey he had consumed. "What is it?" he asked.

"Take a look at who just came in."

Turning his gaze toward the doorway, Brian saw Corrigan's grim-faced stagecoach driver—Ballard, that was his name—striding boldly into Red Mike's. The man stood

49

searching the room until he found the corner table where Brian and Fowler were sitting. Then he squared his shoulders and came toward them.

"Looks like he wants more trouble," Fowler remarked softly.

"Well, if he does, I can give it to him," Brian declared, lurching only slightly as he got to his feet. Facing the Texan as he approached the table, Brian asked sharply, "What the hell do *you* want?"

Ballard glanced around and said with contempt, "I trailed you over here to this dive, Nichols, because I wasn't finished talking to you." He looked at Fowler for a moment before asking, "Where're the rest of your friends?"

"They've gone back to camp," Brian answered. "But that doesn't matter. Your business is with me."

Ballard took a deep breath. "Yeah, my business is with you. Stay the hell away from Lucy Corrigan."

"All I did was compliment her on her riding," Brian said truculently. "There's nothing wrong with that."

"Sure," Ballard scoffed. His tone made it clear that he did not believe Brian for a second.

"You think I could be interested in a girl like that?" Brian retorted, laughing harshly. "Don't be a fool, mister. There're hundreds of girls I could have, just for the asking."

Brian knew that was the truth, for his good looks and his involvement with the Wild West show charmed just about every female he came in contact with. He had turned down more than one subtle proposition from a star-struck young beauty—though some of the propositions were not so subtle. And some of them he had not turned down.

But even as he denied having any romantic interest in Lucy Corrigan, he knew he was lying. Her smile had struck him a different sort of blow from any he had ever encountered before, sort of like a sledgehammer in the belly. Maybe that was what they called love at first sight.

"I just don't want you bothering her anymore," Ballard was saying.

Stubbornness and pride made Brian respond, "She didn't seem bothered to me—at least not until you came barging in. Did the lady seem bothered to you, Quint?" In his slightly drunken state, Brian had forgotten that Fowler had not witnessed the beginning of his conversation with Lucy.

Or maybe the wrangler had, because he confirmed, "No, she didn't seem to mind talkin' to you at all."

"In fact," the sharpshooter went on, resting his palms on the table and leaning forward, glaring at Ballard, "I don't mind saying she's a beautiful girl, and if I want to pay court to her, that's damned well what I'm going to do."

Stiffening, Ballard cautioned, "You do something foolish like that, and there'll be trouble."

"You tellin' my friend what to do?" Fowler demanded.

"Yeah," Ballard said slowly. "Maybe I am."

Brian felt a fresh surge of anger. He said, "Well, maybe I'd better teach you a lesson right now—"

His fist was moving before the words were out of his mouth. But he realized he must have telegraphed the blow, because Ballard dodged smoothly aside, letting Brian's punch go harmlessly past his head. While the younger man was off balance, Ballard stepped around the table and hit him twice in the stomach, hard.

The blows doubled Brian over, but only momentarily. With a roar of rage, he swung wildly at his opponent's head. Brian was fast for a big man, and Ballard was unable to avoid the punch completely. Knuckles scraped his jaw, staggering him.

Grasping the table, the sharpshooter flung it aside, his anger giving him strength. As the furniture went flying, some of Red Mike's customers scurried for cover. Others, long accustomed to brawls there, just looked bored and kept drinking.

Ballard got his hands up in time to block the next set of punches and snap a stinging jab into Brian's face. Stepping back and shaking his head, Brian was amazed at how hard the Texan could hit. But knowing he had the advantage in both height and weight, he figured it was only a matter of time until he crushed his opponent.

Then a blow exploded on his chin, driving him back another step. Ballard was on him like a whirlwind, driving short, brutal punches into his face, chest, and midsection. Surprised, Brian retreated before the onslaught.

He shouted again and flung a careless backhand at his adversary. The blow was not aimed, but it landed anyway, and the impact whipped Ballard's head around and sent the black hat flying from his head. Brian followed it up with a looping right to the solar plexus.

Some of the bar's patrons were crowding around now, shouting encouragement to the two combatants. Ignoring them, the sharpshooter lunged toward Ballard as the Texan stumbled backward and fought to keep his balance.

Just before Brian could wrap his arms around Ballard in a deadly bear hug, the rancher reached up and caught hold of the front of the younger man's shirt. Ballard then let himself fall, hauling Brian around as he twisted sideways. The momentum was too much for Brian to stop, and he found himself flying through the air, then crashing onto a table where a poker game was in progress, scattering beer and cards and money as the table collapsed.

The wind knocked out of him, Brian lay in the wreckage for a moment, trying to catch his breath. He glanced up and saw Ballard standing a few feet away, fists clenched, black hair disheveled, and a trickle of blood coming from the corner of his mouth. But Ballard was on his feet, waiting, and Brian was sprawled on the floor. That thought gave the sharpshooter a new surge of energy, and he rose and threw himself forward, tackling Ballard around the thighs.

Both of them went down, rolling around and knocking chairs out of their way as they grappled. Brian wound up on top, sitting astride the rancher, and he pounded a couple of punches down into the Texan's face, then lifted his right hand for another blow.

Somebody pressed something into that hand. Brian started to swing it, stopping short as he realized he was holding a beer mug. If he smashed the heavy mug into Ballard's face, the blow might well kill him—and Brian had never intended to kill anybody.

The hesitation gave Ballard a chance to recover, and he punched his opponent in the throat, a knuckle driving into the Adam's apple. Dislodged from his position by the blow, Brian toppled to the side, dropping the mug and clutching at his throat as he fell.

Despite his pain, he had the presence of mind to reach out and grab one of Ballard's legs as the Texan scrambled to his feet. He yanked it hard, and the Texan fell again, landing heavily on his rear end. Brian hammered a couple of punches into Ballard's side. The rancher tried to roll away, but Brian caught his shirt collar and held him.

Ballard twisted, writhing around until he launched a kick that slammed into his opponent's chest. That knocked Brian's grip loose, and the Texan was able to put some distance between them this time. He grabbed a table and hauled himself to his feet, and Brian managed to stand a few seconds later.

The men faced each other over about ten feet of empty space. The floor at their feet was dotted with bloodstains, some from Brian's nose and some from Ballard's several cuts and scrapes. Both of them swayed slightly as they drew in deep lungfuls of air.

Brian had only enough strength for one more punch, and he could tell that the black-haired man was in much the same shape. The next blow to hit its target, no matter who landed it, would probably end the fight—and Brian intended to be the winner.

He leapt at Ballard, feinting slightly with his left and then sending a right at the Texan's head. Ballard threw a desperate punch of his own . . .

. . . and both of them missed.

Off-balance, they bumped shoulders and fell. Lying where he landed, breathing heavily, Brian knew there was no way he could get up, no way he could defend himself. If Ballard wanted to continue the fight, he could not stop him.

But as he pushed himself into a sitting position, Brian saw that the Texan was just as bad off. Ballard got a hand under himself, pushed up, but slipped slightly, then managed to lift himself a little more. He said thickly between bruised lips, "You . . . had enough . . . Nichols?"

"What about . . . you?" Brian replied, having to drag the words out. Every muscle in his body was screaming.

"Reckon . . . reckon it's a draw," Ballard rasped.

Brian found himself nodding. "A draw," he agreed.

The spectators who had been avidly watching the battle began to turn away, sensing that the fight was over. Quint Fowler stepped up, grinning, and righted the overturned table where he and Brian had been sitting. "Quite a fracas," he said to them. "I'd almost pay to watch you two go at it again."

Ballard shook his head and climbed to his feet, wincing with pain as he did so. "Not going to be anytime soon," he declared.

"That's right," Brian concurred. He got up, then bent over to retrieve Ballard's hat, which was covered with sawdust and stomped out of shape. He grimaced as he handed it to the rancher. "Sorry about your sombrero."

Ballard batted the hat against his leg to knock off some of the sawdust, then punched it back into shape. "*De nada,*" he said. "It's seen worse treatment." He winced again as he settled the headgear on his skull.

Surprisingly enough, Brian's head was clearer now than before the fight. He waved toward the table and suggested, "Why don't you sit down and have a drink with us, Ballard?"

The rancher hesitated for a moment, then nodded and said, "Don't mind if I do."

Fowler still had the bottle, and as the three men sat down, he signaled for the bartender to bring fresh glasses. The man came over to the table a moment later, and his thatch of fiery hair and equally blazing mustache left no doubt that he was the proprietor, Red Mike. He held three glasses in a huge hand, but before he placed them on the table, he said, "There's a little matter of damages to be taken care of, laddies. I don't mind you settlin' your differences in my place, but you got to pay for what you break."

"Sure," Brian responded, digging into his pocket and tossing a couple of bills on the table. He was reaching for more when Ballard stopped him.

"I'll pay my part, too," the rancher insisted, dropping several gold coins on top of the bills. "That cover it?"

"Aye," Red Mike said, nodding and giving them the

glasses, then scooping up the money. "Drink up, gentlemen."

Fowler poured for the three of them, and Brian lifted his glass. "To a good fight," he toasted Ballard, looking at the Texan over the whiskey.

"A good fight," Ballard agreed with a nod, then tossed back the drink.

Brian regarded the black-haired man. He did not consider Ballard his friend now—far from it, in fact—but the fight had changed things, and he could not deny that he felt a grudging admiration and respect for the man. He asked, "How'd you learn to fight like that?"

"We've got a few saloons in Texas, too, you know," Ballard said dryly. "And I've been in some bunkhouse brawls that would put this one to shame. Although you held your own pretty good." There was respect in Ballard's voice.

Fowler sipped his drink and leaned forward. "I've heard about you, Ballard, and about those horses you brought up from Texas. Mighty bad luck the way it turned out."

Ballard shrugged. "I'll get my money, don't worry."

"How? By waitin' around until Corrigan can pay you?" Fowler's short, derisive laugh was more of a bark. "You may have a long wait." The wrangler's tone became more persuasive as he went on, "Listen, Ballard, the Kid's troupe has been traveling quite a bit, too, and we need fresh mounts the same as Corrigan. How about I buy that herd from you on behalf of Travers? I'll give you a good price."

As Ballard frowned in thought, Brian remembered now hearing some discussion about the Texan's dilemma. Selling the mounts to Travers seemed to the sharpshooter like the ideal solution.

"I don't mind telling you I'm tempted by the offer," Ballard replied after a moment. "I'm a little cash poor right now, 'cause it took nearly all I had to pay off my drovers." He shook his head. "But I can't do it, mister. I gave my word to Corrigan that I'd drive that stagecoach for him until Dawkins can handle the job again. Besides, I've seen for myself now that Corrigan puts on a good show. Folks'll come to see it. It may take a while, but I figure I'll get my money."

Fowler shrugged, taking Ballard's decision in stride. "It's up to you. If that's what you want to do, I won't try to talk you out of it."

"Thanks," Ballard stated. "I appreciate that. And I appreciate the offer."

"Sure." Fowler pushed his chair back. "Well, I may not have waltzed around like you boys did, but I'm still tired. Reckon I'll head back to camp. You comin', Brian?"

"In a few minutes," the young man said. "Don't worry, Quint. I can find my way back."

Fowler nodded, raised a finger to his hat brim, and went out of the tavern, leaving Brian and Ballard facing each other across the table. Turning his glass around idly in his fingers, Brian asked, "Was there anything else you wanted to say to me, Ballard?"

The Texan shook his head. "Nope. I reckon we understand each other."

"I suppose so," the sharpshooter agreed with a nod, well aware that there could be more trouble between the two of them in the future. For starters, he intended to see Lucy Corrigan again. Their conversation had ended too abruptly and too badly for Brian to leave things as they stood. And Ballard had to know what he was thinking. But for the time being, they were both just too blasted tired to do anything except continue the truce.

Each of them had another drink in companionable silence, then Ballard announced, "I'd better be getting back."

"I'll stay and settle up with Red Mike for the booze," Brian remarked.

"I'll pay for my share," Ballard said, but Brian waved off the suggestion.

"It's on me," he insisted. "Come on, Ballard. We don't want to start slugging each other again over something as stupid as this, do we?"

Ballard grinned. "No, I reckon we don't. Thanks for the drinks."

"You're welcome."

Ballard walked to the door and pushed through the

batwings, vanishing into the night. It had been quite an
evening, Brian thought as he climbed slowly to his feet
and started toward the bar. Several surprising things had
happened, from his reaction to Lucy Corrigan to the battle
with Wes Ballard.

Too many evenings like this, Brian thought wryly,
would just about be the death of him.

Wes Ballard paused outside Red Mike's and suppressed a groan. He did not know what part Brian Nichols
played in the Yakima Kid's show, but the youngster could
certainly hit. Brian felt as though he had been kicked all
over by a mule.

And speaking of beasts of burden, where had he left
his horse? With a frown he looked up and down the
narrow waterfront street. He would have sworn he had
left his mount tied to a hitch rail in front of the saloon, but
it was not there now. In fact, the horse was not anywhere
in sight.

Ballard cursed bitterly under his breath. After everything else that had happened tonight, being victimized by
a horse thief would be the last straw. Suddenly he heard a
faint whinny from up the street and he started walking
toward the sound, hoping his horse had simply jerked its
reins loose and wandered off.

He was passing the mouth of an alley about a block
away from the tavern when someone reached out of
the shadows and grabbed him. Ballard was not expecting the
assault, and the attacker was able to yank him into the
blackness of the alley before he could set himself and fight
back. Then something slammed against the side of his
head.

As Ballard fell to one knee, the thought raced through
his brain that he had been set up by riverfront thugs out
to rob him. Well, they would not find much, since he only
had a few coins left—not that he was going to let these
men get their grubby paws on that.

Ignoring the pain in his head, he reared up and
lashed out at the sound of footsteps. His fist sank into a
soft belly, and breath that reeked of whiskey was expelled
into his face. Someone grabbed his shoulder from behind,

but Ballard drove his elbow back into his assailant's torso. Spinning around, he looped a left punch into the shadows.

It connected, the impact sending a satisfactory shiver up Ballard's arm. But before he could strike another blow, more arms wrapped around him from behind, pinning his own. A man ordered, "Hang on to the bastard!"

Another man giggled, a deranged sound. "Hit him, Mace! Hit him!"

A fist smashed into Ballard's face, driving his head to the side. More blows rained across his body, and coming on top of the damage that had already been done in the fight with Brian, these punches made agony explode all through him. Slowly, though, he began to go numb as the men kept hitting him, and he realized that none of them had gone for his money yet. They seemed more concerned with dealing out misery to him.

Just then he knew with chilling clarity that they intended to beat him to death.

That thought made a burst of desperate strength surge through him, but it was not enough to shake himself out of their grip. Soon he would pass out, and then he would die here in this filthy alley, far from the high blue skies and beautiful open ranges of his home in Texas.

One of the men let out a yelp of pain and surprise, and then there was a sound like something being thrown against a wall. Ballard heard the thud of fists on flesh, and abruptly he was free, his attackers' cruel grip releasing his body. He staggered, almost falling before he put out a hand and caught himself against the brick wall of a building. He heard more cries and more blows, and he twisted his head around in an attempt to see what was happening.

Ballard's eyes had adjusted somewhat to the darkness, and he could see the looming shape of a man against the dim light from the street. The tall stranger wore a broad-brimmed hat and lashed out left and right, driving back the assailants. A punch sent one of the thugs in Ballard's direction, and the Texan was ready for him. Setting his feet, he grabbed the man's coat and smashed him face first into the wall. As the man fell limply from Ballard's grasp, another member of the gang tried to run past. But a booted foot thrust between his calves sent him sprawling, and Ballard pounced on him, lacing his fingers together and clubbing his hands down on the back of the fallen man's neck. Maybe such tactics were not very fair, Ballard thought fleetingly, but considering that these men had just tried to kill him, the hell with fairness!

Someone grasped his arm, and he started to whirl around, cocking a fist. A familiar voice said sharply, "Hold it, Ballard! It's me! The rest of them are either out cold or long gone."

"Nichols?" Ballard gasped in surprise. "What are *you* doing here?"

"Saving your bacon, from the looks of things. And if you're as tired as I am, we'd better get out of here before any of these gents come to. If I hadn't taken them by surprise, they might have done us both in."

With Brian Nichols beside him, Ballard hurried back to the street. "They were trying to kill me, you know."

"I thought that's what the commotion coming from that alley sounded like," Brian agreed. "Didn't know it was you on the receiving end until I'd already pitched in to help."

"Or you might have walked on?" Ballard asked sharply as they headed back toward Red Mike's.

"I didn't say that. You're mighty touchy, Ballard—but then, I'd heard that about you Texans."

The rancher chuckled grimly. "Sorry. I appreciate the help. Reckon you're not a bad sort, even if you do work for Travers."

"Thanks," Brian said dryly. "Where's your horse?"

Ballard shook his head, which made his skull ring. Wincing, he replied, "I don't know. I thought he'd wandered off or been stolen, but maybe those fellas took him to put me on foot so they could jump me."

"Sounds reasonable," Brian agreed, nodding. He turned to a horse at the hitch rail. "Come on. We can ride double while we try to scout up your mount."

"What if those river rats come after us again?"

Brian swung up into the saddle and patted his horse. "They won't be able to catch this beauty, even carrying double."

Ballard nodded and climbed on the animal's back,

perching behind the saddle. It was an uncomfortable position, mainly because he had to hang on to Brian to keep from falling off. The sharpshooter did not seem to care for it either, and he sounded greatly relieved when they located Ballard's horse behind an abandoned store a block away from the alley.

"They stashed the horse back here, I reckon, just like you thought," Brian remarked. "Who'd want to kill you that bad, anyway?"

Sliding down off the horse, Ballard caught the reins of his own mount. "I don't have any enemies here in Kansas City—except you," he said bluntly.

"And I'd have to be a damn fool to hire somebody to beat you up, then jump in and nearly get myself killed saving you," Brian pointed out.

Ballard nodded. The other man's words made sense. "Maybe we'll never know," he said. "I reckon this is where we part company. Thanks again for the help, Nichols."

"No problem. Just watch your back trail, all right?"

Ballard forced a laugh. "Sure." He mounted up and sat there while Brian rode off, thinking about what he had said about not having any enemies in these parts. Obviously that was not true. Somebody had wanted him dead.

And as a thoughtful frown crossed his face, he recalled that Quint Fowler had left Red Mike's before him and Brian. Could his refusal to sell the herd to Travers's wrangler have prompted Fowler to set up the ambush? That seemed highly unlikely to Ballard.

Unless there was a lot more going on here in Kansas City than most folks knew about. . . .

Chapter Six

That same evening, inside the bright yellow wagon that served as both home and office, John Travers sat going over the ticket receipts from that night's performance. Staring down at the deskful of paperwork, he put a finger on the bridge of the spectacles perched on his aquiline nose and pushed them up for the dozenth time that night, thinking about the days when there had been no better tracker anywhere in the West than the Yakima Kid. No one was his equal at reading sign, and his keen eyes could spot the flick of a squirrel's tail a quarter of a mile away.

That was a time long gone, Travers mused. Now it took these blasted chunks of glass to enable him to read something only a foot in front of his face. Maybe it had been a mistake to keep his own records; maybe he should have hired a bookkeeper as Cactus Corrigan had done. Still, Travers was a well-educated man, perfectly capable of keeping track of his own accounts, and he had never really been comfortable with the idea of trusting his money to somebody else. Sighing, he leaned forward, frowning as he concentrated on the paperwork.

The creak of a board made him look up. Somebody was coming up the steps at the rear door of the wagon. A second later, a knock sounded on the door, and Travers instinctively glanced at the desk. But tonight's receipts were already locked up in the small safe he kept under his bunk, and besides, it was doubtful that anyone would try to rob him right here in the middle of his own camp.

"Come in," he grunted.

The door opened, and a white-haired man stepped into the room, although the prematurely aged hair was actually quite deceiving, because the man was no more than thirty-five. He was slightly above medium height, with broad shoulders, and he moved with an easy grace as he shut the door of the wagon behind him. Dressed in a tweed suit and a bowler hat, he was rather handsome in a rough-hewn way. He smiled and said, "Good evening, Mr. Travers."

Travers frowned. "What are you doing here, Hayden?"

"I attended your show's performance tonight. It was excellent, as usual, and I thought I'd congratulate you."

"That's all you came to say?" Travers sounded dubious.

"Well . . . at the risk of becoming tiresome, I'll repeat my offer. I want to buy your show—or at least a percentage of it."

"That's what I thought," Travers muttered. "You're wasting your time and mine, and you damn well know it."

The old frontiersman was getting very tired of Neal Hayden showing up with an offer to buy the Wild West show. He had been a persistent visitor while the show was stopped in St. Louis, frequently trying to persuade the Kid to sell. Travers had been annoyed at the time, since he had no intention of selling, and he had done some checking into Hayden's background. What he had discovered reinforced his decision to have nothing to do with the man.

Originally from the East somewhere, Hayden was deliberately vague about his background. Since arriving in Kansas City several years earlier, however, he had become well known as a speculator and promoter, getting involved in some deals that were rather shady. Nothing criminal had ever been proved against him, but the general impression was that he was a dangerous man. He could make a living as a gambler when he had to, and he moved in many different circles, from fancy society balls in mansions on the bluffs overlooking the Missouri to smoky taverns and waterfront dives. Why he was interested in a Wild West show, Travers had no idea—unless it was simply a matter of greed. Perhaps Hayden wanted to cut himself a slice of every successful operation in this part of the country.

Feeling himself growing angry, Travers snapped, "I thought I made it perfectly clear that I have no intention of selling out to you, Hayden."

The white-haired man shrugged. "Your refusals in St. Louis were clear enough, and I didn't press the point because I knew you'd be coming on here to Kansas City. I was hoping you might've changed your mind since then."

"There's no chance of that," Travers stated bluntly.

Hayden's jaw tightened. "I can be pretty stubborn when there's something I want, Travers," he stated, his voice containing a hint of menace.

The quick-tempered Travers did not take kindly to threats. Shoving back his chair, he stood to face Hayden. "I think you'd better get out now," he bristled.

Smoothly Hayden tried to soothe Travers's ruffled feathers. "Your show's been very successful, and if it continues to grow, it's going to be as big as William F. Cody's. I want to be a part of that."

"Thanks for the compliment," the Kid said dryly. "Every showman would like to be as successful as Buffalo Bill. But I'll do it on my own, Hayden, with no help from you. Now, I think you'd better get out before there's trouble."

Hayden regarded him stolidly for a long moment, the promoter's face slowly turning red with anger. "Are you threatening me, Travers?" he finally asked.

"Were you threatening me?" Travers shot back.

Hayden laughed humorlessly. "I was just warning you, old man. You're the one being stubborn now, but you're going to change your tune sooner or later."

Travers took a deep breath and told himself to stay calm. Time was he would have knocked Hayden on his rear end and then thrown the man out of the camp. But he had heard rumors that Hayden carried a pistol and a knife and knew how to use both of them. Travers was not afraid of Hayden, but he *was* reasonable.

"If I call for help, there'll be a couple of dozen men here in less than a minute who'd be perfectly happy to beat the hell out of you," he finally stated. "Why don't you leave peacefully instead?"

Hayden smirked. "It figures an old-timer like you would have to have other people fight his battles." He reached out and poked Travers in the chest with a blunt finger. "This isn't over. Sooner or later you'll get smart and sell out to me."

With that Hayden turned on his heel, stalked over to the door, and left the wagon. Travers waited for the door to slam behind the man before letting out a long breath. Lifting a hand, he saw that it was trembling slightly.

"I could have taken him," he murmured aloud. "I wasn't afraid of him."

But deep down, Travers knew that he had been frightened. Once he had faced marauding Indians and desperate outlaws with ice water in his veins, never flinching from danger. Of course, in those days he had had Cactus Corrigan and Jackrabbit Dawkins at his side, and all three of them had firmly believed that there was no danger they could not overcome.

Times had changed. Men like Hayden were a new breed of snake, and Travers was not sure how to go about stomping him. He wished Corrigan was not so blasted muleheaded about things, for it would be mighty nice to be able to sit down with his old friend and try to figure out what to do about this mess.

Earl Corrigan dropped the thick stack of handbills on the table. "There they are," he announced. "We were lucky to have such a good opening crowd last night without any advertising. Once we plaster these all over both sides of the river, we'll really draw the folks in."

"But where did you get them?" Lucy asked. "The newspaper was supposed to provide us with advertising. That was part of the deal with them."

"Had these printed up myself," Corrigan replied. "I found a fella with a printing press who didn't mind waiting for his money."

Jackrabbit Dawkins was sitting at the table studying the gaudy handbills. "We goin' to have any *dinero* left over once we pay off all these bills we're runnin' up?" he queried.

"If we bring enough people to the show, we will," the showman answered. "I figure we'll stay here at least a week and get as much out of it as we can."

Jackrabbit got to his feet, leaning on his walking stick and tucking the handbills under his other arm. "I'll pass these around and get the boys started tackin' 'em up." The old jehu grinned. "We'll show the Kid a thing or three 'bout attractin' an audience."

"I hope you're right, Jackrabbit," Lucy remarked. "It's very important."

Corrigan and Jackrabbit nodded without saying anything. All three of them knew what was riding on the next few days: the very existence of Cactus Corrigan's Great Wild West.

Acting under Jackrabbit's direction, cowboys and roust-abouts from the troupe spread out all over both cities and spent the day tacking up the handbills on poles and buildings. That night the grandstands were nearly full again, and Corrigan felt a warm glow of satisfaction as he surveyed the audience. The handbills and word-of-mouth were working. Even though the show was set up on the west bank of the river, a location not nearly as prime as the one occupied by Travers's troupe, if they could continue to pull crowds like this, there was a good chance the show would be able to survive.

He had beaten long odds before, Corrigan thought, so there was no reason he could not beat these as well.

The show went smoothly, and the audience seemed pleased. Once again Wes Ballard drove the stagecoach and did a fine job. Ballard had been sporting some cuts and bruises that morning, as if he'd been in a fight, but Corrigan had not pressed him for details. What the Texan did was none of his business. And for that matter, Corrigan realized, a bruise or two still was visible on his own face from his little set-to with Travers.

He was in the arena the next afternoon, watching Ballard practice with the coach, when Jackrabbit came hobbling quickly through the opening in the grandstands.

"Cactus!" the old-timer called, sounding worried. "We got trouble again!"

Corrigan frowned as he hurried over to his friend. Ballard brought the stagecoach over as well, hauling the team to a stop. "What's up, Jackrabbit?" the Texan asked.

"Some of the boys went across the river on an errand, and they found a bunch of rowdies tearin' down all the handbills that was put up yesterday," Jackrabbit replied. "When our fellers tried to stop 'em, those hooligans handed 'em a purty good lickin'."

"Travers," Corrigan muttered bitterly. "He's got to be behind this."

Ballard frowned. "You think Travers hired some thugs to tear down the handbills? Would he do a thing like that?"

"I wouldn't put anything past him," Corrigan replied with a snort of disgust. "He's stolen performers from me; he's spread lies about me; he's done everything he could to hurt my show. He wouldn't hesitate to have some handbills torn down."

"What're we goin' to do about it?" Jackrabbit asked.

Corrigan sighed and shook his head. "I don't want to go any further in debt to have more fliers printed up. I guess we'll have to get by without any advertising."

"You mean you ain't goin' to see the Kid?"

"What good would it do? He'd just deny having anything to do with it. He's too slick to have left a trail leading back to him."

"Maybe so," the old man groused, "but it sure irks me to let somethin' like this pass."

"Me, too," Corrigan said with a sigh. "But right now, let's get back to work. The best way to repay Travers is to draw more customers than his penny-ante exposition."

The showman knew it was wrong to characterize Travers's organization that way, for the unpleasant truth was that the Yakima Kid had a better show. But had he achieved that advantage through unfair means? Corrigan was convinced that he had, and one of these days he was going to settle the score—once and for all.

They had not heard the last about handbills, though. An hour later, while Corrigan was in his wagon, a frantic knock came on the door. Not waiting for a response, one of the show's cowboys jerked open the door and exclaimed, "Riders comin', boss! Looks like Travers and some of his outfit!"

Corrigan got quickly to his feet, wincing as he felt a sudden twinge of pain in his belly. All day he had felt as though another attack was coming on, but he had been trying to ignore it. This was impossible to ignore. He waved the cattle puncher away from the wagon, saying harshly, "Shut the door! I'll be there in a minute!"

He managed to stay upright until the door was closed, although he was pale and sweating. As soon as he was alone again, he doubled over, gritting his teeth and willing the pain to depart. After a moment the agony eased, and Corrigan straightened, took a deep breath, and sleeved sweat off his forehead. He might still be a little pale, but he thought he could successfully hide his pain now.

Stepping out of the wagon, he strode toward the edge of the camp, where quite a crowd had gathered. His people parted to let him through, and he found himself facing Travers and several of his men, all on horseback. The Yakima Kid, who cut a dashing figure in his fancy fringed outfit, bore a definite resemblance to William F. Cody, and he used that resemblance to his advantage whenever possible.

"Hello, Cactus," Travers began, nodding to Corrigan. "I've come to see you about some trouble."

"If there's trouble, you caused it," Corrigan said flatly. "And my neck's sort of stiff. If you've got anything to say to me, you can alight and say it."

Travers hesitated, then swung down from his saddle and stood beside the big horse, reins held loosely in one hand. "It's about the handbills," he stated.

"Come to apologize for tearing mine down, have you?"

Travers frowned. "What the devil are you talking about? I came to tell you you'd better have your people stop tearing *mine* down."

Corrigan glared at him in surprise. "You're saying that *my* people tore *your* posters down?"

"And roughed up some of my men who saw them doing it," Travers confirmed. "I'm surprised at you, Cactus. I never thought you'd hire a bunch of thugs to give me trouble."

"You're crazy," Corrigan declared with a shake of his head. "That's exactly what happened to *my* handbills and *my* men. *You're* the one causing the trouble, dammit!"

Travers studied his rival intently for a long minute. Finally he asked, "Do you really believe that, Cactus?"

"Damned right I do."

"Then there's no point in talking any longer," Travers said with a sigh. "I'm sorry I wasted my time coming up here." He turned back to his horse and swung into the saddle, then gave the angry Corrigan one last glance. With a slight shake of his head, the Kid wheeled his horse and urged it into a gallop away from the camp, his men following.

Corrigan was mumbling, "The gall of that son-of-a—" when someone touched him on the arm. Turning his head, he found himself looking into Wes Ballard's eyes. "Well, what is it?" the showman snapped.

Ballard seemed reluctant to speak, but finally he said, "This may be none of my business, Mr. Corrigan, but it sounded to me like Travers was telling the truth."

Impatiently Corrigan shrugged off Ballard's hand. "You don't know the man like I do," he growled. "John Travers is a natural-born liar. He could say the moon was green and make it sound like the truth."

"I don't know," Jackrabbit Dawkins spoke up from Corrigan's other side. Corrigan had not noticed the old jehu before, but obviously Jackrabbit had witnessed the confrontation with Travers. "I know you've had plenty of run-ins with the Kid in the past," Jackrabbit said, "and I been on your side all along, but I've never known John to lie overmuch."

"You're both crazy," Corrigan barked. "Of course Travers is behind the trouble! He's always behind it! And I don't want to hear another damned word about it!"

He turned and stalked away, but he could feel Jackrabbit's and Ballard's eyes watching him. They just did not understand about Travers, he told himself, but sooner or later they would. The day would come when everyone would see what a low-down scoundrel the Yakima Kid really was.

Late that afternoon Ballard drove the stagecoach over to the corral and began to unhitch the horses so the team could rest and eat before the performance that night. Concentrating on his chore, he did not hear the visitor come up behind him, and he jumped slightly when a female voice asked, "Might I talk to you for a few minutes, Mr. Ballard?"

He turned around and saw Morgan Dixon standing there, a smile on her striking face. She went on, "I didn't mean to startle you, Mr. Ballard. Goodness, I'm glad you're a rancher and not a gunman, or your surprise might have led you to . . . perforate me? Is that the expression?"

Ballard ignored the gibe and said flatly, "What do you want, lady?"

She held out a folded newspaper toward him. "I was just wondering if I could get your reaction to a story I've written for tomorrow morning's edition of the *Clarion*. This is an early copy."

"Why would I be interested in something like that?" he asked without taking the newspaper.

"Because it's about the brawl you had with a member of the Yakima Kid's troupe, a man named Brian Nichols."

"What?" Ballard snatched the paper out of Morgan's hand and located the front-page story. With a frown, he quickly scanned the account, and after a moment he looked up and said, "This is all wrong. You make it sound as if we were trying to kill each other. It was just a fight. Shoot, you might even say we parted on good terms." He did not mention that Brian had saved him from being beaten to death in an alley. "According to this, we're still enemies."

"Indeed," Morgan murmured.

"And this . . . this insinuation that we fought over Lucy Corrigan! How in blazes did you find out about all that?"

"Then you're saying it's true?" Morgan asked quickly. "You and Nichols *did* fight over Miss Corrigan?"

"I'm saying this story is a damned outrage!" Ballard replied coldly. "You had no right to drag a lady's name into your filthy gossip. I reckon you'd know that if you were a lady yourself."

He had been about to decide that this Dixon woman's journalistic façade was impenetrable, but she paled, and Ballard knew that he had landed a blow. However, she recovered quickly, smiling and asking, "Can I quote you on that, Mr. Ballard?"

"You can go to the devil," the Texan snapped. She started to turn away, but he reached out and grasped her arm, stopping her. "You still didn't tell me how you found out about that."

"I have my sources," Morgan responded, her tone as icy as his now, "and no journalist ever reveals her sources."

"Well, just leave me out of your stories from now on. And leave Lucy out, too."

She shook her head. "I can't do that. This rivalry between the two Wild West shows is news, Mr. Ballard, and the *Clarion* reports the news. I think the citizens of Kansas City have a right to know that these two troupes of wild cowboys may start shooting at each other at any moment, don't you?"

"Nobody's going to start shooting—"

"Oh?" she cut in. "Can you guarantee that?"

He sighed. As a matter of fact, he could guarantee no such thing. Corrigan had looked mad enough earlier this afternoon to start blazing away at Travers if he had had a gun—but Morgan Dixon did not have to know that.

Somebody plucked at his sleeve. Irritated, Ballard looked down to see Jackrabbit Dawkins standing there. "I got to talk to you, Wes," the old-timer said urgently.

"Is it important?" Ballard asked. "I was talking to this . . . woman."

"Oh, that's all right, Mr. Ballard," Morgan said, purring sweetly now. "I think I have plenty for another story."

"Durned right it's important," Jackrabbit said, his voice testy. He pointed with a gnarled finger. "Lookee there."

The jehu was indicating the heavy nut that held the front axle of the stagecoach in place, and while Ballard was no expert on these old coaches, something struck him as wrong. Frowning, he asked, "That's not right, is it?"

"Durned tootin' it's not right! Somebody's loosened that nut."

The Texan reached down and turned the nut with his fingers. It moved fairly easily, but only for a fraction of an inch. "There," he grunted. "It's snugged back down."

"Now it is, but if you hadn'ta done that, it could've worked loose durin' the performance." The jehu's leathery old face was grim. "If that wheel'd come off durin' the chase, you would've wrecked for sure, boy. Somebody would've got hurt, maybe killed."

"Mr. Dawkins," Morgan spoke up, "do you think it's likely that that nut came loose on its own?"

Jackrabbit shook his head, not noticing the warning look that Ballard gave him. "Not likely a'tall. Somebody must've loosened it."

"Then that's sabotage," the journalist stated excitedly. "Deliberate sabotage."

"Now, hold on a minute," Ballard cautioned. "Jackrabbit didn't say anything of the sort, and you don't have any right to say in your paper that he did."

Morgan ignored him as she asked, "Mr. Dawkins, has anyone been around this stagecoach today who could have loosened that nut?"

Jackrabbit tugged at his beard. "Why, there's been folks around this coach all day, ma'am. But I don't know of anybody who'd want to fool with it, unless . . ."

Pouncing on his hesitation, Morgan asked quickly, "Were any of the Yakima Kid's men here today, Mr. Dawkins?"

"Now, I didn't say that. . . ."

"But they were, weren't they?" Morgan's questions bored in on the old man. "You think John Travers is behind this attempt to damage Mr. Corrigan's show and perhaps risk the lives of the performers, don't you?"

"That's it," Ballard said, his hand closing around Morgan's arm again. "You're leaving right now, Miss Dixon, and you're not going to bother us anymore."

"You can't do this," Morgan protested as Ballard steered her away from the stagecoach. "Blast it, let go of me, you . . . you big cowboy!"

Ballard chuckled grimly. "I would've thought a writer

could come up with something stronger to call somebody
she was mad at." Spotting a small one-horse carriage parked
at the edge of the camp, he assumed that it was Morgan's.
As he shoved her toward the little vehicle, he went on, "I
may be out of line speaking for Mr. Corrigan, but you're
not welcome here anymore, Miss Dixon. Please don't
come back."

"I'll find somebody who'll talk to me," she warned.
"I'll get the story, Mr. Ballard, I promise you—and you'll
regret tossing me out like this."

"I don't think I'm likely to lose any sleep over it.
Good-bye, Miss Dixon."

He stood there, his hands on his hips, until she got
into the carriage and drove away. He knew he had probably not accomplished a thing by running her off, but at
least it had made him feel good for a moment.

When he returned to the stagecoach, Jackrabbit was
straightening from the wheel where the nut had been
loose. He had a pair of pliers in his hand, and he said, "I
got that nut tighter, Wes. It ain't goin' nowhere now."

"Thanks, Jackrabbit." Ballard stared down at the wheel.
"Do you really think one of Travers's men loosened it this
afternoon?"

The old man shrugged. "Could have. One of 'em
could've slipped over to the coach whilst everybody was
watching Cactus and the Kid jawin' at each other."

"Was Quint Fowler with Travers? I can't remember."

Jackrabbit frowned. "Seems like he was, if'n my mem-
ory ain't playin' tricks on me. Why? You suspicious Fowler
might be the one who did this?"

"I don't have any real reason to think so," Ballard
admitted. "But I'd keep a close eye on him if he happens
to show up again." He took a deep breath. "By the way,
Jackrabbit, thanks for noticing that. If there had been a
wreck, it probably would've been my neck that got busted."

"I'm just glad I seen it. Well, come on, son, we got a
show to put on tonight."

As he resumed the chore of unhitching the team,
Ballard glanced at the river. It was flowing lazily in the
late-afternoon sunlight, broad and brown with silt and
deserving of its nickname—the Big Muddy. At the mo-

ment, being on opposite sides of the stream was one of the things keeping a full-scale war from breaking out between the two Wild West shows. But if the trouble kept up, Ballard reflected gloomily, not even the Big Muddy could keep them apart.

Chapter Seven

Wes Ballard was not surprised when copies of the Kansas City *Clarion* circulated around the camp the next day. Evidently Morgan Dixon had made it back to the newspaper's offices in time to add material to her original story for the later editions, for there was mention of the sabotaged stagecoach as well as a thinly veiled implication that someone connected with the Yakima Kid's organization had been responsible.

Also on the front page, which had been remade from the one Ballard had seen the day before, was a boxed editorial by Jasper Morton Prescott. The publisher's high-flown rhetoric detailed the rivalry between the two shows, from the original brawl between the troupes when Cactus Corrigan had arrived in Kansas City, to the alleged sabotage touched on in Morgan Dixon's article. The tone of the editorial was highly inflammatory, painting the conflict as a classic Western feud. If the people in Travers's camp were reading the same thing—which was very likely, Ballard thought—this was just going to lead to more trouble.

And that was probably exactly what Prescott wanted. By playing this to the hilt, the newspaper could keep things stirred up—and keep their circulation figures up as well. Ballard had heard about the "mistake" that had led to both shows being in Kansas City at the same time. Maybe he was getting overly suspicious, Ballard thought, but he wondered if there had been a mistake made at all. Perhaps Prescott had arranged this whole thing just to have a good story for his paper.

It would be impossible to prove such a thing, the

Texan knew. All Earl Corrigan could do was keep on trying to make the best out of a bad situation.

And the situation was growing worse. After two good nights at the box office, the grandstand had been less than half full the previous night. A drop in attendance was to be expected, but not such a dramatic one. If it kept up, Corrigan was going to be in trouble.

Ballard realized he was truly worried about the show, not just about getting the money owed him. Maybe Jackrabbit was right. Maybe show business did get in a man's blood.

Walking toward the arena, Ballard had a copy of the *Clarion* folded up and stuck in his hip pocket when he spotted Lucy Corrigan leading her horse from the corral. He increased his pace and caught up with her as she reached the arena. " 'Morning, ma'am," he said, smiling and nodding.

"Hello, Mr. Ballard." Lucy returned his smile with a brilliant one of her own. Noticing the paper in his pocket, she gestured toward it, her expression tightening. "I guess you've seen what that . . . that woman had to say. She's just going to cause more trouble."

"Could be she's just doing what her boss is telling her to do," Ballard heard himself saying, surprised that he would defend Morgan Dixon in any way, shape, or form.

"I suppose you could be right," Lucy remarked. "That Mr. Prescott is certainly full of himself, isn't he?"

"He is," Ballard agreed. To change the subject, he patted Lucy's horse on the flank and asked, "You planning to practice for a while?"

"Of course. I practice every day. That's the only way I'm able to perform the tricks I do."

"Mind if I watch?"

She smiled again, making his heart beat a little faster. "Of course not."

"Miss Lucy . . ." Ballard hesitated, then plunged ahead, "I've been thinking. I'd sure like to see you sometime, maybe take you out for a bite to eat."

"You mean court me?" Lucy asked, sounding startled.

"Yes, ma'am. I reckon that's what I mean."

Lucy did not reply for a long moment. Then she said, "I'm very flattered, Mr. Ballard, but I never really thought of you as a potential suitor, I'm afraid. I thought you intended to go back to Texas as soon as you can."

"Well, you never know—" he began desperately, sensing that this had gone wrong.

Lucy shook her head. "I'm sorry. I just don't think it would be a good idea."

Ballard took a deep breath and nodded curtly. "Sure. Sorry I brought it up, ma'am. Didn't intend to offend you."

"But you didn't— Oh, you men just don't understand!"

She sounded as exasperated as he felt. It would be better just to get away from her for a while, he decided. "I'll be seeing you around," he said, touching a finger to the brim of his hat.

"But I thought you were going to watch me practice."

"I just remembered some things I've got to do. So long, Miss Lucy."

He strode away without looking back. He could not blame Lucy for feeling the way she did. After all, when you got right down to it, he was just a cowboy.

Several more days passed, and if anything, the crowds were smaller each night. Earl Corrigan watched the dwindling audiences and tried to tell himself that attendance would pick up again, but he knew that was a lie. The bad location and the lack of advertising were taking their toll. The show was getting some publicity from Prescott's editorials and Morgan Dixon's articles in the *Clarion*, but Corrigan reasoned that the people who were interested in the so-called feud were probably going to see Travers's show.

Corrigan was in his wagon one afternoon when he heard raucous laughter outside. Getting up from the table where he had been studying the accounts, he went to the open door and looked out to see several of the cowboys having some sport with Nathan Sanford. The men had lassos, and every time Sanford tried to take a step, one of them would throw a loop in front of him. A couple of times Sanford failed to avoid the ropes and had the loop jerked tight around his ankles, almost spilling him to the ground. That provoked more hilarity from the cowboys, and the studious-looking bookkeeper joined nervously in the laughter. "Please, fellows," he begged as he clumsily freed his legs from one of the ropes, "I've got to get to work."

"Shoot, you're helpin' us practice our ropin', Sandy," a cowboy called Gilliam hooted. "You're just about as feisty as a little calf that misses its mama!"

"Please . . ." Sanford began again.

"That'll be enough, boys," Corrigan ordered from the doorway of the wagon. "I sent for Nathan, and you're holding us up."

Immediately the men began to coil their lassos. "Sorry, boss," Gilliam said, ducking his head. "We was just havin' a little fun with Sandy."

"I know," Corrigan replied. "Come on inside, Nathan."

Sanford hurried gratefully into the wagon and placed the ledger he had been carrying on Corrigan's desk. "Here are those records you wanted, Mr. Corrigan," he stated shakily.

Shutting the door, Corrigan turned to face the bookkeeper. "Sorry the boys were tormenting you, Nathan. I know they're pretty rough on you sometimes, but they don't mean any harm."

"I suppose not." Sanford took off his glasses and massaged the bridge of his nose. "And I suppose I should be used to such treatment by now. After all, I've been with the show a long time; I know how cowboys are. To them I'm just a dude, a tenderfoot—an object of scorn."

It was unusual for Sanford to be this upset over the harassment he took from the cowboys, Corrigan thought. Things added up, though, and a man could only take so much. He decided he would have to have a talk with the boys sometime soon about leaving the bookkeeper alone.

In the meantime, though, there was bookwork to be done, and after an hour of going over the numbers that were scrawled in various ledgers, Corrigan and Sanford reached the same conclusion.

"We're not going to make it, are we?" Sanford asked grimly.

Corrigan shook his head. "Doesn't look like it. If we could've kept the stands full the whole time we were here, there would have been a chance." The old scout shrugged his broad shoulders. "But with the way the audiences are dropping off, there's just no way to pay all the bills." He sighed. "Without a miracle, we're going to have to shut down for good."

Someone knocked on the door of the wagon.

Sanford frowned. "Maybe that's your miracle now."

Corrigan pushed himself to his feet, chuckling humorlessly as he stood. "What're the chances of that, Nathan?"

"I don't know. Such things happen all the time in those melodramatic dime novels the men are so fond of."

"Don't tell me you read the Yellowback Library, too?" Corrigan asked, summoning up a smile.

The knock came again, and Sanford ignored his employer's question, saying instead, "Whoever it is, they're liable to go away if you don't let them in, sir."

Corrigan nodded and chuckled again, and this time the sound was more genuine. He went to the door and swung it open, looking for a long moment at the stranger who stood there. "Yes? What can I do for you, mister?"

The man smiled and said, "Actually, I think I may be able to do something for you, Mr. Corrigan." He took off the expensive soft felt hat he wore and asked, "May I come in, please?"

Corrigan stepped back and held the door open. "Sure. Come on in, Mr. . . ."

"Hearst," the stranger said as he entered the wagon. "William Randolph Hearst."

In his mid-thirties, he was a handsome dark-haired man in a sober, well-cut gray suit, and his intelligent eyes shone with a peculiar intensity. Corrigan recognized the name immediately, as would just about anyone else in the country. The flamboyant, influential owner and publisher of the San Francisco *Examiner* and the New York *Journal*, among others, William Randolph Hearst was one of the best-known newspaper tycoons in the United States, second only to Joseph Pulitzer. And if Hearst had his way, he would not occupy second place for long.

"You may have seen me at the offices of the Kansas

City *Clarion* several days ago," Hearst went on, holding his hat.

Corrigan shook his head. "Sorry. I was a mite upset at the time."

"I could tell," Hearst said with a soft laugh. "At any rate, *I* noticed *you*, and I was intrigued by what your dealings with Jasper Morton Prescott might be. You see, I was meeting with Prescott on a business matter myself."

"I don't reckon there was any connection between why I was there and the dealings you had with Prescott, Mr. Hearst," Corrigan said dubiously. "But I hope you came out better than I did."

"Well, actually, I didn't. I came to Kansas City to buy the *Clarion* from Prescott—I want to expand my newspaper domain to this part of the country—but Prescott has refused to sell it to me." Hearst's voice hardened, and his air of affability dropped away. "Some people have accused me of being monumentally prideful, but so be it. To put it bluntly, I don't like it when I want something and people refuse to let me have it—and I *want* the *Clarion.*"

With a baffled frown on his face, Corrigan said, "I'm sorry to hear about your difficulties, Mr. Hearst, but I don't understand why you're telling me about them."

"Because, Mr. Corrigan," Hearst responded, "you're going to help me get my hands on the *Clarion*, and I'm going to help you get the upper hand on the Yakima Kid at long last."

The showman stared at the newspaper magnate for several seconds, shocked into speechlessness. Glancing at Sanford, he saw that the bookkeeper looked equally confused.

"Why don't we sit down, Mr. Corrigan?" Hearst suggested. "I'll explain what I have in mind."

"Reckon you'd better," Corrigan agreed, "because none of this makes a whole lot of sense to me so far."

Hearst picked up a chair and carried it over to the table, obviously not being one to stand on ceremony when there was business to discuss. As he sat down, he looked at Sanford and said, "I don't believe I know this gentleman."

"This is Nathan Sanford, my bookkeeper."

"Pleased to meet you, Mr. Sanford," Hearst announced,

extending his hand across the table to the small man. Sanford took it, his expression one of awe.

"Now, Mr. Corrigan," Hearst continued when Corrigan had settled down opposite him, "as for the matter of your problems with John Travers, also known as the Yakima Kid . . . I've been told that I have a natural flair for publicity, and I've come up with an idea that may be just what you need. What would you say to a competition between the Wild West shows owned by you and Mr. Travers?"

"A competition?" Corrigan repeated.

"Exactly. The two of you are already rivals, so this would merely be taking that rivalry to its logical conclusion. The competition would take the place of the final regular performance of both shows, and it would pit the members of both troupes against each other in tests of skill. Your sharpshooters, for example, would compete against Travers's sharpshooters. Your trick riders would vie against his trick riders. You could extend the contest to virtually every act that both of you have in your shows."

The showman turned over the proposal in his mind. Glancing at Sanford, he saw that the bookkeeper was equally deep in thought. Finally, after several moments of considering the idea, Corrigan said cautiously, "It sounds like it might be interesting, all right, and I imagine it would draw the best crowd yet. But frankly, I'm not sure I can even keep operating that long, Mr. Hearst, let alone come up with any extra money to advertise this contest of yours."

"The latter would not be necessary," Hearst said quickly with a shake of his head. "And as to the former, I'll provide whatever financial backing you need, Mr. Corrigan, both to keep your troupe solvent until the competition and to prepare for it as well." He paused, then added, "On one condition, that is."

"And just what condition would that be?" Corrigan asked warily.

"That I can get that bastard Prescott to accept a wager I'm going to propose to him," Hearst replied. "I want him to back Travers, just as I'm going to back you."

"Ah," Sanford spoke up, obviously grasping what Hearst had in mind. "An excellent idea, Mr. Hearst."

The newspaper tycoon smiled proudly and went on, "It will be a simple bet: If the Yakima Kid's show wins the Wild West competition, I will pay Prescott one hundred thousand dollars in cash. But if your troupe prevails, Mr. Corrigan, Prescott will turn the Kansas City *Clarion* over to me—lock, stock, and barrel."

Corrigan stared at Hearst, dumbfounded by the audacity of the man's plan. But that was what separated men like Hearst from the crowd—the guts to come up with such brazen schemes and then carry them through.

"It's an interesting idea," Corrigan finally concurred. "But what makes you think Prescott will accept the bet?"

"He can't afford not to," Hearst replied with a smug smile. "I've heard rumors that he is having financial trouble, which is why I came to Kansas City in the first place. I thought Prescott would jump at my offer to buy the paper. But he seems determined to hang on, and a hundred thousand dollars would solve any problems he might have. With a lure like that, Prescott can't help but bite."

The showman leaned back in his chair, considering everything he had heard. He sensed that for all Hearst's surface friendliness, underneath, the publisher was about as cold-blooded as a rattlesnake, and Corrigan was a bit leery of aligning himself with anyone that ruthless. Yet as he mentally added up all the troubles facing the show, he realized he had little choice but to agree to the plan. He looked at Sanford again, and the bookkeeper ventured a small nod.

"I'm not convinced that either Prescott or Travers will agree to your bet, Mr. Hearst," Corrigan finally said, "but I'm willing to go along with you when you propose it to them. After that, we'll just have to see what happens."

"Fair enough," Hearst said enthusiastically. The thought that everything would not go his way clearly never entered his head.

"I've got one more question, though. . . . Why me? Why would you take such a big chance on my show?"

Hearst merely smiled. "I always like to root for the underdog, Mr. Corrigan. Or should I call you Cactus, now that we're partners?" He held out his hand.

Corrigan drew a deep breath and shook the magnate's hand. "Cactus it is," he said.

Chapter Eight

Earl Corrigan was nervous as he and William Randolph Hearst entered the *Clarion* building the next morning. Hearst had insisted that the showman wear the fancy outfit he wore during the show's performances. Corrigan would have been more comfortable in his old range clothes, but he understood Hearst's request when the two of them were ushered into Jasper Morton Prescott's office: John Travers was there in all his buckskinned finery, and Hearst had wanted his man to look equally impressive.

"Hello, Prescott," Hearst boomed heartily. "I appreciate your seeing me again on such short notice."

"Always happy to oblige a man of your stature, Hearst," Prescott replied, not sounding overly sincere. "But if you've come to renew your offer to buy the *Clarion*, I'm afraid you've wasted your time."

"Not at all," the magnate replied. He sat down in an overstuffed armchair in front of Prescott's desk, and as the other three men took their seats as well, Hearst took out a long, fat cigar. He clipped the ends and lit it, then slid another one from his pocket and offered it to Prescott, who shook his head.

Corrigan shifted in his chair, wishing these formalities were over with. The sooner Hearst got to the meat of the matter, the better.

Hearst exhaled a cloud of cigar smoke and explained, "The reason I asked you and Mr. Travers to meet us here, Prescott, is that I have a sporting proposition for you."

Prescott looked surprised, and Travers glanced over at Corrigan in puzzlement. The showman just shook his head slightly and lifted his shoulders a fraction of an inch. All would be clear soon enough.

"A sporting proposition," Prescott repeated. "Go on."

"What I'm proposing," Hearst continued, "is a competition between Mr. Corrigan's Wild West show and the show owned by Mr. Travers here."

Travers sat up straighter. "Competition? You mean like a contest?"

"That's exactly what I mean, Mr. Travers. One troupe against the other, in a winner-take-all contest of Western skills."

Corrigan could see the flare of interest in Prescott's eyes. With a newspaperman's instincts, the publisher had to sense that this would make a good story, and he leaned forward and remarked, "That certainly sounds like an intriguing notion, Hearst, but what does it have to do with the two of us?"

Hearst smiled lazily. "I had in mind a certain wager that you might care to make. . . ."

The eyes of both Prescott and Travers widened in surprise as the magnate outlined the terms of his bet. When Hearst was finished, Prescott sat back in his chair and regarded the newspaper magnate in silence for a while. Finally he said, "I must admit I've never heard of anything quite like what you're proposing, Hearst. It's . . . it's outrageous!"

"Not to mention a bad bet for you, Mr. Hearst," Travers put in. He waved a hand at Corrigan. "I think the world of ol' Cactus here, but his people couldn't get the better of mine in a contest like that on their best day."

"You think not, do you?" Corrigan snapped.

Travers smiled confidently. "I know they couldn't."

Prescott regarded the Yakima Kid intently. "Are you saying I should take this bet, Mr. Travers?"

"That's up to you, Mr. Prescott." Travers's eyes glittered with excitement as the idea took hold of him. "But I'd sure enjoy having the opportunity to show the world once and for all who has the best Wild West show."

Prescott hesitated, obviously torn between being cautious and accepting the wager. If Hearst was right about Prescott's money problems, Corrigan thought, it was going to be hard for him to turn down a chance at a hundred thousand dollars. And there was also a matter of the *Clarion* publisher's pride, of which he had plenty.

Abruptly Prescott slapped the top of his desk with a sharp crack. "Done," he said, giving in to the impulse. "I accept your wager, Hearst. One hundred thousand dollars against the *Clarion*, the winner to be determined by the outcome of the competition between the two shows."

Hearst cocked the cigar in his mouth at a jaunty angle and extended his hand across the desk. "Done," he agreed.

Corrigan felt his own pulse beginning to race with excitement as he looked over at Travers. After all this time, there was finally going to be a showdown between them.

"I'd planned on wrapping up my show and leaving a few days before Cactus," Travers stated. "But under the circumstances, I don't mind waiting. I've got a question for you gentlemen: Where's this contest going to be held?"

"Mr. Corrigan and I have discussed that, Mr. Travers," Hearst replied, "and we're agreed that the arena where your troupe is performing would be more suitable. It is larger and in a better location."

Prescott nodded. "That's all right with us," he concurred, speaking for Travers as well.

The rival showmen sat there and regarded each other coolly as the two publishers wrapped up the rest of the details of the competition. A date of a full week from the current day was decided upon, giving both shows ample time to prepare—and ample time for the event to be publicized.

Hearst turned to Travers and said, "Now that we've gotten that out of the way, Mr. Travers, I think it's interesting that you mentioned showing the world who has the best Wild West show, because, you see, that's exactly what I mean to do."

Prescott leaned forward, clearly sensing that something unexpected was about to happen. Corrigan also wondered what Hearst was talking about, for the newspaper magnate had said nothing like this in their discussions.

"I've sent for an employee of mine named Garrett Kingsley," Hearst went on. "He's a reporter for my paper the New York *Journal*. My star reporter, you might say."

"I've heard of him," Prescott admitted. "I remember seeing his byline on some of the stories you did last year about the Spanish-American War. That conflict brought up some interesting allegations about you and Pulitzer."

"That so-called yellow journalism business?" Hearst scoffed with a shake of his head. "Nothing to it. And what would it matter if there was, eh? Our circulation figures skyrocketed."

Corrigan knew vaguely what Hearst and Prescott were talking about. Some people seemed to think that the war in Cuba had been nothing but the result of a circulation war between Hearst's *Journal* and Pulitzer's New York *World*. Both men had run a number of stories openly inciting the United States to go to war against Spain, and the sinking of the American battleship *Maine* in Havana harbor had been the last straw needed to set off the short-lived but brutal war.

"At any rate," Hearst continued, "Kingsley is going to be covering this competition for my papers. His dispatches will be sent to every one of them, and the whole country will be following the story of this contest before you know it." Hearst made a show of taking out his pocket watch and checking the time before he stated casually, "He should be here tomorrow night, having left New York early this morning on a special express train I chartered for him."

Prescott was obviously taken aback by Hearst's announcement. He blinked his eyes rapidly for a few seconds, but then his expression hardened. Within seconds a smooth, urbane mask that rivaled Hearst's own was firmly in place on Prescott's face. "Your reputation for publicity is well deserved, Hearst," he said calmly. "But you're not the only one who can play that game. I was already planning on assigning my best reporter to this story before you even mentioned bringing in Kingsley."

"Oh? You have a reporter to equal Kingsley?"

"I have a reporter who'll go him one better," Prescott declared. He pressed a button underneath his desk, and a buzzer in the outer office summoned the male secretary who waited there. When the man opened the door and stepped into Prescott's inner sanctum, Prescott ordered firmly, "Simms, have Morgan Dixon sent up here—right away!"

Morgan was sitting at her desk in the city room of the paper, going over the notes she had made for her next day's story about the Wild West show rivalry, when a copy boy hurried over to her and said excitedly, "Miss Dixon, Mr. Prescott wants to see you upstairs in his office immediately!"

Frowning prettily, Morgan laid her notes on the desk and asked, "What?"

"Mr. Prescott's office—now!"

"All right," she agreed. "Thanks, Ben. I'll get right up there."

She stood up and went out of the city room toward the stairs, knowing that her colleagues were watching her curiously as she left. It was unusual for any of the reporters to be summoned to the publisher's office. Usually their orders and assignments came through old Webb, the editor. Morgan herself had probably spoken to Prescott more lately than any of the other journalists on the staff because she was covering his pet story, the Wild West shows.

Still, she had to wonder what he wanted. Was he displeased with her work? Did he intend to assign the story to another reporter? Morgan shook her head as she climbed the stairs. There was no use speculating. As owner and publisher, Prescott could follow any whim he chose.

Finding the outer office empty, she crossed the room and was about to knock on the door to Prescott's private office when it jerked open. Simms, the publisher's secretary, came hurrying out, and he told her, "Go right in. They're expecting you."

Morgan stepped into the room, not knowing what she was going to find. Her eyes instantly noted the four men waiting for her, as well as the fact that Cactus Corrigan and the Yakima Kid quickly stood when she entered the room, getting to their feet in a show of Western manners. Prescott and the other man remained seated.

Morgan's heart suddenly thudded in her chest as she recognized that fourth man. What was William Randolph Hearst doing here? Was it possible he could have come to offer her a job? She felt a leap of hope at the thought. Her ambition had always been to write for an important paper, one where hundreds of thousands of readers would see her words. Loyalty to Prescott was one thing; advancing her career was another.

"Hello, Mr. Prescott," she said softly. "You wanted to see me?"

"Yes, indeed, Miss Dixon . . . Morgan." Prescott put a smile on his face that did not exactly ring true to his employee. Morgan kept her own face carefully expressionless as Prescott went on, "I think you know Mr. Travers and Mr. Corrigan here. And this gentleman is Mr. William Randolph Hearst."

Morgan held out her hand to Hearst. "Of course I know you, sir. I've been an admirer of yours ever since you took over your first paper."

"Why, thank you, my dear," Hearst said, shaking her hand briefly. "I hope you'll be as kind to me in the stories you'll be writing over the next few days."

"Sir?" Morgan frowned and looked at Prescott in confusion.

"I have a new assignment for you, Morgan," Prescott stated. "It's the biggest one yet, and I'm sure you're not going to let me down. You're going to cover the first ever Great Wild West Show Competition."

The journalist merely stared.

Over the next few minutes Prescott explained the situation, including the bet between himself and Hearst and the fact that the magnate was importing a star reporter of his own to write the story of the contest.

"I'm flattered that you'd trust me with this job, Mr. Prescott," Morgan said when the publisher was finished. "And honored that you rate me as an equal with Garrett Kingsley. I've read many of his dispatches concerning the late war."

"Well, I'm certain you'll do a fine job." Prescott glanced at Travers and Corrigan. "I assume it will be all right with you gentlemen if Miss Dixon visits your camps."

"It's all right with me," Travers said, and Corrigan nodded his acquiescence.

"Just as long as Kingsley is accorded the same privilege," Hearst spoke up.

"Of course."

Morgan studied Travers and Corrigan for a moment. Both of the older men looked as though they were caught up in the excitement of the upcoming competition, and she wondered if either of them realized they were just pawns to men like Prescott and Hearst.

That was their worry. She had just had the best story of her career dumped in her lap, and she did not intend to waste the opportunity. "Now, gentlemen," she said, pulling her ever-present notebook and pencil from one of the voluminous pockets of her skirt, "if I could get your initial reaction to this challenge. . . ."

Being assigned to this story was not the last surprise awaiting Morgan Dixon. She was called to Jasper Morton Prescott's office again the next day and found the publisher sitting back in his chair, a cigar in his mouth and a very satisfied expression on his face. "Sit down, Morgan," he said, waving a hand expansively at one of the chairs in front of the desk.

She sat and waited for Prescott to continue, knowing that the publisher had to go at his own speed in these things.

"I got a telegram this morning," he said after a moment. "Do you know who that telegram was from, Morgan?"

"No, sir," she said, swallowing her impatience.

"It was from Joseph Pulitzer," Prescott announced proudly. "He wants to contract with me for someone to wire stories concerning the contest back to his paper. You're that someone, Morgan."

Morgan's eyes widened as a mixture of emotions surged through her at the news. First and foremost, she was thrilled by this opportunity. Her stories would be read not only in Kansas City but also in New York, in Pulitzer's newspaper, the *World*. There was no more widely read or better-known paper anywhere.

But she was also nervous. It had been difficult getting people to respect her as a serious journalist, for she was a woman—and a very pretty woman at that—in a profession populated almost entirely by men. She had never let her sex stop her, but neither had she used it to try to further her career. The daughter of a small-town newspaper publisher in Ohio, she had been determined from the start of her career that she would rise or fall solely on the basis of her talent. What if—now that she had the biggest chance of her life—her talent proved to be not enough?

Without realizing it, she gave a slight shake of her head at such negative thinking, which could defeat her before she was hardly started.

"Anything wrong, Morgan?" Prescott asked. "You look as though something is bothering you."

"Oh, no, sir," she replied quickly. "I was just thinking about the story. I'm sure Mr. Pulitzer's readers back in New York will be enthralled."

"That's the spirit!" Prescott exclaimed. "Now you'll want to get back to work. . . ."

"Yes, sir," Morgan said, standing up. "I was planning to pay another visit to Mr. Corrigan's camp today, and I believe I'll do it right now."

Prescott nodded and looked down at some of the documents spread out on his desk, signifying that the meeting was over. Morgan hurried out, stopped at her desk only long enough to pick up her hat and her bag, and then went to fetch her horse and carriage from the nearby stable.

She drove straight to the ferry, crossed the Missouri, then headed up the river road to Corrigan's camp. As luck would have it, the first person she saw after parking the carriage and going in search of Corrigan was Wes Ballard.

The Texan glared at her. "I thought I told you you weren't welcome around here," he growled.

"I suppose you've heard about the contest between Cactus Corrigan's show and the Yakima Kid's," she replied coolly. "I'm covering it for the *Clarion,* and Mr. Corrigan himself gave me permission to visit his camp whenever I see fit." That might have been stretching the terms of the agreement just a bit, but Ballard did not have to know that.

He frowned dubiously and said, "I've heard about the competition, all right, but I might just check with Mr. Corrigan about that other business."

"You do that."

Ballard turned and stalked away without another word, and Morgan sighed in exasperation as she watched him go. There was something about Wes Ballard, something . . . compelling. He was not a particularly handsome man, and he was arrogant and accustomed to getting his own way, but she still found herself intrigued by him. Like Corrigan and Travers, the Texan seemed to be something of a throwback to an earlier era, an era that was now gone. She wondered if she would ever get him to consent to an official interview.

Morgan walked toward Corrigan's wagon, thinking that she wanted details of exactly how the troupe would be preparing for the competition. Putting on their regular shows would, of course, keep their skills honed to a certain extent, but the performers might also want to put in some extra practice, given the circumstances.

Something, some instinct perhaps, made Morgan glance over as she passed one of the other wagons. She hesitated as she spotted the two pairs of legs visible on the other side of the vehicle. Two people, both of them wearing buckskins, were standing awfully close together. . . .

The feeling that she was about to pry into something that was none of her business briefly crossed Morgan's mind, but she dismissed it. She was a journalist, after all, and anything that might interest the public was her business. Moving very quietly, she edged to the corner of the enclosed wagon and peered around it.

Lucy Corrigan, her back partially to Morgan, was standing with just enough of her face visible for the reporter to recognize her. The man with Lucy had his arms around her and was kissing her passionately. He wore a more elaborate buckskin outfit than she, and his hat was pushed back so that it hung by the thong around his neck, leaving his long blond hair visible.

Morgan eased back—not that it was likely either of the people she had just been spying on would have noticed her. They were too wrapped up in each other. Literally. Morgan vaguely recognized the young man, and then his identity popped into her mind. She had attended one of the performances of John Travers's show, and the man who had been kissing Lucy Corrigan was none other than Brian Nichols, Travers's star sharpshooter.

Catching her breath, Morgan smiled. *This* was certainly an unexpected angle. Another wagon was parked close to the one she had just peeked around, and the narrow gap between the vehicles was an effective hiding place. Brian must have been sneaking over here to see Lucy, and a romance had developed between them, despite his working for the enemy of Lucy's father.

Just like the Montagues and the Capulets, Morgan thought, remembering the Bard's work from the finishing school she had attended at her mother's insistence. Maybe something good could come of that education after all. She had long believed that growing up in the rough-and-tumble world of newspaper publishing was all the education she really needed, but Shakespeare's doomed couple provided an added twist to the Wild West–show story.

The question she asked herself was: What should she do with the information she had just stumbled upon? Corrigan probably would not take it very well if he found out his daughter was being romanced by one of Travers's men. It might be better to tell Ballard. She had gotten the impression that the young rancher from Texas was interested in Lucy Corrigan himself. If Ballard knew that Brian was winning Lucy, it would certainly foster discord between the two camps—and that could make for an even better story.

Frowning slightly as she pondered the situation, Morgan slipped away from the wagons and resumed her search for Corrigan. She would have to wait and mull this over— and spring her surprise at the right time.

Chapter Nine

Jasper Morton Prescott made a habit of working late at the *Clarion* offices, since there were always a great many weighty matters to occupy the publisher's attention—decisions to be made and plans to implement. But if the truth were told, staying most nights at the office until very late was simply, for Prescott, preferable to going home.

His coat off and his tie undone, he had financial reports spread out on his desk. Downstairs, reporters were still on duty, even though it was approaching midnight, and the presses in the basement were running, churning out late editions of tomorrow morning's paper. Prescott could hear the thumping sound and feel the vibration from the great machines coming up through the floor as he sat behind the desk. The noise and the vibrations were somehow comforting to him, making him feel less alone here on the second floor.

The sudden creak of a floorboard in the outer office told Prescott he was *not* alone. Sitting up straighter, he reached for the middle drawer of his desk, where he kept a short-barreled Colt .32 revolver, fully loaded. "Who's there?" he called firmly, not letting his nervousness show in his tone.

"It's just me," a man's voice replied as his shadow thrown by the light in the corridor filled the doorway. "If you're reaching for that gun you keep in your desk, you might as well stop."

Prescott grunted and leaned back in his chair. This visitor might not be the most welcome one in the world, but he did not represent a direct threat.

The man strolled leisurely into the room, his bowler hat thrust back on his thatch of prematurely white hair. Prescott looked at him levelly and asked, "What are you doing here, Hayden?"

"Don't worry," Neal Hayden said. "Nobody saw me come in, so nobody's going to wonder what the connection is between the respected newspaper publisher and a shady character like me."

Prescott grimaced at Hayden's sarcasm. Still, he supposed he deserved it. After the events of the last few months, could he really consider himself any better than Hayden?

The white-haired promoter pulled up a chair and settled into it. Studying him across the desk, Prescott saw that although Hayden was smiling, his eyes were cold and angry. Something was bothering him.

"I heard about this bet between you and Hearst," Hayden said abruptly. "I'm not sure I like it, Jasper."

Keeping a tight grip on his composure, Prescott replied, "I don't see what the wager has to do with you."

Hayden leaned forward. "When we arranged to have both Wild West shows here in Kansas City at the same time, the idea was to put enough pressure on Travers to get him to sell out to me. Any publicity your paper got out of it was merely supposed to be extra. I don't see how this contest makes Travers any more likely to give me what I want."

Under the pressure of Hayden's icy gaze, Prescott felt his nerves grow even more taut. "I suppose I didn't think—"

"Damn right you didn't," Hayden snapped, no longer bothering with the phony smile. "If this stupid contest doesn't work out right, we could lose everything—and I'm talking about your wife losing everything, too. Don't forget what I know about her."

As if I could ever forget, Prescott thought with a sigh. The horrible events of that night several months earlier would be burned into his brain as long as he lived. He had known for a long time that Cynthia drank too much, going far beyond the occasional brandy commonly taken by the wife of a prominent man. But he had also suspected that from time to time she had taken lovers. He had never been a passionate man except when it came to his work, so he did not begrudge Cynthia her pleasures, as long as she was discreet about them.

But he had known as soon as he answered the door that night and found a dazed Cynthia in the arms of Neal Hayden that she had been far from discreet. Cynthia was almost in a stupor, but she confirmed the story that Hayden told: She had been in an upstairs room in a seedy riverfront tavern, having gone there to meet her latest lover. The man was drunk and began to abuse her, and doing the only thing she could to keep him from beating her, she had pulled the small lady's pistol from her purse and shot him one time, very neatly, in the center of the forehead.

Though the pistol's report had been fairly quiet, Neal Hayden, who had happened to be in the tavern, had heard it and investigated. He had found a distraught Cynthia Prescott, wife of the wealthy Jasper Morton Prescott, standing over the body of her dead paramour.

Hayden had not wasted an instant in seeing how he could turn this situation to his advantage. After calling on one of his contacts who could easily dispose of a body and turning that chore over to him, the promoter brought Cynthia back to the Prescott mansion. Told what had happened, the publisher had had no choice but to go along with whatever Hayden wanted, for even though the killing might have been legally justified, its sordid circumstances assured that Cynthia's reputation—and Prescott's— would be ruined if details of the death were ever made public.

Since that night Hayden had extorted a considerable amount of money from Prescott, a sum large enough to cause trouble for the newspaper. But Hayden was not just a simple blackmailer. He had bigger ideas in mind—one of which was to take over the Wild West show owned by John Travers.

"Well," Hayden said sharply, jerking Prescott back from the unpleasant memories, "what are you going to do about this mess?"

The publisher shook his head. "There's not a great deal I *can* do. The wager is already set up, and all the publicity for the contest is under way."

"You'd better hope that Travers wins," Hayden warned. "If you have to turn this paper over to Hearst, you'll be just another nobody, and I won't have any use for you—which means I'll have no reason to continue protecting Cynthia."

"I understand," Prescott muttered, nodding bleakly.

"All right." Hayden stood up. "Maybe I can fix things so it won't matter what you've done. Travers could still change his mind about selling out to me, and I would think that the bet would be off then."

Prescott did not know whether to hope that Hayden was successful in his bid for the Wild West show or not. He supposed that would be the simplest outcome—but Prescott's pride had been wounded by that pirate Hearst, and it would be worth almost anything to see the expression on Hearst's face if the unthinkable happened and he lost.

Almost anything. If only he did not love Cynthia, Prescott thought as his head drooped and he stared unseeingly at the top of his desk, barely hearing the door shut as Hayden left. If he did not love Cynthia, he could turn her over to the police, divorce her, and put this entire ugly business behind him. But—God help him—Jasper Morton Prescott loved his wife, and he could not stand by and see her hurt more than she already had been.

The evening performance was over, once again playing to a good crowd, and John Travers entered his wagon satisfied with the way this stopover in Kansas City had gone so far. Oh, there had been some trouble, of course. All kinds of minor things had gone wrong, from the troupe's handbills being torn down early on, to the cinches on the saddles of his trick riders mysteriously giving way during one performance, to several of his men being roughed up in bar fights that Travers suspected had been deliberately provoked. Somebody was trying to cause trouble for his show, all right, and Travers suspected it might even be a traitor in his own troupe. But the Yakima Kid's Ace-High Pioneer Exposition and Wild West had always triumphed over the odds before, and it was going to this time, too.

Travers had just taken a turn around the camp, making sure that his people were all right before turning in himself. He was still wearing his costume, and there was a jauntiness in his step that nearly always evidenced itself when he wore the fancy beaded and fringed garb. Going lightly up the steps to the rear door of his wagon, he opened the door and went in.

Inside the doorway he stopped short, staring in dismay at the man sitting on the brocaded divan on one side of the room. Four other men were also in the wagon, and their bulk seemed to fill the compartment. "What the hell are you doing here, Hayden?" Travers asked harshly.

Neal Hayden looked up from the divan and said, "I came to make you one last offer, Travers. If you're smart, you'll accept it and sell me your show. You'll clear enough money to settle down and take life easy from now on."

"Take life easy?" Travers echoed with a snort. "What gave you the idea I'd want to do a fool thing like that?" He gestured at the other men. "And who are these boys?"

"Just some associates of mine," Hayden answered smoothly.

"Hired muscle, you mean," Travers snapped. "Well, take your bullyboys and get out of here, Hayden. I've always said that the public is welcome at my shows, but that doesn't include vermin like you."

Hayden's lips tightened into a grim line. "You'd better reconsider, Travers," he said slowly. "I said this is my last offer."

"Why in blazes do you *want* the damned show anyway?" Travers burst out. "It's profitable enough, but I reckon a man like you can always find a way to make money."

Hayden came to his feet. "Let's just say that I'm tired of people regarding me as a cheap con man. Society tolerates me because I know a lot of secrets, and those people know not to cross me. But they don't respect me, and they never will. The lower classes respect me, but only because I'm rumored to be a dangerous man. Well, I *am* dangerous. I know what I want, and I go after it. That's why I'm telling you you'd better go along with my offer, Travers. For your sake as well as mine."

That was the longest speech Travers had ever heard Hayden make, but it did nothing to change his opinion of the man. Hayden was still a low-life scoundrel, and he was proving it by bringing these strong-arm bruisers with him.

"I'll not be threatened," the old frontiersman said harshly. "I don't care how many men you bring with you, Hayden, I won't sell you my show. In fact, I won't have anything more to do with you. Get out! Now!"

Hayden sighed, but he did not look particularly disappointed. "All right, men," he said softly. "Persuade the old man to come around to our point of view."

The four thugs took a step foward, moving almost as one. Travers's heart was threatening to leap up his throat. Why had he been so muleheaded as to get himself into a brawl with men who would have no compunctions about breaking his bones, maybe even killing him? Swallowing as they came closer, Travers suddenly realized they would not kill him, since he could not give Hayden what he wanted if he was dead. But he could still manage to sign over a deed even if he was in pretty bad shape. . . .

Anger washed through him, and he heard himself saying, "Come on, dammit. What's the matter, afraid of an old man?" He might be a fool, he thought with a grin, but by God, he would not back down.

Complying, one of the men leapt at him, and a knobby, hamlike fist swept toward Travers's head.

Nearby, Brian Nichols held Lucy Corrigan tightly in his arms and wondered how he had lived before he met her. Ever since the night they had met, he had been haunted by thoughts of the young blonde. He could not forget her beauty, her grace, her presence—and he could not stay away from her.

She had been shocked the first time he had shown up at her wagon late at night and asked her to go for a walk with him. She had refused, of course, and warned him to leave before her father or any of the troupe's cowboys spotted him. Brian had been insistent, though, and Lucy had finally agreed. As she shut the door of her softly lighted wagon—quietly, so as not to disturb her father, sleeping in the main wagon not ten feet away—Brian had caught a glimpse of its interior by the lamplight. Its furnishings were a curious mixture of lace and leather, as if Lucy could not decide if she was a young woman or a cowboy who had just happened to be born female. He knew now that she was a woman . . . a vibrant, lovely woman.

They had talked aimlessly for a while as they walked beside the river, downstream from where Corrigan's show was camped. And then Brian had surprised both of them by reaching up to touch her hair in the moonlight, gently caressing the spun-gold strands. His hand dropped to her shoulder, pulling her toward him with a soft but insistent urgency, and her face had tilted back to receive his kiss. Both of them had felt the power in that kiss and the embrace that followed. There was no way they could deny what they felt for each other, but Lucy had insisted that she had to go back to the camp. She was afraid, and he did not blame her.

Since then they had stolen every moment they could together, mostly late at night after the performances of both shows were over and the camps were asleep. But occasionally the need to see Lucy, to hold her and kiss her, had been too much for the young sharpshooter, and he had risked riding over to visit her during the day.

Tonight, for the first time, she had come to him, slipping into his camp and knocking softly on the door of the wagon where he slept. He had been surprised to see her, but he was very glad she had come.

"We're going to have to tell folks about this sooner or later," Brian whispered to her now. "We can't just keep on sneaking around this way."

"Why not?" Lucy murmured, resting her head against his broad chest and hugging him tightly around the waist.

Her warm embrace was doing crazy things to him, making it difficult for him to think, but he finally managed to say, "For one thing, once the contest is over, both shows will be moving on. We couldn't see each other again."

Lucy shook her head slightly. "I couldn't stand that."

"So you see, we have to tell somebody."

"But my father . . . He'd never understand. . . ."

Brian sighed. She was right, of course. And although Travers was not his father, the Yakima Kid would never understand either. He would probably regard Brian's involvement with Lucy as a betrayal. It was a problem to which he saw no answer. "Maybe we'll think of something," he said, stroking her hair. "We've got to—"

The crash that came from somewhere nearby made his head jerk up. Hard on the heels of that shattering impact came several thuds and some muffled words that might have been curses.

"What in the world?" Brian muttered, putting his hands on Lucy's shoulders and holding her away from him.

"It sounds like somebody's scuffling," Lucy replied, a worried look appearing on her moonlit face.

"That's more than just a scuffle." Brian turned his head, trying to locate the source of the sounds. "That sounds deadly serious—as if somebody's going to get hurt."

At that moment, the door of Travers's wagon burst open, and a man came tumbling out of it. The Kid's wagon was about fifty feet from where Brian and Lucy had been standing in the shadows of a storage wagon. In this light, Brian could not make out who the man was, but one thing was certain: It was not John Travers. And that meant the Kid was in trouble.

"Stay here," he ordered Lucy. Out of the corner of his eye, Brian saw the stranger scrambling to his feet and lunging up the steps into the wagon again.

The young woman caught at her lover's arm. "Brian—"

"I've got to help the Kid! Now, stay here where you won't get hurt."

Without waiting to see if she did as he told her or not, the sharpshooter turned and dashed toward Travers's wagon. Still wearing his costume, he reached for the ivory-handled Colts in the double-holster rig strapped around his waist, loading cartridges into first one, then the other as he ran. The shells were blanks, the kind he used in the show, but in close quarters a black-powder blank could still be quite dangerous.

Skipping the wagon's steps, Brian vaulted to the doorway and plunged through, his keen eyes taking in the scene. A knot of big men in city clothes surrounded Travers, doling out punishment to him with fists and feet while another man in a suit stood nearby.

Travers had gotten in at least one good punch—the blow that had knocked one of his assailants out of the wagon—but he was badly outnumbered and about to go down. Slowing only for an instant as he dashed in, Brian leapt across the room and grabbed the shoulder of one of the men. As he yanked the stranger around, he put all the weight and power of his big form behind the punch he threw. His fist caught the man perfectly on the jaw, lifting him off the floor of the wagon and sending him crashing down on an overturned table.

Brian's momentum almost carried him past the struggling group, giving one of the other men a chance to jump him from behind. An arm went around his throat, closing tightly and cutting off his air, but as he gasped for breath, he drove an elbow backward into the stomach of the man who held him. The man's grip loosened, and Brian twisted around and threw a jab at his opponent's face, feeling it connect. His opponent staggered back a step, and the sharpshooter followed closely, peppering the man with more punches.

The unexpected arrival of help had allowed Travers to break free of his captors, and the wiry ex-frontiersman whipped a blow to one man's chin, then whirled around to throw a punch at one of the other thugs. When that man's hand slipped beneath his coat and came out clutching a small pistol, Travers flung himself to the side just as the man fired. The gun roared, and Brian could not tell if Travers had been hit or not.

Acting purely on instinct and anger, Brian shoved aside the man with whom he had been trading blows. His right hand dipped to the holster on his hip, the speed of his draw turning the motion into a blur, and he fired from the hip, just as he did during his act in the arena. The wadding from the blank hit the gunman in the hand, and at such close range it was almost as good as a bullet. The man's pistol sprang out of his fingers, and he let out a howl as he clutched his suddenly bloody hand to his body.

The white-haired man who had been watching the

fight yelled, "No!" but the other toughs were already reaching for guns. As Brian's left hand flashed, drawing his other Colt, he spotted Travers on the floor of the wagon, rolling out of the line of fire.

And then there was no time to think. This was the first time in his life that anyone had shot at Brian, the first time he had ever fired back at a human being. His silver-plated Colts bucked and roared as he triggered shot after shot, driving his opponents back. He had just a glimpse of the white-haired man diving through the door at the front of the wagon, the one that opened onto the driver's box. Then the thugs followed the man in a mad rush, ready to run through a wall if that was what it took to get away from the big blond man with the fancy guns.

Brian was half-deafened by the blasts, and it was suddenly impossible to see anything through the thick pall of gun smoke inside the wagon. He felt someone pulling on the sleeve of his buckskin shirt and let himself be led out of the vehicle. Coughing, he stumbled out into the clear, warm night air along with John Travers.

"Take it easy, son," the older man said, coughing a bit himself as he pounded Brian on the back. "Those boys are long gone, and I bet they don't stop running till they reach St. Louis!"

"Who . . . who the devil were they, and why were they trying to kill you, Kid?" Brian managed to ask.

"They weren't going to kill me," Travers said grimly. "I wouldn't have been able to give them what they wanted if I was dead. But they would have handed me a hell of a beating if it wasn't for you— Here! What's this?"

Hearing hurried footsteps behind him, Brian turned around in time to see Lucy running toward him. She leapt into his arms, obviously having abandoned her hiding place when she saw him emerge from the wagon.

"Oh, God, Brian, are you all right?" she asked frantically, clutching at him and searching for wounds.

He holstered his guns in order to put his arms around her. More people from the troupe were running up now, drawn by the gunfire, and Brian reflected that the events of the night had at least solved one problem for them: They no longer had to worry about their romance being discovered. The way Lucy was holding on to him made it clear for everyone to see.

"I'm fine," he told her quietly. "Not a scratch."

With a frown on his face, Travers asked, "Lucy? What are you doing over here, girl?" Without waiting for an answer, he took in the way Lucy and Brian were embracing and went on, his voice colder, "Never mind. I think I can see what you're doing here."

Brian began, "Look, Kid, we need to talk about this—"

"Damn right we do." Travers turned to face the anxious group that had gathered around them. "Go on back to your bunks, folks. There's nothing here to see. Somebody was snooping around, but Brian and I ran them off."

The cowboys and roustabouts lingered for several moments, but when it became obvious the fight was over, they drifted away. One man said loudly, "I'll bet it was some of that Corrigan bunch trying to make trouble again." Brian was glad that he had moved in front of Lucy, shielding her from view as much as possible.

When they were alone with Travers, Brian began again, "I can explain—"

"In my wagon," Travers cut in. "You can explain all you want to, boy, but do it in my wagon."

Shrugging, Brian led Lucy into the wagon, keeping one arm around her shoulders. When Travers had the door shut behind the three of them, Brian said firmly, "There's no point in being mad, Kid. Lucy and I are in love, and that's all there is to it."

"Hell, I can see that," Travers snapped. "My eyes may not be what they once were, but I'm not blind, boy. What I want to know is how long you've been working for Corrigan behind my back."

"Working for Corrigan!" Brian exclaimed. "Why, I wouldn't work for . . . I mean . . ."

Travers grimaced. "Sort of hard to say anything bad about the daddy of the gal you love, isn't it? Did he hire you to cause trouble for my show, or have you been doing it just to get in good with him?"

Brian regarded Travers's weathered, angry face for a long moment, then said softly, "If I didn't respect you more than any man alive, Mr. Travers, I think I'd be

throwing a punch at you right about now. I may love Lucy
Corrigan, but I have never done anything to hurt this
show and I never will. You've got my word on that."

"That's right," Lucy added, angry herself now. "Brian
ran right in here to help you when those men were
attacking you, Uncle John. Have you forgotten about that?"

Travers paled slightly. "Uncle John . . ." he repeated
softly. "I'd almost forgotten what that sounded like, Lucy.
It's been a long time since you called me that."

She flushed slightly and said, "Well, you were like
my uncle once."

"You're right, I was." Travers took a deep breath.
"And you're right, Brian, it *is* ridiculous to think that
you'd be working against me. I'm sorry, son."

Brian nodded. "Apology accepted. But that still doesn't
explain what happened here, Kid."

"A fella named Hayden paid me a visit," Travers
explained glumly. "He wants to buy this show, and he's
not willing to take no for an answer. Tonight he brought
along some help to try to change my mind."

Quickly Travers recounted his previous meetings with
Hayden, all of which he had kept to himself until now.

"Hayden wasn't expecting to run into so much trouble," Travers finally concluded. "It's possible we scared
him off for good—but I doubt it."

All the while the old frontiersman had been talking,
Brian had been thinking, and now he remarked, "I know
I'm not the one responsible for the troubles that've been
plaguing us, Kid, but this Hayden could have somebody
working on the inside."

"And so could Corrigan." At the look of censure on
Lucy's face, Travers waved a hand and went on, "I'm not
saying he does, mind you. It's more likely that Hayden
paid somebody off to make things difficult for us, thinking
that would make me more likely to sell out." The Yakima
Kid clenched a fist, promising, "If that's what he thought,
he's dead wrong. And the next time I see Neal Hayden, I
may just shoot the low-down skunk on sight!" He took
another deep breath and eyed the young couple. "But you
two have got another problem entirely."

"What's that?" Brian asked, holding Lucy tighter and

sure that he already knew what Travers was going to say.

"Sooner or later you're going to have to tell Cactus what's going on between the two of you." Travers managed a grin. "And that's liable to be a show to put this Wild West contest to shame!"

Chapter Ten

Earl Corrigan leaned back in his chair and intently regarded the studious face of Nathan Sanford. "You really think we can do it?" the old scout asked.

Sanford nodded and turned around a document in front of him so that Corrigan could see it better. "If the attendance at the competition is as good as everyone is anticipating, the share we'll get from this contract Prescott and Hearst drew up will enable us to pay our bills. Especially since our own crowds have been up a bit the last few nights."

Corrigan looked out through the open door of his wagon at the late-afternoon sunlight. In just a few hours the contest would begin, and everything was riding on it. Corrigan had never been a man given to nerves—fighting Indians and owlhoots had taught him how to stay calm even in the worst situations—but there were butterflies in his stomach. His show's share of the gate receipts would be enough to stave off imminent disaster, but in the long run the troupe needed a fresh start, enough money to let it grow and prosper, and winning the competition—and the prize money that Hearst had put up—would accomplish that.

Corrigan had faith in his people. They would do their best . . . or at least most of them would. He had never been able to shake the nagging feeling that somebody in the troupe was working against him, helping to set up all the trouble that had come their way in recent days. If there was one thing Corrigan could not abide, it was a traitor. But between putting on the regular shows and getting ready for the competition, there had just not been any time to root out the troublemaker.

As Sanford was putting away the ledgers, Lucy came up the steps and into the wagon, already dressed in her trick-riding outfit. Corrigan knew she was as anxious as he was for the contest to begin, for it seemed as if the last week had taken a month to pass. Absently Lucy said hello to her father and then sat down on a straight-backed chair and began toying with the fringe on her short skirt.

Something was bothering her, Corrigan suddenly realized as he noticed the distracted look on her face. He wondered if the problem, whatever it was, was a recent one or something that had been disturbing her for several days. He had been so busy, he might not have noticed anything was wrong.

"Are you all right, sweetheart?" he asked now, ignoring Sanford as the bookkeeper stood up and left the wagon.

"I'm fine, Father," Lucy replied. She hesitated, then continued, "I was just talking to Wes Ballard."

Corrigan waited, letting her take her time.

"He still seems to have some sort of romantic interest in me," she blurted after a moment.

"Nothing surprising in that," Corrigan remarked. "He's a young fella, and you're a mighty pretty gal, Lucy. A gal could do worse than a man like Ballard. He's really pitched in to help around here."

"I know that. And I appreciate everything he's done for the show, from not demanding his payment for those horses to taking Jackrabbit's place on the stagecoach. I'm fond of Wes, and I've told him so. But I just don't like him . . . that way."

Corrigan shrugged, feeling slightly uneasy. He could ride a bronc, throw a loop, shoot a gun, and do just about everything else necessary for a man to survive on the frontier in wilder times. But affairs of the heart were another matter entirely. "I reckon folks can't really help what they feel," he said slowly. "You feel one way and Wes feels another, and the two of you will just have to work that out."

"I suppose so," Lucy murmured with a sigh. "With

everything else that's going on, though, couldn't just one thing be simple?"

"Not in this life," Corrigan said wryly, chuckling. "Simple is one thing you don't run into very often."

But winning this contest tonight would help simplify a few things, Corrigan added silently. And then he could worry about all the other problems—the ones that would not go away.

A few minutes earlier, Wes Ballard had watched Lucy disappear into her father's wagon. Then he'd turned away and stalked toward the corrals. His mind was in a turmoil, and when that was the case, nothing calmed him down like working with horses.

Walking swiftly, he vowed that he was through being a stubborn fool. Lucy Corrigan might be the prettiest, sweetest girl he had seen in a long time, but he had to face facts. She was not attracted to him and was never going to be—in fact, it was almost as if she was already in love with somebody else.

That thought made Ballard's step slow, and a frown appeared on his face. Brian Nichols, that sharpshooter from Travers's show, had been interested in Lucy from the first, and Ballard wondered if it was possible—

"Well, Mr. Ballard, are you ready for the big contest?"

The question took Ballard by surprise, but the voice asking it did not. He recognized it immediately and turned to face the woman who had asked it. "I'm ready, Miss Dixon," he said flatly. "Are you?"

"Of course," Morgan Dixon replied, looking as smart and stylish as ever despite having been at the show's dusty camp all day, watching their preparations. *Getting in the blasted way*, was how Ballard put it to himself. She went on, "I saw you talking to Lucy Corrigan a few minutes ago, and I must say, you don't look very happy, Mr. Ballard. I take it the course of true love is not running smoothly?"

"My conversations with Miss Corrigan are my own business, lady," Ballard snapped. "Anyway, you're barking up the wrong tree. Lucy and I are friends, and that's all."

Morgan's tongue darted out of her mouth and wet her

full lips. She started to speak, then stopped abruptly before any words came out, as if she had decided against what she had been about to say. Ballard was grateful for small favors.

He tugged on the brim of his hat. "Now, if you'll excuse me, I've got work to do—"

The sounds of a scuffle nearby made him turn around quickly. A high-pitched voice yelped, "Dammit, get away from me!" The demand was followed by coarse laughter.

About twenty yards away, Nathan Sanford was surrounded by four of the show's cowboys. They were roughly shoving him back and forth, and his normally mild face suddenly contorted in rage. Balling his fists, he swung a punch at one of the cowboys.

The bookkeeper's resistance was so unexpected that the cowboy did not even try to dodge the blow. It landed flush on his nose, and blood spurted. The man howled in pain, dancing back a step and holding his hands to his injury. "The little bastard hit me!" he exclaimed. "Grab him!"

Ballard's mouth tightened. Ever since he had temporarily joined the Wild West show, he had seen various cowboys giving Sanford a hard time. Sanford had never fought back, but the Texan supposed the little bookkeeper had finally gotten his fill of the harassment, and the cowboys had forgotten that even the smallest dog will turn and bite when pushed hard enough.

A couple of the wranglers grabbed Sanford's arms and jerked him back as he tried to dart past them. The one with the bloody nose growled, "Hang on to him. I'll teach him a lesson he won't ever forget." With clenched fists he moved in on the feebly struggling Sanford.

Ballard vaguely heard Morgan Dixon say, "Shouldn't somebody help that poor man?" But the rancher was way ahead of her, his long legs already carrying him quickly across the gap between him and the cowboys. As the man with the bloody nose drew a fist back, intending to slam it into Sanford's belly, Ballard stepped beside him and grabbed his wrist.

"You're not teaching anybody a lesson, mister, unless it's how to be a damned fool," Ballard grated.

The cowboy spun around, furious at having his revenge interrupted, and used his other hand to throw a punch at Ballard's head. The Texan ducked the blow easily and let go of the cowboy's wrist, driving his own fist into the man's midsection. The cowboy grunted and started to double over, which put his chin in perfect position for the left cross Ballard smashed into it. Staggering to the side, the cowboy collapsed onto his knees.

Only a few seconds had passed. Ballard faced the other three wranglers. "Clear out," he ordered coldly.

The two holding Sanford released him abruptly. Stepping back, they and their companion hoisted their injured friend to his feet. "Sure, Ballard," one of them said nervously. "We didn't mean no harm. We was just funnin'—"

"It had gone past that, and you know it," Ballard cut in angrily. "Now, git!"

The cowboys hurried away, leaving Sanford to catch his breath and regain his composure. Drawing a handkerchief from his pocket, the bookkeeper wiped it across his face, then said, "My thanks, Mr. Ballard. Those ruffians would have handed me quite a beating if you hadn't stepped in."

"Reckon you must have known that before you threw the first punch," the Texan said, a tinge of admiration in his voice. "But you did it anyway."

Sanford nodded shakily. "I . . . I was just so tired of the way they treat me. I'm not like them, so that gives them license to make me the butt of their jokes and physically terrorize me," he said bitterly. He shoved the handkerchief back in his pocket, his hand still trembling. With a sigh, he went on, "I appreciate what you just did for me, Mr. Ballard, but I curse the fate that brought me among such barbarians."

Ballard did not know how to reply to that, so he just nodded and said, "Well, maybe they'll leave you alone for a while." He turned, intending to go on about his business.

But he had forgotten Morgan Dixon. She was standing nearby, and she regarded him for a moment, then politely clapped. "Bravo," she declared, and he could hear the cynicism in her tone. "That was quite an exhibition of gallantry, Mr. Ballard."

"I didn't much like the odds," he said brusquely. "You can make of that whatever you want to, Miss Dixon. I'm sure you will anyway." Brushing past her, he muttered, "As for me, I've got work to do."

He walked away, feeling her eyes on his back. She was probably figuring out how to use this incident in one of her newspaper stories, he decided, and that would just embarrass Nathan Sanford that much more. Not that Morgan would care, he added to himself. It was a shame there was no heart to go with the woman's beauty and brains, Ballard thought.

Music and laughter came floating on the early-evening air as Cactus Corrigan's wagons rolled southward on the road along the eastern bank of the Missouri. They had crossed over on the ferry and were now on their way to Travers's arena for the contest, and from the sound of things as they approached, the crowd was going to be a huge one.

From the driver's box of the stagecoach, second in line in the procession, Wes Ballard could see throngs of people streaming into the grandstand. The place was an oasis of light in the rapidly gathering darkness, brilliantly illuminated by some of those newfangled electric lights. The glare of the artificial lights seemed harsh to Ballard, but he had to admit they were a lot brighter than torches and kerosene lamps.

"Ye gads! Look at all them people!" Jackrabbit Dawkins exclaimed from his seat beside the Texan. "Did you ever see so many folks?"

"Not lately," Ballard replied. The grandstands were going to be packed, probably with people left standing in the aisles.

"Don't worry 'bout drivin' the coach in front of so many people, Wes," Jackrabbit remarked. "Once you get started, you won't pay them no mind."

"Thanks," Ballard responded dryly. "I wasn't worried about that . . . yet."

The old jehu was getting around on his sore leg without much trouble now, but he still had to use his cane, and Corrigan had decided that Ballard should continue to handle the driving chores during the competition's final event, a stagecoach race around the arena—if that was all right with Ballard. The rancher had agreed. After spending more than a week with Corrigan's troupe, he knew and liked most of them, and he wanted to see them win this contest tonight.

With Corrigan's wagon in the lead, the procession circled the outside of the arena and came to the area where Travers's troupe was waiting for the contest to begin. Ballard felt himself tensing as he reined in the team. He could see Brian Nichols, tall and handsome and resplendent in his fancy outfit. In contrast, Ballard was wearing the same well-worn range clothes he had sported from the first, and he felt decidedly drab next to some of the flashily garbed performers.

A cowboy rode up alongside Corrigan's wagon, leading the old scout's saddle horse. The showman took the reins and stepped into the saddle, leaving the wagon for Lucy to handle. She took over expertly while Corrigan rode ahead to meet Travers.

Then the Yakima Kid loped forward on his gorgeous palomino, and the former partners met and shook hands briefly. Ballard was not close enough to hear what was said, but the two of them seemed civil enough, if not overly friendly. Travers waved a hand toward the entrance to the arena, and Corrigan nodded, and the rancher knew they were discussing the opening ceremonies for the evening's entertainment, which had already been worked out. Both troupes would enter the arena at the same time, circling in opposite directions in front of the grandstands and then meeting and passing each other on the far side. It would have been nice to be able to rehearse the routine, but it was simple enough, and Ballard did not think they would have any trouble with it.

As he watched Corrigan and Travers both taking out pocket watches and flipping them open, a grin tugged at Ballard's mouth. He had heard his father speak of Cactus Corrigan and the Yakima Kid many times, and the old-timers had turned out to be everything he had expected. Looking at the two of them together, a man could see how much alike they were. They should have remained friends rather than turning into bitter rivals, Ballard thought, but there was no arguing with fate.

Corrigan snapped his watch shut, and Travers did likewise. Turning in their saddles, both men swept their hats off, held the Stetsons high, then waved their people forward into the opening procession.

The Great Wild West Competition was under way.

Cheers erupted from the audience as both troupes entered the arena. Waves of applause washed over the performers, showering them with the crowd's adulation. This contest was the biggest thing to hit Kansas City since the arrival of the railroad, and from the way the spectators were crammed in, practically everybody in town seemed to be in attendance.

Ballard tried to keep his mind on his work as he drove the stagecoach around the dirt-floored arena behind the lead wagon, but his eyes strayed over to glance at the crowd. An area in the middle of the stands was roped off for dignitaries, and sitting there were Prescott and Hearst, both applauding politely. Each man had quite an entourage with him, including the reporters from their respective newspapers. Ballard saw Morgan Dixon seated near Prescott, and beside her was a man with thick brown hair and an impressive handlebar mustache. Garrett Kingsley, the reporter Hearst had imported from New York, no doubt, Ballard decided. The man leaned over to say something into Morgan's ear, and she laughed in response. Ballard could not hear her, of course—not in the pandemonium that filled the arena—but he could see the merriment on her face.

It was too bad Morgan worked for Prescott, Ballard thought. Too bad she was part of the enemy camp—and such an annoying part at that. But did she have to be so damned amused by what that Yankee jackanapes had to say?

Ballard's mouth tightened as he told himself there was no reason for him to be angry about whomever Morgan Dixon was talking to. No reason in the world.

As the two troupes met and passed each other, Ballard got a good look at the other stagecoach and its driver. A Concord of about the same age and seemingly identical in its construction to the one he was driving, the vehicle appeared to have only one variation, which was that some of its trim was painted differently. Travers's driver was a barrel-chested, middle-aged man, who was handling his team with ease. Given the similarities of the two coaches, Ballard figured that the real difference in the race would probably come down to the drivers. Whichever man could coax the greatest speed out of his team would win.

The two groups wound up at opposite ends of the arena, and they stopped to bow and let the audience clap and shout some more. When the noise finally subsided, a frock-coated man stepped down from the box where Prescott and Hearst were sitting and walked to the center of the arena. The man was the mayor of Kansas City, and he was scheduled to open the competition with a few remarks. Ballard hoped the speech would not last too long, for like everyone else here, he was anxious for the contest to begin.

The mayor waved for silence, and when he got it at last, he lifted his orator's voice, which filled the arena. "Welcome, ladies and gentlemen, to a spectacle the likes of which our fair city has seldom seen! Tonight we are privileged to witness a competition between two of the finest troupes of entertainers in the country, the Yakima Kid's Ace-High Pioneer Exposition and Wild West . . . and Cactus Corrigan's Great Wild West! It is a great honor for me to introduce the two men who have brought this incredible event to us—from San Francisco, Mr. William Randolph Hearst, and our own Jasper Morton Prescott!"

There was applause for the two newspaper publishers as they strolled out into the arena and lifted their top hats to the crowd, but the volume was considerably less than that which had welcomed the two Wild West shows. The audience had come to see cowboys, not publishers. A moment later, that became obvious as a thunderous ovation greeted the mayor's introduction of Corrigan and Travers.

The two men rode their prancing horses into the center of the arena, waving their hats to the crowd. Ballard felt an unexpected tingle as spotlights played over the mounted figures. He was looking at history, he realized, at men who had helped to create a world that had flourished briefly but gloriously, then disappeared. These Wild West shows were the last vestiges of those days, and men like Cactus Corrigan and the Yakima Kid were living relics.

Not that Ballard would ever call them that to their faces. No, sir, he thought with a grin.

"Nice seein' the two of 'em out there together like that, ain't it?" Jackrabbit asked, leaning forward on the seat with an intent expression on his bearded face.

"Yep, it is," the rancher replied.

"Too bad it can't stay that way. You never saw two partners better suited than Cactus an' the Kid, but I don't reckon it'll ever be like that again. Durned shame."

Ballard nodded in agreement.

The actual competition got started quickly. Ballard and Jackrabbit climbed down from the stagecoach and watched from beside it as the two troupes pitted their best performers against each other. The contest was something like a rodeo, as cowboys from each side demonstrated their skills at riding bucking broncs, roping steers, and bulldogging calves. But interspersed between those activities were events such as trick roping, sharpshooting, and trick riding. Ballard felt his excitement grow as Lucy Corrigan stunned the crowd with her acrobatic feats on horseback, winning easily over the trick rider from Travers's show. But Brian Nichols put on a dazzling display a little later, shooting what seemed like a hundred glass balls and spinning plates out of the air in the wink of an eye. Ballard could not deny the young man's skill with a pair of six-shooters. Brian put to shame everyone else Ballard had ever seen, including the trick-shot artist from Corrigan's troupe.

Suddenly, almost before Ballard realized it, nearly two hours had gone by, and the final event of the night was fast approaching. Jackrabbit nudged him in the ribs and said, "Get on up there, boy, and get ready! Looks like the whole shootin' match may be ridin' up there with you!"

Ballard's eyes widened as he realized the old jehu was right. The finals of the steer roping were drawing to a close, and as Ballard watched, Corrigan's man won, throwing the score for the evening into a tie.

A tie! That meant that whoever won the stagecoach race would determine the outcome of the entire contest.

Ballard's nerves felt like rawhide thongs that had been dipped in water and then left out in the sun. If they were drawn any tighter, he thought, he would fly apart like a busted watch. It had come down to this: Outsider or not, he was suddenly responsible for the fate of something that involved dozens of people.

Corrigan galloped over to the coach as several cowboys drove the steers from the previous event out of the arena. "Good luck, son," the showman said, leaning over in the saddle to shake Ballard's hand. "Just do your best."

"I will, sir," the rancher promised solemnly. He thought Corrigan looked unusually pale, and he supposed the tension of the situation was getting to the old scout, too.

"You all right, Cactus?" Jackrabbit asked suddenly, a worried frown on his grizzled face.

"I'm fine," Corrigan insisted. "At least, I will be once Wes here shows Travers's man how to drive a coach. Leave him in the dust, boy!"

Ballard forced a grin, and Corrigan wheeled his horse and rode back toward the center of the arena. Travers was on his way there, too, so that they could announce the score and start the stagecoach race.

As he turned to step up onto the driver's box, another voice said, "Good luck, Mr. Ballard." Glancing around, he saw that Morgan Dixon had left the publishers' box. She was standing next to the coach and looking up at him with a serious expression on her pretty face, and her words had sounded sincere.

"If I didn't know better, Miss Dixon, I'd think you meant that," Ballard remarked, tugging on his mustache.

"Strangely enough, I do," she responded. Her dark eyes met his, and he found himself frowning in confusion.

"Thank you," he said gruffly. "But if your boss loses that bet, you might not have a job anymore."

"I'd like to see you win anyway."

Hoisting himself onto the seat, Ballard looked down at her. "Going to do my best," he declared, then picked up the reins and got the team moving. He headed the coach toward the mark where the race would begin, where Travers's stagecoach was already waiting.

He was only about halfway to the appointed spot when the sound of the cries coming from the crowd suddenly changed. Most of the shouts were still of excitement, but there was an abrupt undercurrent of something else, and Ballard looked up, scanning the grandstand to see if he could spot what was wrong.

His eyes widened in shock as he saw the spectators stampeding out of one section, flames licking up behind them from the wooden bleachers. People screamed and ran and trampled each other in their mad rush to get away from the fire. Even worse, the same scene was being repeated in locations all over the grandstand.

Within seconds, the huge crowd that had been so happy and thrilled turned into a fear-crazed mob, and Ballard watched in horror as shrieking spectators pushed toward the exits. Those openings were clogged with people, and as the fires began to spread, more and more of the audience leapt over the railing into the arena itself, heading for the big main entrance used by the performers.

Ballard would not have thought that anything could be louder than the chaos already going on, but suddenly he heard something else, something that sounded almost like the rumble of faraway thunder. Almost, but not quite, and a few seconds later he recognized the sound for what it really was: *hoofbeats*—hundreds of hoofbeats, and they were coming this way.

Standing up on the driver's box, Ballard shouted, "No!" to the people who were rushing toward the arena entrance. But none of them could hear him, of course, and it was doubtful they would have stopped if they had as they continued their blind charge toward the opening.

The stampeding horses reached the entrance first. The galloping animals thundered through the opening, and the people in the vanguard of the mob never had a chance. They fell beneath the sharp hooves, their screams drowned out by the stampede.

Sickened, Ballard finally snatched up his whip, lashing the frightened team until they started moving again. He guided the coach toward the side of the arena, and as he drove, he searched the frenzied crowd for familiar faces—Corrigan, Lucy, Jackrabbit, Morgan Dixon. . . .

He did not spot any of them, but he abruptly saw through the clouds of dust and smoke filling the air that the horses had not stampeded by accident. Men on horseback, wearing bandannas over their faces and firing guns into the air, were driving the horses into the arena. This was a deliberate stampede, and Ballard suddenly realized that the fires had been no accident either. To have been so widely spread around the arena, the blazes must have been started on purpose. Whoever was behind this was already a murderer on a grand scale.

Ballard saw a familiar head of dark hair in front of him. The raven-black tresses were now rather disheveled, but they belonged to Morgan Dixon, who was stumbling along in the middle of the mob, trying to stay on her feet. If she fell, she would be trampled either by the crowd or by the horses, but Ballard could not move his own team any faster for fear of running over someone, so his progress toward her was maddeningly slow. He glanced up at the grandstand and saw that virtually all of it was in flames now.

Finally the coach reached Morgan's side just as she stumbled and started to fall. Ballard threw himself half off the seat, hanging on to the reins with one hand while thrusting the other toward her. His fingers closed on the shoulder of her dress for an instant, and then he shifted his grip to her arm. Holding her more solidly now, Ballard shouted to her, "Climb up! It's safer up here!"

Nodding in understanding, she scrambled up to the box with his assistance. As she settled beside him, breathing deeply and raggedly, she managed to gasp, "Th-thank you!"

"Are you all right?" he asked over the tumult. She nodded, and Ballard turned his attention back to the scene in the arena. The force of the stampede had been broken by the relatively small confines of the enclosure, and the horses were now milling around, a few of them still galloping but most of them slowed to a canter. The masked riders were trying to goad them into running again, but were having little success.

"Ballard!" someone shouted nearby, and the Texan looked over to see Brian Nichols forcing his way closer to the stage on horseback. Perched on the saddle in front of him was Lucy Corrigan, his strong arm around her waist holding her tightly.

He had been right about the two of them, Ballard thought, but at the moment there was no time to think about romance. He waved Brian over. The stagecoach was the safest place for Lucy.

Brian brought his horse beside the coach, and Lucy reached over, caught the railing around the vehicle's roof, and pulled herself aboard with the same lithe ease she had demonstrated in her horseback-riding stunts. Twisting his head, Ballard asked her the same question he had asked Morgan, and Lucy nodded that she was all right.

"Have you seen Corrigan and Travers and Jackrabbit?" Ballard called to Brian. The sharpshooter started to shake his head, but a fresh crackle of gunfire made all of them look around quickly.

Still mounted on their magnificent horses, Corrigan and Travers were exchanging shots with the men who had started the stampede. Ballard caught his breath at the sight of the two old frontiersmen routing the villains who had caused this death and destruction. The electric lights had all shattered from the heat by now, but the flames from the grandstands threw a hellish glare over the scene.

Ballard turned and asked Lucy, "Are your father and Travers shooting real bullets?"

Lucy nodded. "He's no trick shooter. His guns are usually unloaded, but he doesn't carry any blanks, just live rounds."

"Same with Travers," Brian said, leaning in from his saddle.

Suddenly scrambling up the rear boot of the coach to the roof, with the agility of a man thirty years younger, was Jackrabbit Dawkins, an old Henry rifle in his hands. Ballard had no idea where Jackrabbit had gotten the weapon, but it looked natural in his grip. "Head over yonder!" he barked at Ballard. "We gotta give Cactus and the Kid a hand!"

The mob had thinned out some, as most of the spectators had fled—the ones who could, at least. Quite a few lay sprawled in twisted attitudes of death on the sandy floor of the arena. Swallowing the bile that rose in his throat at the sight, Ballard sent the coach rolling toward the battle between Corrigan, Travers, and the masked thugs.

Jackrabbit scuttled up to the front of the roof, thrust the barrel of the Henry between Ballard and Morgan, and pulled the trigger. Ballard flinched slightly at the blast, while Morgan clapped her hands over her ears and let out a cry of surprise. One of the masked men went flying out of his saddle, landing in a limp sprawl.

A path was opening up now, and Ballard whipped the team into a faster gait. Brian Nichols rode alongside, guiding his horse with his knees as he filled both hands with his ivory-handled Colts and began to fire. The thought darted across Ballard's mind that they must really look like something out of a Wild West show now, charging into a gun battle this way. But this was no performance. It was real—deadly real.

The masked men were running, wheeling their horses, and doing their best to get away. As Ballard brought the coach alongside Corrigan and Travers, he heard the Kid shout, "Hayden's mine!" Ballard had no idea what Travers was talking about, but the silver-haired frontiersman spurred his horse forward and took off after one of the fleeing men. Travers's quarry was wearing a derby, and the headgear flew off from the force of the wind to reveal a head of close-cropped white hair. The man turned and emptied a pistol at Travers, who leaned forward over the neck of his racing horse to let the slugs go harmlessly over his head.

The gun in Travers's hand boomed once, and the man he was after suddenly clutched his right shoulder and swayed in the saddle. His feet slipped out of the stirrups, and he fell with a cry of dismay, landing hard and rolling over and over several times. He managed to come up into a crouch, however, and with his uninjured arm started to lift another pistol he had snatched from under his coat.

Travers squeezed off two more rounds, both bullets catching the man in the chest and throwing him backward. Thumbing back the hammer of his revolver, the Kid looked for a moment as if he were going to continue firing, but there would have been no point in it. Taking a deep breath, he let down the hammer of the gun and slid it back in his right-hand holster.

Sirens and bells clanged in the night, and Ballard saw firemen and police officers fighting to bring both the blaze and the resulting chaos under control again. Travers turned and trotted his horse back toward the stagecoach, where Corrigan was having a relieved reunion with his daughter. She assured him she was all right, but Ballard noticed she did not say anything about Brian Nichols being the one who had plucked her out of danger.

As Travers rode up, Corrigan turned toward him angrily. "What the hell happened here?" Corrigan demanded. "I saw you take out after that fella. This was personal between you and him, wasn't it?"

Travers was grim-faced as he replied, "I'm afraid it was, Cactus. That bastard's name was Hayden, and he'd been trying to get me to sell him my show for months. Things got rough last time he came around, and I reckon he decided he'd rather settle the score than do business with me."

"So you're to blame for all this," Corrigan shot back, waving a hand at the carnage surrounding them.

"The devil I am!" Travers countered. "Would you have sold your show to some underhanded skunk like that?"

Corrigan did not answer for a long moment, but then he shook his head. "No, I reckon I wouldn't," he admitted.

In the center of the arena as they were, the small group was relatively safe from the fire, although the heat from the flames was extremely uncomfortable. It was a miracle, Ballard thought, that they had all come through this unharmed. They had kept their heads rather than panicking, and that had made the difference.

"Reckon this means the contest is off," Jackrabbit commented. "Can't very well finish 'er now."

Ballard had not even thought about the competition since the fires had broken out, signaling the start of the nightmarish last few minutes. Now he nodded, along with Corrigan and Travers.

Brian Nichols spoke up, pointing out, "Hayden was an Easterner, and those hired thugs of his were mostly city boys. They couldn't have stampeded those horses without some help from somebody who knew what he was doing."

"You're right," Travers agreed. "And those were our horses they used."

Brian grimaced. "Anybody seen Quint Fowler around here tonight?"

Ballard lifted an eyebrow as the others all shook their heads. He understood what the sharpshooter was getting at, and his own suspicions followed right along in stride. Ever since he had refused Fowler's offer to buy his herd and then shortly thereafter had almost gotten beaten to death in that alley, Ballard had thought Fowler might be involved. Now he was sure of it.

He looked over at Corrigan and Travers and asked, "Who's counting the money from tonight's show?"

"Why, Nathan Sanford's taking care of that," Corrigan replied.

"He's using my wagon for the chore," Travers added. "One of my men is there to help him and show him the safe."

"To keep an eye on him, you mean," Corrigan snapped. "You didn't trust Nathan because he works for me."

"Now, dammit, Cactus, it's just good business—"

Ballard ignored the rest of the exchange. Turning to Jackrabbit, he asked, "Can I borrow that Henry for a few minutes?"

"Sure thing, son," the old driver said, handing the rifle to Ballard. "Just take good care of her. She's always took mighty good care of me."

Ballard nodded, then looked at Brian Nichols and said, "Let's go."

Ballard stepped down from the coach, ignoring Morgan Dixon's questions of where he was going and what was happening. Brian dismounted, and he and the Texan wove a path through what was left of the crowd, staying out of the way of the firemen and police. Things were rapidly getting under control again, although the grandstands and the arena were a shambles.

Both men strode rapidly through the camp, Brian slightly in the lead as they headed for Travers's gaudy yellow wagon. A light was visible through the window in the rear door as they approached. Not many people were in this part of the camp now; most were still over at the arena, doing what they could to help out in the devastation.

"I'll go in first," Brian said quietly, and before Ballard could argue with him, he had bounded up the steps and thrust his left hand against the door. With his right, he scooped the Colt from the holster on that side. The Texan was right behind him, clutching the Henry rifle, and the sight that greeted their eyes did not come as a surprise to either man.

Nathan Sanford was sprawled on the floor of the wagon, blood oozing from a gash on his head. A few feet away was the man Travers had left to assist the book-keeper, and he was unconscious as well. Crouched just beyond them, Quint Fowler pointed the gun in his hand at the newcomers and regarded them with wide-eyed surprise. A bulge under his shirt was probably a money bag full of stolen gate receipts.

"Hold it, Fowler!" Brian commanded. He leveled his gun at the wrangler, and Ballard moved up beside him to do the same.

Fowler spat a curse, then insisted, "You fellas have got this all wrong—"

"The hell we have," Ballard cut in. "We caught you red-handed robbing the gate receipts, Fowler. Now, drop that gun."

Fowler shook his head and licked dry lips. "Back out of here and nobody else has to get hurt," he growled. "You're not stoppin' me. I'm tired of hoppin' every time Hayden says jump. This money will get me free of him."

"You're already free of him," Brian said dryly. "Hayden's dead. He was killed during that riot and stampede after the place caught fire." He did not mention that Travers had killed the shady promoter.

"Dead?" Fowler echoed. "Hayden's dead?" An ugly grin pulled at his mouth. "Then I can keep all this loot instead of using most of it to pay off those IOUs of mine he had. I don't know how the hell he got most of 'em. He must've followed me around for months buyin' them off the people I gambled with."

"So Hayden wanted a man on the inside to cause trouble for the Kid and force him to sell," Brian said, putting it all together now. The gun in his hand did not waver as he went on, "You've been behind all the bad breaks we've had, Fowler. You turned on your own friends."

"Friends?" the wrangler snarled. "You people were never my friends, you stupid bastard!"

Ballard took up the line of reasoning. "You knew what Hayden had planned for tonight, and you decided to take advantage of the confusion to pull this robbery. The money would let you make a new start." The Texan's voice hardened. "But folks got killed in that mess, Fowler. It's not just robbery anymore. You'll be facing murder charges, too."

"Like hell I will!" the wrangler cried, triggering the gun in his hand. Brian and Ballard threw themselves to opposite sides of the wagon, trying to get out of the line of fire. A slug burned across Brian's upper left arm, cutting a fiery trench in the flesh and throwing off his aim as he let go with a shot. Ballard fired the Henry as he hit the floor, but the impact disrupted his aim, too, and the rifle bullet whined past Fowler's head and buried itself in the far wall of the wagon.

Then before either of them could fire again, Fowler lunged forward, diving between them and heading for the rear door. He slammed through it as Brian and Ballard both tried to twist around for a second shot.

A gun cracked outside before either of them could pull the trigger. Fowler let out a cry of pain, and then they heard something heavy fall to the ground. Scrambling to his feet, Ballard reached the door a step in front of Brian. Both of them saw Fowler lying behind the wagon, curled up in death, a hand pressed to the bullet wound in his chest.

A few yards away, Cactus Corrigan stood with smoke curling out of the barrel of the revolver in his hand. "Didn't give me time to do anything but kill him, blast the luck," he said with a sigh.

"That's all right, Mr. Corrigan," Brian said as he and

Ballard stepped down from the wagon. "We know who he was working for."

"Brian!" a female voice called anxiously. A second later Lucy ran up, followed by Travers, Morgan, and Jackrabbit. "You're hurt!" she cried, throwing her arms around him.

"Lucy!" Corrigan exclaimed. "What are you doing, girl? That boy works for Travers!"

Lucy looked over her shoulder at her father and said fervently, " 'That boy' is the man I love, dammit, and he's hurt! Now, quit trying to run my life for a few minutes!"

Corrigan stared openmouthed as the young blonde inspected the bullet crease on Brian's arm and reassured herself that it was not a serious wound.

Ballard had to chuckle as he looked at Corrigan. All of his suspicions were being confirmed tonight. Lucy and Brian were in love, just as he had thought they might be, so the revelation did not come as a complete shock to him. But the same could not be said of the showman, who looked as if he had just been poleaxed.

Travers laughed, too, and laid a hand on Corrigan's shoulder. "That's about how I must have looked when I found out, Cactus. Come on inside and we'll talk about it."

"Sanford and that other fella are in there," Ballard told them. "Looks like Fowler just knocked them out, but they'll need a doctor to check them over." He stooped and pulled the money bag out of Fowler's shirt, then tossed it to Travers. "You'll be wanting that, too."

"Thanks, Ballard," Travers said as he led the still-stunned Corrigan toward the steps, with Jackrabbit trailing along behind. "You know, Cactus, even with all the awful things that happened tonight, it was sort of fun to be fighting on the same side with you again. It's been a mighty long time since we cleaned out a nest of owlhoots together. . . ."

Although Corrigan seemed somewhat loath to admit it, the twinkle in his eyes made it clear that he was in agreement. The three old saddle mates disappeared inside the wagon and closed the door behind them.

Taking his gaze from the wagon, Ballard saw that

Lucy and Brian were still wrapped up with each other, and he realized that his presence was no longer needed here. As he turned away, Morgan Dixon fell in step beside him and said, "Well, this was a pretty exciting night, even if it didn't turn out the way it was supposed to."

"Maybe so," Ballard grunted, looking at the smoldering remains of the grandstand. "But I reckon a dozen or more people were killed in that fracas, and plenty more were hurt. That's a high price to pay for an exciting story."

Morgan stopped and caught his arm, taking him by surprise and swinging him around to face her. "That's not what I was talking about, and you know it," she said angrily. "I'm not worried about some damn story right now. For all I know, Prescott and Hearst both got trampled in that stampede and I don't even have a job anymore."

Ballard saw her point. "Sorry."

"Just don't be so quick to judge, cowboy. Until everything gets sorted out, I'd say there's only one thing certain about this whole mess."

"What's that?" Ballard asked.

"This much-ballyhooed Wild West show competition is over—and it ended in a tie. Now we'll never know which show was the best."

Chapter Eleven

Earl Corrigan looked around at the men gathered inside his wagon the next morning. A few days ago, he would have thought it highly unlikely that he would be meeting this cordially with some of them. Jackrabbit Dawkins and Wes Ballard were his friends, of course, but John Travers and Brian Nichols . . . well, that was different.

"It's a little early in the day," Corrigan said as he broke out a bottle of whiskey, "but since we were up most of the night, I reckon it'd be all right to have a drink."

Travers nodded. "That's a good idea, Cactus."

The five of them had come back to Corrigan's camp a short time earlier, bringing Lucy with them. Brian had come along to spend a few more minutes with her, and Travers had invited himself because he wanted to continue discussing the tragic events of the night before with his old colleague. Across the river at what was left of Travers's camp, police and firemen were still sifting through the rubble of the arena for more bodies. So far, the total was fourteen dead and uncounted dozens injured.

Hearst and Prescott had not been hurt in the melee, and both publishers had thrown their influence behind Travers. Once it was revealed that Neal Hayden and his hired thugs were responsible for setting the fires and starting the stampede, the police had overlooked the fact that Travers had killed the promoter in a gunfight. As far as the authorities were concerned, the Yakima Kid had saved them the time and expense of a trial by disposing of Hayden.

Corrigan got out glasses, spilled liquor into them, and

passed around the drinks. Settling down in a chair, he sipped the whiskey and said to Brian, "I reckon you and me have a lot to talk about, mister."

"Not so much, sir," the young man replied. "It's pretty simple: I love your daughter, and she loves me."

"And you work for the fella who's been making my life miserable for years now," the showman pointed out.

"Dammit, Cactus," Travers spoke up, "I thought you were getting over that. I never did anything to hurt your show, and if you'll just stop and think about it, you'll see I'm right. Hayden was the one stirring up trouble, and *I* was the target, not you."

"Then why did we have the same sort of bad breaks you did?" Corrigan asked sharply.

"Because Hayden wanted you and me at each other's throats. It makes perfect sense, Cactus. You got your feelings hurt years ago when my show started doing better than yours—which was nothing but luck, blast it—and Hayden took advantage of that. He caused problems for both of us so the feud would heat up, but what he was really after was driving me out of the business so he could take over."

Corrigan nodded slowly, reluctant to agree with Travers but unable to deny the logic of his reasoning.

Ballard took up the theory. "That's probably why Fowler hired those fellas to jump me in that alley. He was not only getting back at me for refusing to sell him those horses, but he must have figured that Brian would get the blame if I turned up dead, since there were plenty of witnesses to that fight the two of us had. That would have caused even more trouble between the two of you."

Earlier, Ballard had told Corrigan and Travers about the brawl between Brian and himself and the ambush that had occurred shortly thereafter. Corrigan had to admit that what Ballard was saying now made sense.

"All right, Travers," he concurred. "Maybe you and me have been at odds for too long."

"That's what I've been trying to tell you. For God's sake, Cactus, if anybody had a right to be mad all these years, I did. After all, you took Lucy's mother away from me."

"I did no such thing," Corrigan bristled. "She never loved you."

"The hell you say! We talked about getting married, and then you came along—"

Jackrabbit moved between the two old frontiersmen and cried, "Here, now! I thought you fellers was goin' to stop actin' like a couple of banty roosters! It's time both of you put that old grudge aside."

Corrigan and Travers glared at each other, but they settled in their chairs again. After a moment Ballard said, "This may not be any of my business, but how did the money situation turn out?"

"Bad," Corrigan sighed, feeling a familiar twinge inside. "Thanks to you and Nichols, Fowler didn't steal the receipts, but nearly every ticket buyer demanded his money back. Travers and I figure they've got a right to it, considering what happened. So once we hand out all the refunds, the whole thing will have been for nothing."

"Not to mention the damages," Travers added gloomily. "It's going to cost a lot. I can probably stand it, but I don't know about Cactus."

"Dammit, don't feel sorry for me," Corrigan shot back. "We'll be just fine—" He caught himself, then sighed. "Hell, what's the use in lying? My show's had it, and we all know it. There's no way the troupe can go on."

"I could buy the show from you, Cactus," Travers suggested. "You could stay on with it—" He stopped abruptly as Corrigan shot a look of cold disdain at him.

"Sell the show to you?" the old scout asked incredulously. "Hayden wanted to buy your show, Travers, and you wouldn't sell. You expect me to sell mine?"

Travers tossed down the rest of his drink. "Sorry, Cactus," he said sincerely. "I reckon I wasn't thinking."

Corrigan leaned back in his chair. It was true that he did not feel as much hostility toward Travers as he had in the past, but there was no way he was going to let the Kid take over his show. He would close down for good first.

With Hayden and Fowler dead, the bad luck that had been dogging the heels of both shows should be over, Corrigan mused, but that development had come too late to help him. He also could not shake the thought that

Hayden had had someone inside his own troupe to keep the pot boiling. If that was the case, the traitor was still loose, and while he probably posed no danger on his own, it was still an annoying loose end. Also, from what Corrigan had learned about Hayden from Travers and the police, Hayden had not had enough money to buy Travers's show. Was it possible he had had a silent partner, somebody backing him in his quest?

"You still haven't said what you intend to do about Lucy and me, sir," Brian spoke up, pulling Corrigan out of his reverie.

The old scout took a deep breath and let it out in a weary sigh. "I'm too damned tired to argue with you, boy. I'm not happy with the idea of Lucy getting mixed up with you, but she's a grown woman with a mind of her own. She wants me to let her make her own decisions, and that's what I'm going to do." As the sharpshooter started to smile, Corrigan went on, "But she'll always be my daughter, and I can promise you this: If you ever hurt that gal of mine, I'll track you down and kill you."

"You don't have to worry about that, sir," Brian promised quietly. "I'll never hurt her."

"See that you don't," Corrigan muttered, then turned to Wes Ballard. "Reckon you lost out, son. The gal picked somebody else, and I still can't pay you for those horses you brought up here. But I'll see that you get your money . . . someday."

"Don't worry about that, Cactus," Ballard replied, using Corrigan's nickname for the first time. "I don't mind waiting."

"You won't have to wait very long, Mr. Ballard," a new voice said from the open door at the rear of the wagon.

The men glanced up in surprise as William Randolph Hearst, a jaunty expression on his face and as impeccably groomed as ever, stepped casually into the wagon. Behind him came Jasper Morton Prescott, whose face in contrast seemed rather grim. Trailing the newspaper publishers were their reporters, Morgan Dixon and Garrett Kingsley.

"What do you want?" Corrigan asked, knowing he

sounded ungracious but not particularly caring at the moment.

"We came to tell you our new idea," Hearst explained excitedly. "We're going to salvage this entire dreadful situation."

Corrigan ran a hand through his graying dark hair. He had a feeling that Hearst alone had come up with this new idea, whatever it was, and he was not sure he wanted anything to do with it. But before he could say so, the man from San Francisco went on. "Since the competition ended in a tie, Prescott and I have come up with a way to settle the issue once and for all. The stagecoach race was the only event remaining to be decided, correct?"

"That's right," Travers confirmed with a nod. "But we can't very well finish it now. The place burned down."

"We're well aware of that, Mr. Travers. Our suggestion is that the bet between Prescott and myself will continue and the tie will be broken by an even bigger race."

"What in the blue blazes are you talkin' about?" Jackrabbit asked, expressing the whole group's puzzlement.

"An overland stagecoach race," Hearst explained, "from Kansas City to Denver. Each of you will supply a coach and drivers, and Prescott and I will back you. The prize money that was promised to the winner of the overall competition will be awarded to whoever reaches Denver first, and the stakes remain the same, eh, Prescott?"

Prescott nodded unenthusiastically. "I'm willing to go along with that and wager my paper on the belief that Travers's coach can win."

Travers grinned. "You don't have to worry, Mr. Prescott," he said confidently.

Corrigan found himself surging to his feet. "We'll see about that!" he exclaimed, unable to stop the words from coming out of his mouth. "With Jackrabbit and Wes here as drivers, there's no way we could lose a race like that!"

Travers faced him, thrusting out his goateed chin. "Then you're on!" he announced.

"Excellent, gentlemen, excellent!" Hearst was grinning as if he had never doubted for an instant that the two showmen would agree to the race. "Why don't we sit down and discuss the particulars?"

By the end of the day an agreement outlining all the details had been drawn up: Each coach would carry the same amount of weight and have the same number of fresh teams available along the way. The publishers would travel ahead of the competitors by train—in Hearst's private car—to arrange for fresh horses; since no stagecoach lines ran along the route of the race anymore, each stopover and change of horses would have to be set up individually. Each coach would also have as a passenger a reporter for the other side's newspaper to ensure that no cheating took place, which everyone agreed was a reasonable precaution. Morgan Dixon would ride in Corrigan's coach, and Garrett Kingsley would travel in the Yakima Kid's vehicle. The remaining troupe members would travel on the publishers' train—albeit in regular passenger cars.

With Kingsley covering the race for Hearst's newspaper empire and Morgan's dispatches going back to New York to be published by Joseph Pulitzer, this great overland race would have even more publicity than the Wild West show competition. To celebrate the agreement, Hearst took the entire group to dinner at one of Kansas City's finest restaurants that evening, and he was in fine form as he proclaimed, "This race will capture the imagination of the entire country as never before, gentlemen—and ladies." He nodded to Lucy and Morgan. "The workingmen and women in their tenements back East who dream of the wide-open spaces, this race will be for them. It will be for every store clerk who ever read a dime novel about the West and for every youngster who ever dreamed of being a cowboy. It will be a monument to the Old West, a tribute to the pioneer spirit that made America great." He paused long enough to take a sip of his wine, then rubbed his hands together and continued, "That's why, if everything goes as planned, the race should culminate in a gigantic Fourth of July celebration in Denver. What better way to celebrate the independence of our nation, eh?"

"What if we don't get there by the fourth, though, Mr. Hearst?" Travers asked with a frown.

"I've had the route checked and analyzed, gentlemen. If you leave Kansas City on the proper day and don't encounter any unforeseen delays, at least one of the coaches should reach Denver on Independence Day."

Earl Corrigan exchanged a glance with his rival. Hearst was putting quite a bit of pressure on them by trying to time the conclusion of the race to coincide with Independence Day. But the publisher was right, too: It would be an appropriate way to end the competition.

"We'll give it a try," Corrigan said, followed by a nod from Travers.

"Of course you will," Hearst said smoothly. "You men have the spirit of the Old West within you, and that spirit will not turn away from a challenge." He lifted his glass, and his voice boomed out in the private dining room as he toasted, "To the overland race—and to the Old West!"

It was nearly midnight as Jasper Morton Prescott entered the study in his mansion overlooking the Missouri River. He loosened his tie, tossed his coat onto a chair, and walked across the room to the big windows. Pushing aside the heavy velvet curtains, he peered out at the night and pondered everything that had happened.

Neal Hayden was dead. That thought had been echoing through his brain all day. Hayden was dead, and that meant Cynthia was safe at last from the man's threat.

He should have been relieved, Prescott knew, but worry still gnawed at him. Hayden's blackmail had bled him nearly dry, and unless he could somehow recoup those losses, it would not be long before the last *Clarion* was published.

That was why he had leapt at the chance to continue the bet with Hearst when the magnate had proposed the overland race. Prescott wanted the hundred thousand dollars Hearst had put up as his share of the bet, and if Travers won the race so that Prescott could collect from Hearst, everything would be all right again.

He would do anything, he realized, to get his hands on that money. Anything.

The sound of a door opening behind him made the publisher turn around. His wife came into the room, and he could tell from the slight hesitation in her steps that she had been drinking—as usual.

In her mid-thirties, Cynthia was considerably younger than Prescott, and she was undeniably lovely. Her reddish blond hair flowed onto the shoulders of the silken dressing gown that was gaping enough in the front to reveal the swells of her creamy breasts.

"H'lo, Jasper," she greeted him, closing the study door behind her and leaning back against it so he would not see how she swayed were she to try to stand unsupported. But Prescott knew perfectly well what she was doing.

"Good evening, Cynthia," he responded coolly.

"Where you been tonight? Working at . . . at the paper?"

"Part of the time. I also had a business dinner to attend." Cynthia knew very little of his business dealings, and she never read the *Clarion*. Prescott saw no reason to apprise her of what was going on.

"I had dinner by myself," she said forlornly. "But I waited up for you."

"You shouldn't have. I'm sure you're tired. Why don't you go on to bed?"

She leaned forward and let her gown fall open even more, giving him a leer that was supposed to be a provocative smile. "Why don't . . . why don't you help me to bed?"

Taking a deep breath, the publisher stalked across the room, restraining the urge to slap her. She had been such an appealing woman once—before she had turned into a drunken slattern.

Grasping her arm firmly, he said, "Come along, Cynthia. I'll take you to your room." They slept in separate bedchambers and had done so for quite a while now, at Prescott's insistence.

"Oh, Jasper," she sighed, letting herself sag against him and giving him no choice but to put his arms around her to keep her from collapsing to the floor. Her body under the robe was firm and warm as she rested her head against his chest, and he felt a stirring inside him. Perhaps he could—

Cynthia let out a loud, raucous snore, asleep on her feet.

Prescott began to laugh bitterly as he held his wife. God, how had they come to this? Where had it all gone wrong? But even as he asked the questions, he knew there were no answers.

Chapter Twelve

It was barely nine o'clock in the morning on that late-June day, but already the heat was beating down from the brazen sun overhead. As Wes Ballard sat on the driver's seat of the old Concord coach, sleeving sweat from his forehead, he looked along the street in front of him, taking in the hundreds of people lined up on both sides of the avenue, and he realized that William Randolph Hearst deserved his reputation for knowing what the public wanted. Despite the heat, people had turned out in droves to witness the beginning of what was now being ballyhooed in the Kansas City *Clarion* and the San Francisco *Examiner* as the Great Stagecoach Race and Wild West Extravaganza.

Ballard had been surprised at how quickly the citizens of Kansas City seemed to have forgotten about the disaster at the Wild West show arena. Stories by Morgan Dixon in the *Clarion* had made it clear that criminal activity by an unscrupulous promoter had been responsible for the tragedy. And Hearst had not only helped pay the medical expenses of those injured on that night but also presented cash settlements to the families of those killed.

As a result, although only a couple of weeks had passed, almost everyone's attention was focused on the imminent race. The excitement had culminated the evening before in a lavish society ball given by Hearst and Jasper Morton Prescott to commemorate the beginning of the race.

"I never seen such a fuss," Jackrabbit Dawkins remarked from his place on the seat beside Ballard. Earl

Corrigan was inside the coach, along with Lucy and Morgan. The bearded old-timer went on, "You'd think folks'd never seen a stagecoach before."

"A lot of them probably haven't," Ballard pointed out, raising his voice to be heard over the blare of a brass band playing nearby. "It's been thirty years since the transcontinental railroad opened up, Jackrabbit. The day of the stagecoach is long gone."

Jackrabbit snorted derisively. "Railroads! Why, I've seen these old Concords get into places a train couldn't never think of gettin'! Ain't never been a better means of transportation than a stagecoach."

Ballard did not agree, but he was not going to waste his breath arguing with the man who would be taking turns at the reins with him over the next week or so. Ballard would do most of the driving, but Jackrabbit would spell him on a regular basis as the coach headed toward Denver. Corrigan had told him earlier, "I really appreciate you doing this, Wes. You could have taken your money from Hearst and headed back to Texas, you know."

"I know," Ballard had said to the old scout. "But there may never be a race like this again, and I'd sort of like to see it. No better place to do that than from the box. Besides, I don't want Hearst's money. You'll be able to pay me soon enough, Cactus, with your winnings."

Corrigan had grinned and slapped him on the shoulder.

Now Ballard lifted the reins—part of the all-new rigging for the race—and gave them a last check, as Jackrabbit had done after supervising the hitching of the team. Ballard took a deep breath. They had all been waiting long enough; it was time to get started.

But apparently not just yet. Hearst, Prescott, the mayor, and several other dignitaries climbed onto the reviewing stand that had been built for the occasion—meaning there would be some speeches to sit through first.

Luckily, the politicians proved not to be long-winded. It was too hot and the crowd was too anxious to put up with lengthy speeches. Introduced by the mayor, Hearst and Prescott stepped to the center of the reviewing stand and together parted a curtain that hid a section of the platform from view. A pair of burly men abruptly wheeled out something that made Ballard's eyes widen in surprise: a cannon.

As the massive gun was positioned between the publishers, Hearst slapped the barrel of the cannon and said loudly, "Ladies and gentlemen, this is a genuine United States Army cannon of the kind used for years in forts throughout the West to repel attacks by savages. Today this cannon will serve another purpose: as the starting gun for the Great Stagecoach Race and Wild West Extravaganza!"

Cheers and wild applause burst from the crowd as Hearst motioned for the stagecoaches to come forward. Flicking the reins, Ballard clucked to the team, walking them toward the reviewing stand. Travers's coach came alongside, and Ballard glanced over to see the silver-haired frontiersman himself riding on the box, next to the same man who had been handling the reins the night of the contest. Travers had a couple of other drivers riding inside, along with Garrett Kingsley. The reporter from New York leaned out the window of the coach, smiling and waving to the spectators.

Both coaches drew to a halt in front of the platform. Corrigan hopped out of his coach and walked over to Travers's vehicle. Extending a hand to his rival, the showman said with a smile, "Good luck, Kid!"

Travers stepped down and returned the hearty handshake. "And good luck to you, too, Cactus!" he said ringingly.

Ballard knew they were putting on a show for the crowd, but he thought there was some sincerity in the voices of both men. If nothing else good came out of this whole affair, at least Corrigan and Travers were not the bitter enemies they had been. It might be going too far to call them friends again, but they obviously felt some mutual respect for the first time in years.

"By the way, folks," Hearst added to the crowd, "don't worry about this cannon hurting anything when it goes off. It's loaded with a charge of powder but no cannonball."

That was good, Ballard thought. After everything that

had already happened, nobody wanted to blow a hole in one of the buildings in downtown Kansas City.

Stepping to the edge of the platform, Hearst looked down at Corrigan and Travers. "Are you ready, gentlemen?" he asked.

Both men nodded emphatically and returned to their coaches. "Very well," the magnate declared, and walked back beside the cannon. Pulling a match from his pocket, he held it out to Prescott. "If you would do the honors, sir?"

Awkwardly Prescott took the match and placed the head of it against the barrel of the cannon. "On your mark!" he called.

Ballard bunched the reins in his left hand and gripped the whip in his right.

"Get set!" Hearst announced in a stentorian shout.

Prescott scratched the match into life and held the flame to the short fuse at the breech of the cannon. The fuse caught, sputtering and spewing sparks for a couple of seconds. . . .

BOOM!

Ballard's hand flashed down, the whip popping over the backs of his team. He flapped the reins with his other hand and cried, "Hiii-yahhh! Giddap!"

The horses lunged in their traces, and the coach lurched into motion. Ballard leaned forward as the vehicle picked up speed. Travers's coach was close beside him to the left, the driver using his whip to urge more speed from his team. The Kid's coach pulled ahead of Corrigan's just slightly, and, practically side by side, the two coaches thundered out of Kansas City, heading west.

A determined smile tugged at Ballard's wide mouth under his thick black mustache. Travers might be ahead for the moment, but it was a long way to Denver. A long way, indeed.

The drama of racing neck and neck had been primarily for the benefit of the spectators, and once the coaches were out of the city, both drivers slowed to a more reasonable pace. They crossed the Missouri together on the ferry, then followed the same road toward Topeka. For the most part, their path would parallel the Union Pacific railroad, although each coach was free to take shortcuts or alternate routes if the drivers decided to do so. Corrigan had promised Ballard that he knew some shortcuts, and Ballard imagined Travers had a few tricks up his sleeve too.

The road ran within sight of the railroad tracks at times, and around the middle of the day, a westbound train passed the two coaches, the engineer blowing his whistle as he did. Jackrabbit pointed to the ornate car just ahead of the caboose and said over the clatter of the wheels, "Reckon that's Hearst's private car. They're wavin' to us from inside."

Ballard saw people leaning from the windows of the railroad car and waving, but he did not return the gesture. He was too busy driving the coach. They were fifty yards or so ahead of Travers at the moment, but that meant nothing.

During the day they changed teams at every small town, and that night they camped between Lawrence and Topeka on the banks of the Kansas River. Looking at Morgan Dixon, Ballard thought that while he was tired and sore, Morgan Dixon looked as though she had been to hell and back. She was getting a firsthand introduction to stagecoach travel, with all of its attendant dust and bouncing and swaying, but despite being exhausted and disheveled, she took out her notebook and wrote for an hour after supper, sitting beside the campfire. Ballard got another cup of coffee and sat down cross-legged nearby, studying her face as she intently filled the pages with her precise writing.

Feeling his gaze, she finally glanced up. "Do you need something, Mr. Ballard?" she asked.

"I was just wondering how you found so much to write about. This is just the first day, after all."

She smiled slightly. "Mr. Ballard, this race is history in the making. There's never been anything like it before, and it's doubtful there ever will be again. Have you ever heard of the automobile?"

"I've heard of the contraption," Ballard scoffed.

"Well, some people think that within a few years that

'contraption' will have replaced horses for travel. Why, there's even talk of one day having machines that will fly through the air. The world is going to change completely, Mr. Ballard. Take my word for it."

"We'll see," he said, sounding dubious. "I know one change that I'd like."

"Oh? What's that?"

"I'd like for you to stop calling me Mr. Ballard. Name's Wes."

She started in surprise, then frowned and said, "My goodness, Mr. Ballard, if I didn't know better, I'd say you wanted to be friends."

He snorted and took a sip of his coffee. "Shoot, I thought we'd just call a truce, ma'am. Seeing as how we're going to be together on this trip and all."

"All right . . . Wes. That sounds like a good idea."

Ballard felt his lips curving into a smile and told himself sternly to stop it. The woman called him Wes, and first thing you know he was grinning like an idiot. *Better get your mind back on your job, boy,* he thought.

When they stopped in Topeka the next day, Morgan hurried over to the local Western Union office and left her story to be wired back to the *Clarion* in Kansas City. From there it would go on to Pulitzer's *World* in New York.

Travers's coach was in Topeka at the same time, but it was about ready to pull out just as Corrigan and the others were arriving. "They're gaining on us," Corrigan groused. "Better not let 'em get too far ahead, Wes."

Ballard nodded, watching impatiently as the fresh team was hitched up. "Yes, sir."

Word of the race had preceded them, of course, and in every town they came to, people turned out to welcome the competitors. Some places had bands playing and red-white-and-blue bunting strung across their main streets, while other settlements just had cheering crowds on the sidewalks. On the third day, as they rolled into Abilene, Ballard had to suppress a groan as he saw the speaker's platform set up in front of the Dickinson County Court-house. *More politicians and more speeches,* he thought.

A tall, well-dressed, middle-aged man wearing a marshal's star on his coat stepped down from the platform to greet them, and Corrigan immediately hopped out of the coach. "Well, Cody Fisher," he said enthusiastically, shaking hands with the lawman. "I heard you'd come back to Abilene."

"Yep, I got tired of chasing owlhoots all over the country for the U.S. marshal's office. Figured I could use a nice easy job like this in my old age." The man grinned, relieving what seemed to be a naturally grim cast to his lean face. "Abilene's not like it used to be in the old days, Cactus."

"I remember it well," Corrigan said.

"Will you have time to go down to the Scotsman's for a drink?"

"We'll see, Cody. Can't let the Kid get too far ahead of us, you know."

The town band began playing, followed by the speechmaking, and while that was going on, Ballard and Jackrabbit supervised the changing of the team, both men champing at the bit to get started again. Morgan came over to them as the ceremony in front of the courthouse was breaking up and said to Jackrabbit, "That man Mr. Corrigan was talking to . . . Was that—?"

"It sure was," Jackrabbit said, answering her question before she could finish it. "Me an' Cactus an' the Kid come through here a few times years ago, and that's when we met the feller. 'Course, he weren't as famous then. He was just a deputy here. A few years later he resigned and went to work as a U.S. marshal, and that's when he really started makin' a name for himself. I sure could tell you some stories 'bout him and the other lawmen who toted a badge around here."

"You're going to, Mr. Dawkins," Morgan stated, scribbling furiously in her notebook. "You're going to."

Late that afternoon, as they were pressing on toward Salina, Ballard spotted someone up ahead on the road, riding toward them on horseback. As the man came closer, Ballard recognized him as Brian Nichols.

"Howdy," the young man called as he met them, wheeling his horse to fall in alongside the coach.

"Nichols," Ballard said with a noncommittal nod. "What are you doing here?"

"You mean you didn't miss me?" Brian asked, grinning.

"*I* did, you big galoot!" Lucy called, leaning out the window in the coach's door with a big smile on her face.

"Might as well stop the coach, Wes," Corrigan said from the other side of the vehicle. His tone was a mixture of dry amusement and impatience.

Ballard hauled back on the reins and brought the coach to a halt. Lucy opened the door and sprang out, and by the time she hit the ground, Brian had swung down from his saddle and was waiting to greet her. He took her into his arms and kissed her.

"Shameful," the old driver muttered from up top.

Ballard glanced over at him. "I thought you approved of that romance, Jackrabbit."

"Well, I reckon I do. But it's the middle of the afternoon, dag-nab-it! Young folks should save their sparkin' for nighttime."

Corrigan and Morgan also got out of the coach, and when Brian and Lucy finally parted, the showman asked, "What are you doing here, Nichols, besides kissing my daughter?"

"I got off the train in Salina," Brian replied, shoving back his broad-brimmed hat. "I didn't particularly want to wait until you got to Denver to see Lucy again, so I thought I'd ride back and meet you. Took my horse out of his boxcar, and here we are."

"You seen Travers?" Jackrabbit asked, trying to sound sly.

Brian chuckled. "He's about two miles ahead. That's his dust you can see up ahead."

"Figured as much," Corrigan said. "We'll catch up to him when we hit rougher country."

"Maybe so. Anyway, I thought if you're agreeable, Mr. Corrigan, I'd offer my services to both of you as a scout. You know, sort of ride ahead and make sure there's no unexpected trouble."

"I *know* what a scout does, boy," Corrigan said dryly. "What did Travers think of the idea?"

"The Kid said it was all right with him—but only as

long as it was all right with you, too. He said he didn't want any unfair advantages."

"Can we trust you?" Corrigan asked flatly.

"Yes, sir." Brian looked down at Lucy, who was snuggled in the crook of his arm. "I've got loyalties in both camps now, Mr. Corrigan. I just want to help out and be part of this race."

Corrigan nodded. "All right. I reckon you're the official scout for the Great Stagecoach Race, Nichols."

Brian grinned broadly and tightened his arm around Lucy's shoulders. The passengers then climbed back aboard the coach, and the sharpshooter rode along with them the rest of the afternoon before galloping ahead to rejoin Travers.

That night Morgan sat down beside Ballard, instead of vice versa. There was a thoughtful look on her face, and when Ballard looked over at her, she remarked, "Brian and Lucy make quite a nice couple, don't they?"

Ballard nodded. "I reckon they do. Lucy's a mighty fine girl, and Nichols seems like a good man—even if he does work for Travers."

Morgan laughed and said, "You sound like Cactus now."

"Thanks. I'll take that as a compliment."

The journalist hesitated for a moment, then said, "I thought that you liked Lucy Corrigan yourself."

"I did," Ballard said frankly. "I still like her, but it's different now. She's a good friend, like Cactus and Jackrabbit. I want to see her happy, if that's what you're getting at, and if Nichols makes her happy, more power to him."

"I knew they were in love, you know. I knew it before any of you."

Ballard grinned. "Reading minds now, are you? Could be there's a place for you in some sideshow."

"No, seriously. I saw them together one day, and there was no mistaking what was going on between them. I . . . I even started to tell you about it once."

Ballard shot a quick glance at her. "Why didn't you?"

"Because it seemed like I'd just be causing some unnecessary trouble," Morgan replied.

"I thought trouble was your business. Makes for a good story, doesn't it?"

She shrugged. "There's more to life than a good story. But I do want to use the irony of the relationship between Brian and Lucy in one of my dispatches about the race."

"Are you sure you want to do that?" Ballard asked sharply.

"Why not? Like you said, Wes, it's a good story. And I still have to do my job."

Ballard abruptly got up and walked away from the campfire. He stood peering off into the moonlit night, his hands in his hip pockets. A minute later Morgan came up beside him, but although he knew she was there, he did not look at her.

"You're angry with me," she accused him, "just because I want to use Lucy and Brian in my story."

"They're my friends," Ballard said stiffly. "I don't like the idea of exploiting their personal business to sell newspapers."

Morgan laughed humorlessly. "Well, you'd better get used to things like that. I told you the world is changing, Wes, and that's part of it."

"I can't stop the world from changing—but that doesn't mean I have to like it."

Morgan regarded him intently for a long moment, then said softly, "My God, you're as much of a relic as those old-timers. Look at you. You're a cowboy. In a few more years, there isn't going to be any place for you, is there? That's why you came along on this race. You're trying to grab a piece of the past, even though you weren't there when most of it happened."

Ballard's head jerked around, and he glared at her. "You're a mighty smart little lady," he said tautly. "But let's leave it at this: I'm asking you—as a favor to me—to leave Brian and Lucy in peace."

Morgan met his gaze, then finally nodded. "All right," she agreed. "As a favor to you."

"Thank you." Ballard started past her. "I've got to see to the horses," he mumbled.

She let him go without saying anything else, but he could sense that she was watching him. Was she angry with him? he wondered. And did he care if she was?

Maybe Morgan was right. Maybe he was as much of a relic, a throwback, as Corrigan and Travers and Jackrabbit. But, considering what he had seen of the so-called modern world, he was going to take *that* as a compliment, too.

Corrigan's prediction was right. Once the stagecoaches reached western Kansas, with its slightly more rugged terrain, Ballard's and Jackrabbit's skill at the reins came into play. They cut down on Travers's lead and even passed him after a day and a half, and as Corrigan's coach rolled past his rival's, the showman grinned and waved at Travers, who frowned in return.

They camped that night between Hackberry Creek and the Smoky Hill River. Travers's campfire was visible about a quarter of a mile away, and as Corrigan regarded the glowing dot of flame in the darkness, he thought about the race and was not surprised at how close the competition had been so far. From here on out, though, the land would become more hilly as the route crossed the Colorado border. Once they reached that stretch, it would be his knowledge against Travers's, and the man who remembered the easiest trails and the shortest cutoffs would win.

Corrigan was leaning against the side of the coach that was not facing his group's campfire. He could hear the animated conversation going on between Lucy, Ballard, Morgan, and Brian Nichols, who was taking his supper with them tonight. The young people sounded happy, as though they were having the adventure of their lives—and that was probably true. None of them had ever been involved in anything like this before, not even Lucy. Corrigan knew from eavesdropping on their earlier talks that Morgan Dixon had grown up in a small town in Ohio, while Brian had been born and raised on a farm in Missouri. Neither of them had any firsthand experience with the real West. Wes Ballard did, having grown up on the Texas frontier, but even that wild and woolly land had settled down a great deal since the old days.

Suddenly Corrigan sucked air between his teeth as pain exploded inside him. He started to double over, grabbing for the sill of one of the coach's windows to hold him up. He refused to give in to the demon that was eating away at his guts. The pain was coming more often now, but so far he had been able to hide it from everyone else—

"Hurtin' bad again, Cactus?" Jackrabbit asked from beside him, his raspy voice little more than a whisper.

Corrigan tried to pull himself upright. "Wh-what are you talking about, you old fool?" he asked harshly. "I feel fine."

"Oh, sure. These eyes may be old, but they ain't blind. I've knowed for quite a while that somethin' was botherin' you, Cactus. Don't you think you ought to see a sawbones about it?"

The old scout shook his head, knowing it was futile to deny his illness to his old friend. They had ridden too many trails together to keep a secret for very long. "What's a doctor going to do for me?" he asked bitterly. "They can't do anything about this."

"Know that for sure, do you?"

"I know," Corrigan said flatly.

The driver scratched at his beard. "Maybe you're just a mite scared to hear what a doc would tell you."

Corrigan surprised both of them by admitting, "Maybe I am. But I'm asking you not to say anything about this, Jackrabbit—especially to Lucy."

The old jehu grumbled and spat but finally nodded. "All right, I'll keep my mouth shut if that's what you want. But I still think you ought to get some help."

"Maybe when this race is over," Corrigan said, although both of them knew he intended to do no such thing. Fortunately the pain subsided a little later, and Corrigan was able to roll up in his blankets and get some sleep.

When they broke camp and hit the trail again bright and early the next morning, Earl Corrigan felt much better—so good in fact that he climbed onto the box with Wes Ballard and told Jackrabbit Dawkins to ride inside for a while.

The morning air was warm and fragrant with the

scent of wildflowers, and above them the clear blue sky arched majestically. All in all, it was about as pretty a day as Corrigan could remember, and he enjoyed being on top of the coach as it rolled along.

Just before noon, as the road passed between two fairly steep hills, Corrigan suddenly felt some instinct trying to warn him. With a frown, he looked around, scanning the terrain, but there was nothing threatening—at least not as far as he could see.

As Ballard drove the coach along the trail between the hills, a low rumble from the left caught Corrigan's attention. The driver heard it, too, and both men whipped their heads around to look in that direction. Several boulders, none of them overly large but still big enough to do damage, were rolling down the slope toward them, bringing more rocks and a shower of dirt with them.

"Dammit!" Corrigan snapped. "Get us out of here, Wes!"

Ballard was already acting. Snatching out the whip, he cracked it above the heads of the lead horses, and the team broke into a gallop. The road was a little rougher than usual here, and the faster pace meant that the coach bounced and swayed even more. Corrigan heard startled cries from inside the vehicle and knew that Lucy, Morgan, and Jackrabbit were being shaken up—but better that than to have some of those rocks crash into the coach.

Leaning forward on the seat, Ballard urged the horses on, keeping a tight grip on the reins. Corrigan had to grab the railing on the side of the box to steady himself. As landslides went, this one was small, but it was loud enough and dangerous enough to start his pulse pounding. Lashing at the team with the whip, Ballard shouted, "Yahhhh!" He had to keep his eyes on the trail, but Corrigan was able to turn his head and watch the rocks sweeping toward them. It was going to be close, mighty close. . . .

The stagecoach raced past just as the landslide reached the road. Ballard and Corrigan ducked as several small rocks pelted them, but that was the extent of the damage. Once they were past, the Texan tugged back on the reins, slowing the team and gradually bringing the coach to a halt. Corrigan half rose and twisted around to peer behind them, seeing that about half the trail was covered with rocks and dirt. A cloud of dust hung in the air above the road.

Ballard also turned to look and said, "That probably would have knocked us over if it had hit us."

Corrigan nodded. "Could've torn up the coach, too. That was a close call, Wes. Reckon you saved our bacon."

"Thank the horses," Ballard grunted. "They're the ones who did the running."

Jackrabbit, Lucy, and Morgan got out of the coach and regarded the results of the landslide. The two young women were pale, but Jackrabbit bounced around in anger. "What the ding-busted blazes happened back there?" he demanded. "Them boulders didn't start bouncin' down that hill by theirselves!"

"I'd say you're right," Corrigan agreed grimly. "Somebody must've started them."

Ballard hopped down from the coach and nodded. "I thought I saw something moving up there on the hill, just before the rocks started falling. It was only a flicker out of the corner of my eye, but it was enough to tell me something was wrong."

"Well, I reckon this'll slow the Kid down a mite," Jackrabbit said, calming down. "They may have to clear away some of that mess 'fore there's room on the trail for the coach to get by."

Corrigan cast a glance at the hills on both sides of them and nodded. "Everybody back in the coach. I want to get out of here before whoever started that slide decides to try again."

"Good idea," Ballard agreed.

"Jackrabbit, you ride up top again," Corrigan continued. "And get that Henry of yours out of the boot. If you see anything suspicious, let go with a warning shot."

"You mean I'm ridin' shotgun again?" Jackrabbit asked with a cackle. "Hot damn! Just like old times!"

The old jehu was right, Corrigan thought. Maybe it was too much like old times.

Chapter Thirteen

The next day, as Earl Corrigan's stagecoach crossed the Colorado border, the travelers looked forward to seeing the Rocky Mountains, which would soon be visible in the distance to the west. Jackrabbit Dawkins, who was doing the driving, swung the coach to the northwest, on a direct line to Denver. Riding beside the old-timer, Wes Ballard held Jackrabbit's Henry rifle across his lap. He turned and looked behind them as the coach rolled up a gentle slope, and about three-quarters of a mile behind he could pick out the moving dot that was John Travers's coach. Obviously the landslide had not slowed down the Yakima Kid very much.

Sooner or later, Ballard thought, one of the coaches would pull away from the other. It did not seem possible that they could cover the hundreds of miles between Kansas City and Denver and still remain so close together.

Ballard was thoroughly enjoying the journey. He had wired his foreman back in Texas not to expect him until he saw him again. Although a part of him hated to leave the ranch in other hands, even trusted hands, for such a long time, he realized that this might be his only opportunity to see these sights. It was surely his only chance to see them from the top of a stagecoach. It could be that Morgan was right; within a few years, those newfangled automobiles might be sputtering around on these plains. The coming of the railroad—the "iron horse" so despised by the Indians—had changed things in the West immensely, and each new contraption would only push the old days further into the forgotten past.

Jackrabbit glanced over at him and asked, "What're you thinkin', boy? You look like you got a heap o' things on your mind."

Ballard shook his head. "Just enjoying the view."

"Mighty nice, ain't it?" the jehu said with a grin.

Nodding, the rancher was looking at a stand of trees at the top of the slope when he saw a flash of sunlight on metal among the growth. Leaning forward, his brow creased in a puzzled frown, he said, "I wonder what that was shining up there."

"Shinin'? . . ." Jackrabbit echoed. His eyes widened. "Get down, boy!"

Ballard ducked. He heard a high-pitched whine, followed an instant later by a sharp crack, and he knew with a chill along his spine that somebody was shooting at them. Another rifle barked as Ballard levered a shell into the Henry's chamber, pointed it at the trees, and squeezed the trigger.

Corrigan stuck his head out the window of the coach and shouted, "What the hell?"

Ballard leaned over and waved him back. "Stay inside!" the Texan yelled. "Bushwhackers!" He had heard that word from his father when the old man had told stories about wild times in the past, but he had never figured he would be using it himself.

He shot two more slugs at the trees, firing as fast as he could work the lever, while Jackrabbit flapped the reins and shouted at the team, sending the horses into a gallop. The canny driver swerved the coach from side to side, a dangerous maneuver that could overturn them but a necessary one to throw off the aim of the hidden riflemen.

"You're charging right at them!" Ballard cried as he realized what Jackrabbit was doing.

"No place to hide if we turn and run," the jehu replied, slashing at the horses with the whip.

Ballard grimaced as he heard another slug slice through the air close to his ear. Trying to ignore the fear he felt, he kept firing toward the trees, peppering them with bullets. As the coach drew nearer, he suddenly realized he had not heard any more shots for several seconds.

"Hold on!" he said to Jackrabbit, and the old-timer

began to slow the coach. When it came to a stop, Ballard listened intently for a second, then said, "Hear those horses? Whoever it was, we ran them off!"

"Better hope you're right," Jackrabbit said grimly. "Otherwise we're goin' to be sittin' ducks out here in the open like this."

But no more shots were forthcoming, and after a few minutes Jackrabbit drove the coach on to the top of the hill. As they crested the rise, they could see a ranch house in the distance, and Ballard remarked, "That must be where we're supposed to change horses next."

Corrigan stepped out of the coach as Jackrabbit brought it to a halt among the trees, the shade a welcome relief from the hot midday sunshine. "What happened back there?" the showman demanded.

"Some low-down skunks ambushed us," Jackrabbit replied. "Wes threw lead back at 'em and run 'em off."

"Looks like we owe you our lives again, son," Corrigan told Ballard. "I don't suppose you got a look at them."

The Texan shook his head and gestured toward a thin haze of dust to the west. "I never saw them at all, but it appears they took off in that direction."

"Chances are they're the same ones who started that rockslide."

Morgan and Lucy had also gotten out of the coach, and the reporter asked, "You mean you think someone is trying deliberately to sabotage you, Mr. Corrigan? I thought that all ended when Hayden died."

Corrigan sighed. "Reckon somebody else must have a reason for wanting me to lose this race. I always wondered if that Hayden fella didn't have somebody working with him, maybe even somebody in my own show."

Lucy's eyes widened, and she exclaimed, "Surely you don't mean there's a traitor in the show, Father! You've known everybody for so long—"

"Quint Fowler had been working for Travers a long time, too," Corrigan pointed out, "but he had his price. Other folks do, too."

"You never said anything about suspecting someone in your show," Morgan commented.

"It's not an easy thing to admit. Besides, I don't have

any proof of anything." The old scout stared toward the west, where the dust raised by the departure of the bush-whackers had now dissipated. "But we've got to get to the bottom of this. Let's get rolling again, and at the next stop we're going to wait for Travers to catch up."

"Catch up?" Jackrabbit barked in a disbelieving voice. "Why'd we want to do a thing like that?"

"Because I want him to tell me to my face that he doesn't have anything to do with this."

Ballard frowned as he climbed onto the box again. From what he had seen of John Travers, landslides and ambushes were not the man's style. But after years of distrust, Cactus Corrigan was obviously having a hard time not being suspicious of the Yakima Kid.

When the stagecoach reached the ranch house less than half an hour later, a fresh team was waiting for them. The rancher greeted them with a grin and explained that a representative from Hearst and Prescott had paid him a visit a couple of days before and given him a hefty sum to have two teams of horses ready at short notice. "You've got folks all over the West talking about this here race," the man told them. "Where's the other coach?"

"It'll be along soon," Corrigan replied. "Is it all right if we wait here for it? I've got to have a talk with one of the gents on board."

"All right? I'll say it's all right. Come on inside. There's coffee on the stove."

Travers's coach arrived after another half hour. Corrigan stepped outside to meet it, followed by Ballard and Jack-rabbit, and Travers gave all of them a surprised look as he swung down from the box. He was wearing his fancy fringed-and-beaded outfit, but it was covered with dust and looked nowhere near as elegant as it had before this journey began. "Good to see you, Cactus," he stated, "but I never expected to run into you here. Why haven't you gone on?"

"I need to talk to you, and I figured it was important enough to give up the lead we had."

"We would have caught up soon enough, anyway," Travers responded with a chuckle. "Well, what's so impor-tant that it couldn't wait?"

"Somebody's tried to kill us twice. Have you got anything to do with that?" Corrigan asked bluntly.

Travers's goateed face hardened. "What the devil are you talking about?"

Quickly Corrigan told him about the landslide and the rifle shots from ambush. Before he had finished, the Kid was shaking his head.

"Dammit, Cactus, I thought you knew me better than that. We've had our differences, sure, but I'd never do things like what you've told me about. Hell, that slide slowed *us* down a little, too."

"Then you deny hiring people to stop my coach?"

"I do," Travers said emphatically.

Corrigan nodded. "All right. I believe you. Sorry I had to ask, Kid, but things have just been getting stranger ever since we hit Kansas City."

"Well, that's true enough." Travers's agreement was grudging. "But what do we do now?"

"I don't know," Corrigan said with a sigh. "I was hoping maybe you'd have a suggestion."

While the two former partners were talking, Brian Nichols swung down from his horse and hurried to Lucy, reaching out to take her hands. "Are you all right?" he asked anxiously, having listened intently while Corrigan related what they had encountered.

"I'm fine," she assured him. "Nothing's going to happen to me, Brian—not with my father and Jackrabbit and Wes around to take care of trouble."

He frowned. "I'm going to be around, too. I'll be riding alongside your coach from now on."

"Are you sure Uncle John will let you?"

"I don't care what the Kid says," Brian answered. "I'm staying with you."

As it turned out, that was Travers's first suggestion. "Brian left his blanks behind on the train," Travers remarked. "He's carrying live rounds now, and we all know you won't find a better shot. Maybe those scoundrels will think twice before trying to ambush you again if Brian is riding next to you."

Corrigan looked at the young fast-draw artist. "Is that what you want to do, son?"

Brian nodded and said, "Yes, it is, sir. I'd just as soon not let Lucy out of my sight again."

"All right. Glad to have you with us."

Off to one side of the stagecoaches, Garrett Kingsley had taken out his notebook and was writing hurriedly in it. He glanced up and grinned at Morgan as she came over to him. "Great stuff, eh?" asked the reporter from New York. "Blazing guns and all that. The dime-novel readers should lap it up like cream."

"This is real life, Mr. Kingsley, not a dime novel," Morgan said tartly. "Don't forget, I was in that coach while we were outrunning the landslide and being shot at."

"I know. That makes it even better. A pretty woman who goes right into the heart of danger to get a story." Kingsley stuck the stub of an unlit cigar in his mouth. "You'll be more famous than Nellie Bly, kid."

At one time, Morgan would have been flattered by the comparison with the famous female journalist who had plunged into all sorts of adventures. But now she was beginning to wonder if she was really cut out to follow in such footsteps. She had been damned frightened during the riot back in Kansas City, as well as during the landslide and the attack on the coach. One of those wild slugs could have easily punched through the wall of the coach and hit her, she knew.

"Go ahead and write what you want to," she told Kingsley. "I couldn't stop you anyway."

He grinned around the cigar. "That's right."

Sighing, Morgan turned her attention back to Corrigan and Travers.

"We've come too far to call the race off now," Travers was saying.

Corrigan nodded. "I was hoping you felt that way. When somebody tries to scare me away from something, I get as stubborn as an old mule. We're going on to Denver, and may the best man win!"

"But let's watch each other's backs along the way, eh?"

Agreeing, Corrigan then smiled slightly and said, "By the way, our team has already been changed. So we're ready to go."

"Blast it!" Travers exclaimed, swinging around and curtly gesturing for his men to get to work. "You old fox! You kept me jawing while you were getting ready to leave!"

Lucy and Morgan had overheard and were scrambling back into the coach. Ballard vaulted onto the box and grabbed the reins, while Jackrabbit clambered aboard on the other side and picked up the Henry from the floorboards. As the showman stepped into the coach, he grinned at his rival and said, "Remember, the best man wins."

Ballard slapped the team into motion, and Corrigan's coach rolled out of the small yard in front of the ranch house, leaving a fuming Yakima Kid behind in the dust.

What a thoroughly disreputable-looking place, Jasper Morton Prescott thought as he stepped into the saloon, a watering hole in a small settlement called Agate, southeast of Denver. It had taken Prescott most of a day to reach the place driving alone in a hired carriage, and he was decidedly nervous about entering the tavern. He was out of place here among cowboys and prospectors and hardcases, and he knew it.

But when the note from Lem Decker had arrived at his Denver hotel, he had had no choice but to answer the summons. There was too much riding on Decker's efforts to ignore the man.

To cover his absence, Prescott had told William Randolph Hearst that he wished to check out a few business deals in the area he had heard about. Hearst had been more than willing to accept the explanation, and the two publishers had parted company. Prescott had then hired the buggy and driven to the settlement.

Now, as he walked to the bar, his gaze darted around the dingy, low-ceilinged room. Perhaps a dozen men were in the saloon, most of them sitting at tables with drinks in front of them and a few playing cards in a desultory fashion. The two men standing at the bar paid no attention to Prescott, and he was grateful for that.

The bartender was short and wide and bald, and he looked up at Prescott without the faintest sign of curiosity

on his face. The publisher said quietly, "Ah, excuse me. I
. . . I'm looking for a man named—"

"No need for names," the bartender interrupted. "The
fella you want is back there." He nodded toward the rear
wall, where one man sat alone in the saloon's only booth.

"Thank you," Prescott said, wondering if he should
give the bartender a coin. He decided against it and
headed toward the rear.

Even sitting, the burly barrel-chested man in the
booth was powerful-looking. He wore a flat-crowned black
hat, a cracked leather vest over a plaid shirt, denim pants,
and high black boots. A cartridge belt and holster were
fastened around his waist, and a Remington revolver with
a well-worn walnut grip rode in the holster. As Prescott
approached, the man looked up and regarded him with
intense pale blue eyes.

"You must be Prescott," he said scornfully. "Nobody
else would show up in a place like this dressed like a
dude." He gestured at the bench on the other side of the
booth. "Sit down. Want a drink?"

Prescott shook his head. The man's blatantly arrogant
attitude struck sparks of anger within him, but he suppressed them. "And you must be Lem Decker," he stated.
"What was so important that you had to disobey my orders
and contact me in Denver?"

Decker leaned forward, clasping his long-fingered hands
on the tabletop. Clearly he regarded the publisher as no
threat, or he would not have done such a thing. "Look,
Prescott," he began, "you hired me to stop that fella
Corrigan from winning that damn stagecoach race. I figure
it must be important to you, or you wouldn't have forked
over the loot. So when my boys had trouble, I thought
you'd want to know."

Prescott closed his eyes and clenched his teeth. It
had been difficult enough to get in touch with Decker; he
had been forced to use several unsavory contacts he had
made over the years among Kansas City's lower classes.
But the publisher had been a reporter himself at one time,
and he still knew how to find someone when he set his
mind to it. After putting the word out that he was looking
for someone in Colorado who was willing to step outside

the law for money, he was eventually given Decker's name. He had not met the hardcase until now, and he would have preferred to keep it that way. Unfortunately . . .

"Do you mean to say that you haven't stopped Corrigan?" he finally asked.

"You got it, mister. In fact, my boys nearly got their hair parted by some lead when they ambushed that coach. I'm afraid this is goin' to be more trouble than I thought. I'll have to handle it myself." Decker shrugged. "So it's goin' to cost you more."

"But we had an agreement!" Prescott protested.

"Doesn't matter. Things change. I want another five hundred."

The publisher grimaced, but even as he hesitated, he knew he would have to give the man what he was asking for. Everything had gone too far for Prescott to back out now. His newspaper, his career, his whole life—it was all riding on the outcome of this race. He had to win the bet with Hearst or lose everything.

"All right," he agreed, reaching into a pocket inside his coat. He brought out an envelope and dropped it on the table between them. "I thought you might want more money, so I took the precaution of bringing this with me. There's five hundred dollars there, in fact."

Decker frowned suspiciously. "How'd you know—"

"Let's just say that great minds work alike, shall we?" Prescott's voice was the one dripping with scorn now. Some of it was a pose, but now that he had paid off Decker again, he felt more in control. He went on, "What assurances do I have that you'll get the job done this time?"

"You got my word on it," Decker stated, and when Prescott looked dubious, he snapped, "My word's good, mister. I may be an owlhoot, but I keep my promises." He grinned. "At least most of the time."

Decker started to stand up, but Prescott reached across the table with uncharacteristic daring and grasped his arm, stopping him. "Are you sure you can prevent Corrigan from winning?"

The outlaw sneered. "That coach is still a good couple of days away from Denver. Corrigan and the others won't ever reach there." He paused. "Not alive, anyway."

Chapter Fourteen

"**J**uly the second," Earl Corrigan said as the group prepared to break camp after a night with no further trouble. "That Hearst fella was right. We ought to be in Denver on the fourth."

"If nothin' else happens," Jackrabbit Dawkins cautiously added as he threw the coffee grounds into the ashes of the fire.

Wes Ballard nodded his agreement. He and the old jehu had already hitched up the team and were ready to travel, anxious about keeping their lead on Travers. Ballard was unsure how far behind them the other coach was, but he figured at least a mile. For the first time he began to have a definite sense that they were going to win this race, that Corrigan was going to collect the prize money and be able to continue with his show.

He also realized that when it was all over, it was going to be a bit hard to return to Texas. He would miss Corrigan and Jackrabbit, and he would miss Lucy, too. But whenever he thought about never seeing Morgan Dixon again, that was when his chest tightened strangely and he got a hollow feeling in the pit of his stomach.

Morgan had changed in the time he had known her. She still wrote her accounts of the race for the newspaper every night, and her career as a journalist was obviously still important to her, but her eyes seemed to have been opened to other things. She knew more about a wider variety of topics than anyone else Ballard had ever encountered, and he was going to miss talking to her.

And there was no point in denying it: He was also

going to miss her beauty and her charm. He was in love with her, dammit.

Before he could carry that thought any further, Corrigan was calling for all of them to board the coach. Nearby, Brian Nichols swung up into his saddle and let his mount prance ahead of the stage.

They had camped on a flat stretch of land between a brush-choked gully on the east and a rather rocky hill on the west. The Texan had just grasped the rail on the edge of the driver's box and was about to hoist himself up when a gunshot shattered the early-morning stillness.

The slug thudded into the side of the coach not six inches from Ballard. He whirled around as more shots rang out, coming from the top of the hill. Several men on horseback boiled over the rise, whooping and shooting.

Brian jerked his pistols out and began blazing away at the attackers, for even though they were too far away to be in the range of handguns, the gap was narrowing with every passing second. Corrigan ran to the boot at the rear of the coach, tore back its canvas covering, and snatched out a couple of Winchester rifles. He tossed one to Ballard, following it a second later with a box of shells. Jackrabbit already had his Henry unlimbered, and it was cracking wickedly.

"Get out of the coach!" Ballard shouted to Morgan and Lucy as he hurried around to the side, putting the stage between him and the attackers. "And stay down!"

The two young women scrambled out and crouched behind the vehicle, using it for cover. Corrigan stayed at its rear, thumbing shells into his rifle and then opening fire on the raiders. As soon as Ballard's rifle was loaded, he fired over the backs of the team, glad that the brake on the stagecoach was solidly set. Otherwise the nervous animals might have bolted by now.

The blast of the guns was deafening, and the air was filled with gun smoke, but except for the first slug, which had struck the coach near Ballard, none of the bullets from either side were finding their targets. Ballard could determine now that there were five men charging down the hill, and as he levered the Winchester and fired again, the group of attackers split up, three riders going to the right, the other two heading left. They obviously planned to flank the coach and expose its defenders to gunfire from the sides.

He swung the muzzle of his rifle to the left, took a deep breath, and squeezed off another shot. One of the men threw his arms up and pitched out of the saddle, rolling over and over as he landed on the grassy ground, and then lay motionless, either dead or badly wounded.

A second later, Jackrabbit let out a whoop. "Glory be! Got one o' the rapscallions!"

"Drilled him plumb center, Jackrabbit," Corrigan said as he laid his cheek on the stock of his rifle and aimed another shot. The old scout fired, then cursed loudly, muttering, "Just creased that son of a buck. Didn't even knock him off his horse."

Brian had reloaded both six-guns, and shooting from horseback, he laid a hail of lead in front of the surviving raiders on the right side. They broke off, yanking their horses around in an effort to dodge the bullets.

Ballard sent another slug screaming toward the last man on the left. The shot missed, but it came close enough to make the raider duck frantically. Ballard grinned. The travelers were putting up more resistance than the ambushers must have expected. Within seconds, he thought, the three men who were left would be fleeing.

A sudden pounding of hoofbeats behind him made him whirl around. Lucy screamed as two men rode up out of the gully a few yards away from the coach. These two must have slipped along the brushy wash for a sneak attack while the others kept them occupied with the assault from the hilltop. Ballard swore and tried to bring his Winchester to bear.

The attackers' revolvers roared, and Ballard felt the wind of a slug going past his ear. Lunging forward, he tried to get between the riders and Morgan and Lucy, but he was too late. The shoulder of one of the charging horses clipped him, and the impact spun him around and made him lose his grip on the rifle.

He fell to the ground, and as he went down, he heard Lucy scream again. Looking up, he saw one of the men lean over in his saddle, throw an arm around the young blonde's waist, and snatch her off her feet. The other man made a grab for Morgan, but the journalist flung herself backward, causing him to miss.

"Lucy!" Corrigan cried as the raiders swept past him, more pain in his voice than Ballard had ever heard. The showman could not fire for fear of hitting his daughter, and neither could Jackrabbit or Brian. All they could do was watch as the riders galloped away with her.

Suddenly Brian spurred his horse into motion. He could not use his guns, but if he could catch up to the kidnappers, he might be able to throw himself from the saddle and tackle the man who had hold of Lucy. It would be risky, but it was the only chance they had.

But before Brian could reach the men, one of the three surviving ambushers who had charged back up the hill fired a rifle shot at the young pursuer. Scrambling to his feet, Ballard caught his breath as Brian's horse suddenly went head over heels, throwing the sharpshooter crazily through the air. The Texan scooped up his Winchester and ran to the rear of the coach, joining Corrigan and Jackrabbit, and they immediately opened fire on the owlhoots, giving Brian the cover he needed to scurry behind the meager shelter of a small tree. By this time the men who had snatched Lucy were almost out of sight around a bend in the trail that led through the hills. Breaking off the fight, the three attackers who had lived through the initial assault wheeled their horses and raced over the hill.

Corrigan cursed fervently. "Come on!" he urged. "We've got to get after them!"

Jackrabbit caught his old friend's arm and said, "Hold on there, Cactus! They got Lucy!"

"I know that, dammit! Why do you think we have to catch them?"

Nodding in agreement, Ballard said, "Jackrabbit's got a point, Cactus. If we go charging after those bastards, they're liable to kill her."

The danger seemed to be over for the moment. Brian's horse, which was sporting an ugly but not serious crease from the bullet that had knocked it down, had gotten back up and was moving around nervously nearby. The sharp-shooter, his face pale and his eyes huge with fear for the woman he loved, caught the animal and led it back over to the stagecoach. With a visible effort he calmed himself and asked, "Why would they grab her like that, anyway?"

"Can't be for ransom," Corrigan rasped, pacing back and forth. "I don't have any money."

Morgan Dixon spoke up. "Couldn't these be the same men who have been trying to stop us? Maybe they kidnapped Lucy as a last-ditch measure to slow us down."

"Damn them!" Corrigan raged. "If they've put my little girl in danger just because of this blasted race—"

"I think Morgan may be onto something," Ballard put in. "It looked like those men were trying to kill us, but we put up a better fight than they expected. Could be the two who snuck up in the gully were there just in case the others didn't have any luck in gunning us down."

"Makes sense," Jackrabbit agreed bleakly. "But what happens now?"

Ballard looked at Corrigan and Brian, then exchanged a glance with Morgan and Jackrabbit. They were expecting him to make the decision, he realized, for the showman and the sharpshooter were too worried to be thinking straight.

"They went in the same direction we're headed," the Texan noted after a moment. "Let's get the coach rolling and head that way, too. They wouldn't go to the trouble of grabbing Lucy and not try to take advantage of the fact that they've got her, so I reckon it's only a matter of time until they let us know what they want us to do."

"That's all well and good," Brian snapped, "but what about between now and then, blast it? What do you think is happening to Lucy right now?"

"I imagine she's scared out of her wits," Ballard said, forcing himself to remain steady. "But they're not going to hurt her—not until they get what they want from us."

"You really believe that, Wes?" Corrigan asked softly.

"I've got to," Ballard replied honestly.

Corrigan heaved a long sigh. "All right. We'll play it as you say. But by God, if they hurt that girl, I'll see that every one of the miserable bastards burns in hell for it!"

"We'll get her back, Cactus," Ballard murmured, putting a reassuring hand on the old scout's shoulder. "We'll get her back."

Moving almost in a daze, the five travelers prepared to get the coach rolling again, but before they could, someone hailed them. His nerves stretched to the breaking point, Ballard whipped around on the seat and brought up the rifle that had been resting across his lap. Brian's guns were out again, and Corrigan and Jackrabbit were both leaning from the coach, bristling with hardware.

Ballard relaxed a little as he saw John Travers's coach bearing down on them at a good pace. Travers was on the seat next to the driver, and he, too, was holding a rifle at the ready. As the coach pulled up next to Corrigan's vehicle, Travers said anxiously, "We heard some shooting. What happened, Cactus?"

"Some riders attacked us just as we were about to pull out," Corrigan replied, stepping down from the passenger compartment. Wearily he rubbed a big hand across his rugged face and went on, "Reckon it was the same bunch as before. We were fighting them off when a couple of them came out of that gully and took us by surprise."

"Sneaky scalawags," Travers grunted. "Looks like you were still able to run them off, though."

"They left on their own," Corrigan said, all the misery of the world in his voice. "And they took Lucy with them."

"My God!" the old frontiersman exclaimed. "What are you going to do?"

"Go after them. Not much else we *can* do."

Travers nodded and slipped one of his Colts out of its holster, spinning the cylinder to check the loads. "We'd better get moving, then. Don't want them to get too big a lead."

Corrigan frowned. "You're coming with us? What about the race?"

"Blast it, Cactus, that girl is a lot more precious to me than winning some foolish race. You ought to know that by now."

"Reckon I should, at that," Corrigan responded, nodding. "Thanks, Kid. We appreciate the help."

"Of course, you know there's a good chance we'll be riding into a trap."

"I know," the old scout agreed.

Garrett Kingsley leaned out the coach window, a concerned expression on his face. "What's this about chasing some kidnappers?" he asked. "You've got a race to win, Mr. Travers."

Travers looked down from the driver's box at the reporter and grinned humorlessly. "I thought you and your boss were rooting for the other side to win, Kingsley."

"I suppose we are, but I wasn't expecting to get shot at along the way."

Morgan Dixon poked her head out the window of Corrigan's coach. "Why, Mr. Kingsley, I thought you sent back dispatches from the war in Cuba. You should be used to getting shot at by now."

"I covered the war, all right," Kingsley replied nervously, "but never from the front lines."

"We goin' to sit around gabbin' all day, or are we goin' after them desperadoes?" Jackrabbit demanded.

"We're going after them," Corrigan answered. "Let's get started, Wes."

Ballard nodded and started the team in motion, and Travers's coach fell in right behind. Kingsley was still muttering, and the Kid told him, "Just stay inside and keep your head down, mister. You'll come through this just fine."

As Ballard guided the coach along the trail, he figured the odds. Travers had a total of three drivers with him, rugged individuals who were veterans of his show. That gave them seven guns in all, not counting the two journalists. Five of the seven raiders had survived the fight, so on the face of it, Corrigan and his friends outnumbered the kidnappers. However, there was no way of knowing if the owlhoots had other cohorts waiting somewhere nearby.

The road was fairly broad and level, and Ballard set a good fast pace. Keeping his eyes peeled, he scanned the surrounding terrain constantly, while Jackrabbit did the same. Their route wound through quite a few small hills, and it was maddening to know there were probably dozens of hiding places within sight. If Lucy's kidnappers were holed up somewhere, the coaches might go right past and never see them.

But that would defeat their purpose in taking her, Ballard reasoned. Now that they had Lucy, they would want to use her to lure the others on.

After about a mile, a small trail that was little more than a pair of grassy ruts led to the left off the main road. It wound up farther into the hills, and Ballard might not have even noticed it—if it had not been for the fringed jacket hung on a bush right next to the trail.

He reined in the team sharply as Jackrabbit exclaimed, "That's Lucy's jacket, by gum!"

Corrigan hurriedly got out of the coach and ran over to the bush, snatching up the garment. "It's my girl's, all right," he confirmed.

Travers's coach pulled up just behind Corrigan's, and the silver-haired frontiersman hopped lithely down from the box. Joining his old friend, he gestured at the old trail and said, "They must have taken her up that way."

"And they want us to follow," Brian said from horseback. "Well, I'm ready." He started trotting along the weather-beaten ruts.

"Hold on!" Corrigan called. "We'll all go together, son. Let's get these coaches turned."

Ballard maneuvered the stagecoach until its wheels were in the ruts, and from the way the iron-rimmed wheels fitted, he knew that this was probably an old stage road. The coach bounced along the trail, with Brian riding a few yards ahead and Travers's vehicle traveling behind.

The path wound around, and within minutes the road was out of sight behind them, cut off from view by several hills. Ballard searched the landscape, but the area seemed to be deserted. There were no ranch houses or farms to be seen anywhere, just rugged, rocky hills covered with scrub brush and hardy grass.

"I'm startin' to get a bad feelin' about this," Jackrabbit said quietly as he squinted at the countryside.

"You and me both, old-timer," Ballard agreed. He could almost feel the eyes watching them—murderous, angry eyes.

*　　　*　　　*

"Dammit to hell!" Lem Decker grated from where he was crouched in a cluster of rocks on a hillside up ahead of the two stagecoaches. "That other coach wasn't supposed to be with Corrigan!"

Behind him, Lucy Corrigan made angry noises through the rag that gagged her. Her wrists and ankles were bound, but otherwise she had not been harmed. However, during the last ten minutes she had been forced to watch as Decker and his men spread out over the hillside, concealing themselves so they could ambush her father's stagecoach.

"Can't hit Travers," Decker muttered to himself. "That'd foul everything up." He began motioning to the other nine men—he had left five behind earlier, just in case the raid on Corrigan's coach did not pan out—trying to get their attention. He had to let them know through hand signals that they should try to avoid Travers's stage when they opened fire on Corrigan.

The coaches were almost within range now. Decker edged forward, tightening his grip on the Winchester. He hoped his men understood about Travers. The object of this whole scheme was for Prescott to win his bet with Hearst, and the bet would be off if both of the old showmen died.

On the other hand, Decker thought, he had already been paid, and there was nothing Prescott could do about it if Travers did catch a bullet. Maybe he was worrying for nothing. If it came down to that, they would just kill everybody in sight and let somebody else sort it all out.

One of the team seemed to be limping a little, as if it had picked up a rock in its hoof, and Ballard leaned over to get a better look at the horse's gait. Just as he did, a bullet screamed past his ear and whined away harmlessly—rather than blowing his brains out.

In one fluid move he kicked the brake to set it and threw himself off the side of the driver's box. Jackrabbit did the same on the opposite side. As the Texan landed heavily, he scuttled toward a small clump of rocks that would give him some protection from the snipers.

More slugs were thudding into the coach, and from

inside Corrigan opened fire. Brian yanked his horse around to the other side of the coach and dropped out of the saddle, pulling his own Winchester from the saddle boot. A few yards back along the old trail, Travers's coach had also stopped, and both the Kid and his jehu dived for cover, but none of the bullets seemed to be coming close to them.

Cursing the fact that he had left his Winchester on the box, Ballard stared up the hill and saw gun smoke floating up from behind rocks and trees and bushes. The ambushers were scattered all across the hillside.

As gunfire erupted from the coaches, Ballard realized that Lucy was probably somewhere up in the hills, and he prayed none of the slugs they were firing hit her. Ultimately, though, she was in more danger from the kidnappers.

About ten yards up the hill and slightly to the Texan's left were some trees. Ballard assessed them for a long moment, then surged to his feet and sprinted toward them. His high-heeled boots were not made for running, but he did the best he could. Bullets kicked up dust around his feet, and he left the ground in a dive that carried him behind the trees. His battered Stetson flew off, and he had no way of knowing if it had been plucked off his head by a slug.

Catching his breath, Ballard lay flat out on the ground, the trunks of several trees giving him cover. After a few moments he wriggled forward so he would have a better view of the hillside. His eyes searched for more cover farther up the slope and found it in an outcropping of rock that would shield him from the bullets being fired from above—if he could reach it.

Twisting his head around, he saw Corrigan and Brian watching him from the corner of the coach. They seemed to be waiting for him to signal, and when he nodded to them, they started firing at the ambushers again as rapidly as they could. Travers and his men had also picked up on what was happening, and they joined the fusillade.

Kicking off his boots, Ballard got to his feet and raced toward the outcropping. Bullets zipped by close enough for him to feel the wind of their passage, but none of them touched him. Reaching the rock, he crouched behind it, safe again for the moment.

He was about halfway up the hill and not too far from one of the spots where he had seen gun smoke. Risking a glance, Ballard located the place again, and he felt his skin crawl. He had at least ten yards still to cover, and in that distance any man who was a reasonable shot could hit him four or five times. Charging the ambusher's position head-on would be suicide—unless he had some sort of distraction to take the man's attention off him.

On the slope above the outlaw was a fan-shaped area of talus, thousands and thousands of small rocks that would slide easily if something started them moving. Grinning, Ballard reached for several of the fist-size stones lying nearby. Without lifting his body enough to expose himself to gunfire, he started flinging the rocks up the hill, arching them over the nearest man so that they would strike the hillside behind him . . . or so Ballard hoped.

He heard a coarse laugh and knew that the owlhoot must have thought Ballard was throwing the rocks at *him* and missing badly. Then suddenly the man cursed, and Ballard heard the sound of the talus sliding. He knew he could not wait. Vaulting over the top of the outcropping, he ran straight up the hill.

The talus was still showering down on the kidnapper when Ballard threw himself over the top of the squat boulder the man had been using for cover. The outlaw was thrashing around with rocks covering his legs nearly to the knees. Ballard's fist smashed into his jaw, and then his other hand closed over the breech of the man's rifle. Jerking the weapon free, Ballard slammed the butt into his opponent's belly, then clubbed it down on his head. The owlhoot collapsed, out cold.

A bullet ricocheted off the boulder, and Ballard snapped his head around to see one of the other men firing at him. However, from this angle Ballard had a clear shot of his own, and he fired the rifle as he threw himself forward. The second outlaw clutched at his middle and fell, rolling out from behind the bushes he had been using for concealment.

Looking past that man, Ballard spotted Lucy in a

cluster of rocks about twenty yards away and a bit higher on the slope. A man was with her, and he had his rifle lined on Ballard. The Texan's breath stuck in his throat as he realized the man had him dead-on.

Abruptly, though, the kidnapper scowled and threw the rifle aside; it had either jammed or it was empty. The man grabbed for the pistol holstered on his hip.

Ballard levered the Winchester in his hands, squeezing off a shot, and the man with Lucy staggered back a step and clutched a suddenly bloody upper arm. Dropping his gun, the outlaw turned to stumble out of the rocks, fleeing toward the top of the hill.

Before Ballard could loose another shot at him, he had to turn his attention to the other owlhoots. Several of them were running now, no doubt having seen their leader deserting them. Ballard felled one of them with a quick shot, then ducked as the fire was returned. He heard bullets thudding into flesh and turned his head to see that several of the slugs had struck the man he had knocked out, riddling him. Ballard grimaced at the ironic death: The owlhoot's own companions had killed him.

Now that the tide of battle had turned, Corrigan, Travers, Brian, Jackrabbit, and Travers's men were able to emerge from behind the coaches and charge up the hill. The sharpshooter especially was a madman, leaping up the slope in great bounds and firing his Colts as fast as he could pull the triggers. A couple of the kidnappers went spinning to their deaths with his lead in them. "Lucy!" the young man shouted.

"Over there, Brian!" Ballard called to him, pointing to the spot where Lucy had been held captive. She was still writhing around trying to free herself, and Ballard felt reasonably sure she was all right. Brian reached her side a moment later, jamming his guns back in their holsters and whipping out the knife he wore in a sheath just behind the right-hand gun. He slashed the ropes, tore the gag out of Lucy's mouth, and lifted her into a tight, thankful embrace.

Ballard got to his feet and scrambled up the slope in his stocking feet as Corrigan, Travers, and the others finished the mop-up. Dead outlaws were sprawled grotesquely all over the slope, but Ballard did not see the man who had been with Lucy. Evidently he had reached the top of the hill and gotten away, for the gang had no doubt had their horses tied nearby.

But except for the one who had gotten away, all the kidnappers were dead. As Lucy shakily described the dreadful experience, she said that her captor's name was Decker. "At least that's what one of the others called him," the young blonde said. "He didn't seem upset that the man used his name. He . . . he obviously figured I'd be dead soon, and it wouldn't matter."

"You're fine," Brian assured her, drawing her into his arms once more as she began to tremble again. "Nobody's going to hurt you."

Morgan came hurrying out of Corrigan's coach to make sure Lucy was all right, but Garrett Kingsley did not emerge from the other one for several minutes. "Is it all over?" he asked when finally he stuck his head out.

"Reckon it is," Ballard told him, pulling on the boots he had retrieved. His feet were bruised from the rocks, but considering that Lucy was safe again, the pain was well worth it. He went on, "That gang's pretty much wiped out. The only one who got away was wounded, and I don't think he'll give us any trouble from here on out."

"I agree," Travers said. "That was mighty brave of you, charging up there like that, Ballard."

The Texan shrugged. "Just worked out that way. I might not have done it if I hadn't forgotten to grab my rifle when I jumped off the coach."

Lucy came over to him and laid a hand on his arm. "Thank you, Wes," she said softly. "I . . . I don't know when my father and I have had a better friend than you."

Ballard just smiled, feeling vaguely uncomfortable from all the praise. Kingsley saved him from having to reply by saying brightly, "Well, I guess we've got a race to get back to, don't we?"

Corrigan looked over at Travers. "This race, this whole competition, has caused us nothing but trouble, Kid. Do we go through with it?"

Travers shrugged and said, "Seems like we're too close to the end to stop now, Cactus."

"All right," the showman agreed with a nod. "We'd best get a move on, then."

Ballard climbed onto the box as everyone else boarded the two coaches. He grinned tiredly. They had been through a lot, but the Great Stagecoach Race and Wild West Extravaganza was not quite over.

Chapter Fifteen

The Fourth of July was clear and warm, another beautiful summer day. No more attempts were made to stop either coach after Lucy Corrigan's rescue from the kidnappers, and that delay had been overcome by some hard driving on the part of both drivers. The coaches were running practically even as they entered the outskirts of Denver that afternoon.

The scenery was magnificent, with the Rocky Mountains thrusting up majestically into the blue sky to the west of the city, but Wes Ballard had no time for taking in the sights. He was only a matter of yards ahead of John Travers's coach, and the other vehicle was steadily cutting the gap. Ballard leaned forward on the seat, using the reins and the whip to coax all the speed he could out of his team, while beside him Jackrabbit Dawkins looked just as anxious.

Cheering throngs lined both sides of Colfax Avenue as the coaches raced into Denver. Outriders from the town had been monitoring their progress all day and carrying word back to the expectant crowds.

As the iron-rimmed wheels clattered loudly on the avenue's paving stones, Ballard glanced over his shoulder and saw that Travers's coach was even closer now. Suddenly Earl Corrigan leaned out the window and ordered, "Stop the coach, Wes!"

Ballard reached for the brake automatically, then hesitated. Had Corrigan lost his mind? Less than a mile ahead the Texan could see the state capitol and the United States Mint. The finish line was in front of the mint, and a huge platform decked in red-white-and-blue bunting had been built there for the two publishers and all the local dignitaries to witness the conclusion of the race. Ballard had heard that several congressmen were also going to be on hand, and it was rumored that a special celebrity was going to serve as the judge in case of a close finish to the race.

"Dammit, stop!" Corrigan shouted again.

Against his better judgment, Ballard hauled the coach to a stop. The showman hopped out, ignoring the questions being thrown at him by Jackrabbit, Lucy, and Morgan.

"Get in the coach, Jackrabbit," Corrigan told the old-timer. "And slide over on that seat, Wes. I'm taking the reins."

"What?" Jackrabbit yelped. "Have you lost your cotton-pickin' mind, Cactus?"

"Just do like I tell you," Corrigan snapped.

Ballard glanced at Travers's coach. It was drawing alongside, but it slowed to a halt instead of passing them. And Travers was taking the reins from his driver, as had Corrigan.

"Ready to finish this race, Cactus?" Travers called over the tumult of the crowd.

"Damn right," Corrigan replied, stepping up onto the box and holding out his hands for the reins.

Ballard gave them to him. A smile creased the Texan's face. He understood now. This last half-mile or so would decide the race, and after hundreds of miles and years of rivalry, it had come down to this: Cactus Corrigan versus the Yakima Kid—one last time, winner take all.

"Better get in the coach, Jackrabbit," Ballard yelled. "And hang on!"

The old jehu's eyes widened with the same realization that had hit Ballard. Letting out a high-pitched cackle, he herded Morgan and Lucy back inside, and just as he pulled himself in, he shouted, "Let 'er rip, Cactus!"

Corrigan and Travers exchanged one last look, each man raising a finger and touching the brim of his hat in a salute to the other. Then, with a yell and a crack of the whip, they were off.

Ballard held on for dear life as the coaches raced

down the street. The cheering rose until it was deafening. Corrigan and Travers leaned forward, driving their teams on. First Corrigan pulled ahead slightly, then Travers. Corrigan drew even again, and the teams were galloping neck and neck, neither a fraction of an inch ahead of the other.

Ballard's heart pounded wildly in his chest. The whole city seemed ready to explode in excitement. There was the capitol, looming up on the left, and just ahead was the mint and the finish line. Ballard caught a glimpse of the men lined up at the railing of the reviewing stand, top-hatted politicians jumping up and down and cheering just like everyone else. Prescott and Hearst were both caught up in the frenzy, and beside them, directly in front of the finish line, was the judge. Ballard felt a shock as he recognized the ruddy, bespectacled face of Theodore Roosevelt, the rough-riding hero of the Spanish-American War. Ballard jerked his gaze back to the horses.

Corrigan's team was ahead . . . and then Travers's took the lead again . . . Corrigan . . . Travers . . . Corrigan . . . Travers . . .

Both stagecoaches flashed past the finish line in a dead heat.

Denver erupted in tumult as both showmen gradually slowed their teams. Ballard looked at Corrigan and saw the broad grin on the man's face. The two rivals swung the coaches around to head back to the finish line, and as they did, the Texan saw the silver-haired Travers wink. To Ballard's shock, Corrigan returned the gesture. The two men looked extremely pleased with themselves.

Ballard felt himself starting to smile as understanding of what had just happened sank in. Sometime in the last couple of days, Corrigan and Travers had worked this out between them, agreeing to finish the race together, just as they had been through so much together in the past. It was a fitting conclusion, Ballard decided, although he was sure Hearst and Prescott would not feel that way.

In fact, both newspaper publishers were hopping mad as the coaches rolled up in front of the platform. They were talking heatedly to Theodore Roosevelt, who did not seem disturbed in the least by their anger. Roosevelt held up both hands, palms out, and Ballard heard him say, "I'm sorry, gentlemen, but in my considered opinion, the outcome of this race was a tie. You appointed me judge, and that judgment will stand. Now, if you'll excuse me . . ." He pushed past Hearst and Prescott and stepped to the edge of the platform, where he leaned over to shake hands with Cactus Corrigan and the Yakima Kid.

"Hello, Teddy," Corrigan said. "Didn't know you were going to be here."

"Wouldn't have missed it," Roosevelt replied. "I haven't seen the two of you since you helped me apprehend those miscreants on my spread in Montana. How are you, Kid?"

"Doing just fine, Teddy," Travers said with a grin. "Or should I call you Governor?"

Roosevelt waggled a finger. "Not yet. Why, I haven't even decided if I'm going to run or not. At any rate, we're not in New York."

Prescott and Hearst came up behind him, still demanding that something be done about the race. Roosevelt turned around and snapped, "Please, gentlemen, I'm talking to my friends. I'm sorry about your bet, but considering how the race turned out, I think you should just call it off."

"But I can't—" Prescott began, then stopped abruptly. With a furious look on his face, he turned and stalked off, heading for the stairs at the side of the platform.

Hearst heaved a philosophical sigh. "Well, I don't like it, Colonel Roosevelt, but I don't suppose there's anything I can do about it." He summoned up a cocky smile. "I may not have won, but no one can say I lost."

"No, indeed, Mr. Hearst. No, indeed."

Jackrabbit climbed on top of the coach and called out a greeting to Roosevelt, who returned it eagerly. Grinning, the old jehu said, "Hear you made a name for yourself down there in Cuba, Teddy. Always said you wasn't a bad cowboy—for a four-eyed tenderfoot."

Roosevelt threw back his head and laughed. "And I see you haven't changed either, you old scoundrel."

Morgan Dixon and Garrett Kingsley scrambled out of the coaches and began an impromptu interview with the war hero and up-and-coming politician, while the crowds who had gathered for the conclusion of the race poured into the street to continue their celebration of Independence Day. Somewhere firecrackers began to go off, and a band started playing. Brian Nichols had ridden up and gotten off his horse to take Lucy in his arms, while Corrigan and Travers sat atop the coaches and basked in the admiration and applause that was still being showered over them.

Ballard leaned back on the driver's seat and grinned. He had seen and done more in the last month than he had ever dreamed possible when he left Texas on a supposedly simple delivery of a herd of horses to Kansas City. He had been a part of something that would never be repeated. For a while, he had held a piece of the Old West in his hands. It had felt good—mighty good. And he knew that as long as he lived, he would never forget Cactus Corrigan and the Yakima Kid.

Wes Ballard almost felt like whistling as he ambled down a hallway in one of Denver's fanciest hotels. The last hour had been a busy one, following the conclusion of the race, but he had managed to get himself cleaned up a little. Hearst had rented several floors in this hotel for the members of both Wild West shows, and Ballard and Jackrabbit were sharing a room that had its own bath with hot running water. Jackrabbit had stared at the claw-footed tub for a long time before daring to enter it. "I ain't used to such highfalutin gewgaws," he had said dubiously.

Down the hall, in the largest suite the hotel had to offer, Earl Corrigan and John Travers were in great demand. Journalists from all over the country were clamoring to interview them, and dozens of politicians wanted to be seen with the two frontiersmen who were now more famous than ever. In fact, Corrigan had told Ballard during a moment snatched from the uproar, it looked as if the show would be able to get on its feet again even without the prize money from the race. All the publicity generated by the race in the past few weeks had promoters falling all over themselves to book both troupes—and tonight they would join forces in Denver's indoor arena for the biggest Wild West show yet.

"We've already got advance money from tonight's gate and half a dozen other bookings," Corrigan had said. "I want you to go see Nathan Sanford and get that cash I owe you for those horses, Wes." Clapping Ballard on the shoulder, he had chortled, "You're finally going to get paid, just as I promised."

"I never doubted you, Cactus," Ballard had replied with a grin.

That was where he was headed now. Nathan Sanford had set up a bookkeeping office in one of the hotel's smaller rooms, around a corner from where Corrigan was headquartered and tucked away in a quiet alcove where Sanford could get some work done. In fact, as Ballard turned the corner into the short hallway leading to the room, he saw that there was no one else around at the moment. He could still hear the commotion down the main hall, but this part of the hotel was a small oasis of peace and quiet.

The Texan was just lifting his hand to knock on the door of Sanford's makeshift office when he heard an angry voice coming from the other side of the panel: "Dammit, you'd better take me seriously. I mean every word I say."

Ballard frowned. The high-pitched tone belonged to Sanford. He had not heard the bookkeeper so angry since the time he had rescued him from the roughhousing cowboys in Kansas City, and he wondered who had gotten him so mad.

Knowing that he should not eavesdrop but giving in to his curiosity, Ballard leaned closer to the door, listening intently as another man replied smoothly, "I'm sure you do mean it, Sanford, but I think you must be badly mistaken. The things you're accusing me of are ridiculous."

Ballard's eyes widened in surprise. The second voice was unmistakably that of Jasper Morton Prescott. What the devil was the publisher of the Kansas City *Clarion* doing arguing with Cactus Corrigan's bookkeeper?

"Ridiculous, am I?" Sanford snorted. "Well, I happen to know, Mr. Prescott, that you were working hand in glove with Neal Hayden to ruin the Yakima Kid's show."

"You can't . . . You're insane, man." Prescott's denial sounded insincere, Ballard thought, even muffled as it was through the door of the room.

Then he remembered what Corrigan had said about Hayden's possibly having a silent partner, and suddenly everything that had happened began to make more sense. If Prescott had been involved all along, that would explain many things.

The revelations were not over, however, and Ballard hoped that no one came along and caught him listening at the door.

"Hayden thought he was so damned smart," Sanford was saying. "He coerced Quint Fowler into working against Travers and then sought me out to help him disrupt Mr. Corrigan's show. Hayden, of course, was only interested in aggravating the feud between the two shows and pushing Travers into selling out to him, but it was my chance to get back at those awful cowboys who were always tormenting me. Does any of this sound familiar, Prescott?"

It certainly sounded familiar to Ballard. That was exactly what they had theorized after the riot at the arena in Kansas City. Sanford's involvement in the plot came as a surprise, but not a very big one considering all the trouble he had experienced with Corrigan's cowboys.

"Go on, Sanford," Prescott said quietly. "You're telling this story."

"That's right, I am. Hayden liked to pretend that he was running everything, but he let enough things slip while he was talking to me that I was able to figure out he had someone rich and powerful backing him. I looked into the matter and found out that someone was you, Prescott." Sanford sniffed smugly. "I assumed Hayden was blackmailing you; I can't see a man such as yourself becoming involved with a greedy scoundrel like him otherwise. So I continued to investigate. No one pays much attention to someone like me. Most men simply despise me—if they even notice I'm there. I heard some rather interesting stories about your wife and a dead man in a tavern. . . ."

"You bastard." Prescott's voice shook with emotion. "What do you want of me?"

"I'm not finished with my story yet," Sanford snapped. "I kept an eye on you after we got to Denver, and I know about your meeting with a man named Lem Decker—the same man whose gang kidnapped Lucy Corrigan, I believe, after they failed to stop her father's coach a couple of other times. You had to win that bet with Hearst to recoup the money that Hayden took from you in blackmail, I imagine. Decker seems to have disappeared after that debacle . . . but you're still here, Prescott."

The newspaper publisher sighed heavily. "How much, Sanford? How much blood money do you want?"

The bookkeeper tittered, more sure of himself now that Prescott had surrendered. "Oh, I'm not as greedy as Hayden was. I'll settle for a thousand . . . for now."

Ballard heard Prescott start to count out bills as he paid off Sanford's blackmail demand. The Texan leaned away from the door, trying to absorb all the information he had just overheard. His pulse thudded angrily in his head. So Prescott was behind all the trouble they had had during the race. He might have been able to forgive the publisher for his involvement with Hayden in Kansas City; from what he had heard, Prescott's part in that had occurred under duress. But hiring Decker and nearly getting all of them killed just to win the bet with Hearst—that was different, a lot different. Ballard's hands clenched into fists.

He heard footsteps approaching the door and darted away from it, half-running back down the short hall and reaching the corner just before the door opened. Ballard hugged the wall until Prescott emerged into the corridor and stalked away angrily in the opposite direction, never noticing Ballard. The Texan heaved a sigh of relief.

When Prescott was gone, Ballard went back down the hall, and this time he rapped sharply on the closed door. Sanford called, "Who is it?"

"Wes Ballard. Cactus sent me."

"Oh, yes." Sanford sounded distracted—and with good reason, Ballard thought. "Come in."

The bookkeeper had papers spread not only all over the desk that had been brought into the room but also on the bed. His coat was off, his tie and collar were loosened, and the sleeves of his shirt were rolled up. He looked as harried as ever, but there was something else sparkling in his eyes. Ballard might not have even noticed it if he had not overheard the conversation with Prescott, but now he knew what he was seeing: Greed. Triumph. Vindication for all the ills, real and imagined, that had ever been visited on this meek little man.

Sanford barely glanced at Ballard and did not notice the grim look on the Texan's face. "I suppose you've come about your money for those horses," he remarked.

"That's right," Ballard snapped, "and there's something else, too." He shut the door of the room solidly behind him.

Sanford looked up from his ledgers, and an expression of alarm abruptly appeared on his face. "Wh-what?" he stammered.

"I think it's time you and I had a long talk, mister," Ballard growled.

Wes Ballard looked around the arena. Later, once the combined Wild West show began, it would be full of happy, cheering people, but at the moment it was practically deserted. The handful of people clustered together stood on the dirt surface of the arena itself, but the grandstand was empty.

Ballard glanced at the others. Earl Corrigan and John Travers were talking quietly to each other, with Jackrabbit Dawkins standing nearby. Brian Nichols and Lucy Corrigan were there, too, holding hands and giving each other little smiles from time to time. Garrett Kingsley was chewing on his habitual unlit cigar and looking puzzled, while Morgan Dixon chatted distractedly with Ballard. There was obviously more on her mind than the chilled bottle of champagne and the tray of glasses sitting on a table that had been set up near the group.

There was one other person in the arena, his hands shoved in his pockets and a miserable expression on his face—Nathan Sanford.

"Do you think Hearst and Prescott will show up?" Morgan asked Ballard.

"No reason for them not to," the Texan replied. "Seems

likely enough that Cactus and the Kid would invite them for a drink before the show starts, seeing it was the two of them who got all this started in the first place." Ballard nodded at the tunnel that led underneath the grandstand and into the arena. "In fact, here they come now."

The two newspaper publishers strolled out of the tunnel and toward the group waiting for them. Keeping an eye on Prescott, Ballard thought he saw the man hesitate slightly when he caught sight of Sanford and apparently wondered what the bookkeeper was doing there.

"Good evening, gentlemen," Travers greeted Hearst and Prescott.

Hearst nodded. "Mr. Travers, Mr. Corrigan. Thank you for inviting us."

Prescott mumbled something. His gaze kept darting toward Sanford. The publisher would not have made much of a poker player, Ballard decided.

Corrigan opened the champagne while Jackrabbit passed around the glasses. The old-timer was wearing a suit for a change, even though it was a garish plaid, and his beard had been combed and his hair slicked back. He looked almost respectable. Corrigan followed along behind his friend, filling the glasses from the big bottle. When he reached Ballard, one eyelid drooped in a wink, and the Texan knew that everything was going ahead as planned.

Sanford was the last one to have his glass filled with champagne, and his hand shook as he held it out. He looked as though he wanted to gulp down the drink without waiting for the others, but he restrained himself. When everyone had been served, Corrigan replaced the bottle in the ice bucket, picked up his own glass, and lifted it for a toast. "To the Yakima Kid," he said simply.

"And to Cactus Corrigan," Travers replied.

"An' to the old times we ain't never forgot," Jackrabbit chimed in.

"To old times," the others echoed, and then everyone drank.

Corrigan lowered his glass after taking only a sip. Looking directly at Prescott, he remarked, "I don't normally drink with skunks like you, but I figured I could make an exception in this case."

"That's right," Travers said. "We wanted to see how long you could keep up the act, Prescott."

The publisher scowled. "What the hell are you talking about? You bring me here and then insult me? I thought you gentlemen of the Old West had a code of honor that prohibits such behavior."

"Honor is something you wouldn't know anything about, Prescott," Corrigan snapped. "Otherwise you wouldn't have hired those outlaws to kidnap my daughter and nearly kill all of us."

Prescott's eyes widened in shock for a moment, and then he stared angrily at Sanford, who was intently studying the dirt floor of the arena. "I don't know what you're talking about," Prescott barked, obviously intending to try to brazen it out.

"I thought we made that clear. We're talking about kidnapping and attempted murder," Travers shot back. "There was a time when we would have just strung up a varmint like you and saved some time, but I reckon those days are over. We'll turn you over to the law and let them handle you."

"You're insane," the publisher declared, forcing a laugh. "You're all insane."

Hearst was regarding his fellow publisher with consternation, while Garrett Kingsley's mouth had dropped open, letting his cigar fall out. The reporter recovered his wits enough to take out his notebook and pencil and start scribbling. Unlike Morgan and the others, he had not been warned about what was going to happen.

"What is this, Prescott?" Hearst demanded. "Is there anything to these outrageous charges?"

"Nothing! Nothing at all, I tell you," Prescott insisted. "It's all a bunch of rubbish—"

"Sanford has already talked to the police," Ballard cut in. Pointing toward the tunnel through which Hearst and Prescott had entered the arena, he indicated several men in the blue uniforms of the Denver police now standing there, waiting patiently. "Those fellas have a heap of questions they want to ask you, Prescott. I reckon you'd better go along with them peacefully."

The empty champagne glass slipped from Prescott's fingers, falling unnoticed to the floor of the arena, and he shuddered as the blood drained from his face. His mouth opened and worked for a few seconds before words finally came out. "I . . . I never really meant for anyone to . . . to be hurt. It was Hayden's fault, all Hayden's fault. . . ."

Knowing what he did about the situation with Prescott's wife, which had given Hayden his hold over the publisher, Ballard could almost feel sorry for Prescott. *Almost*. But remembering Lem Decker and the way bullets had come close to ending the race—not to mention lives—prematurely, the Texan could not quite manage sympathy.

Neither could the others. Hearst had stepped away from the other publisher, revulsion appearing on his well-bred features. Corrigan took hold of Sanford's arm and led the bookkeeper over beside Prescott. Motioning to the waiting policemen, the showman said, "Take these two out of here."

Prescott stiffened as the officers approached. With a hint of his former arrogance on his face, he proclaimed, "You won't get away with this! I'm an important man! I own a newspaper!" His voice rose. "The public will think what I tell it to think!" His wide-eyed gaze fastened on Morgan, and he demanded, "Miss Dixon, I want you to write a story immediately, absolving me of all blame in this situation and explaining how I've been framed. The headline can read: 'PUBLISHER INNOCENT.' "

Morgan shook her head. "I can't do that, Mr. Prescott."

"But . . . but I'm ordering you to!" Prescott sputtered. "I'm your publisher. You have to write what I tell you to."

"Not anymore." She smiled. "I'm tendering my resignation, effective here and now." She turned to Ballard. "I think I'll look elsewhere for a newspaper job. In Texas, perhaps."

Ballard stared at her in surprise. She had said nothing to him about making such a decision, but as his heart leapt in his chest, he knew he was glad that she had. He reached out and took her hand.

The police led their two prisoners away, Sanford's shoulders slumping in defeat but Prescott still loudly proclaiming his innocence. As they entered the tunnel, the publisher's voice echoed for a few moments, then faded away.

"Well, dad-gum-it, we'd better get busy," Jackrabbit reminded everyone with a grin. "We still got us a Wild West show to put on."

Chapter Sixteen

This was the loudest crowd he had ever heard, Earl Corrigan thought as he waited in the tunnel for the grand entrance to begin. The show had not even started yet, and already the spectators were cheering and yelling and clapping to beat the band. Corrigan grinned. He missed a lot of things about life in the old days, and sometimes he thought that putting on these shows was just a sham; but at moments like this he realized just how much entertainment and enjoyment he and Travers and all the other old-timers who remembered the West were bringing to people. That made it all worthwhile, Corrigan mused, knowing that folks enjoyed what you were doing.

Pain suddenly slammed into him. The attack was the worst one yet. Corrigan was standing next to his horse, so he clutched the stirrup to hold himself up. Maybe with everything that was going on in the tunnel as the two troupes prepared for their entrance, no one would notice what was happening. If he could just hold on until it passed, he thought. . . .

But maybe this time it would not pass. The showman knew that had to happen sooner or later. The disease had been eating up his insides for months now. They had called it consumption in the old days, because it seemed to consume a man once it got started, but no matter what name was put on it, it was a killer.

Jackrabbit was suddenly at Corrigan's side, slipping a hand under his other arm and supporting him. "Dammit, Cactus, you got to do somethin' about this," the old-timer insisted in a low voice.

Corrigan shook his head. "Nothing I can do, pard."

"But you're dyin'!"

"Happens to the best of us." Corrigan summoned up a grin from somewhere deep inside.

"What about Lucy?" Jackrabbit asked grimly.

"She . . . she'll be fine. Brian's a good man, and he'll take care of her, what taking care of she needs. I raised my gal to be strong, Jackrabbit. But . . . if they ever need help, either of them, you'll look after them, won't you?"

Making his voice rough to conceal the tremor in it, the old jehu said gruffly, "Reckon you know I will."

Corrigan fumbled for the saddle horn. "Now, just let me . . . get mounted up . . ."

"You can't go on like this!" Jackrabbit exclaimed.

"The hell I can't. There's folks out there waiting to have a good time—but I reckon this'll be my last performance, Jackrabbit. We always said we'd go out in a blaze of glory, didn't we?"

"We was just talkin', you dad-blasted ol' fool—"

Travers rode up alongside Corrigan's horse as the old scout pulled himself into the saddle. "You ready, Cactus?" he asked.

Corrigan forced another grin. "Ready as I'll ever be," he declared.

The music coming from the band in the arena swelled, and the two old showmen heeled their mounts into a trot that carried them through the tunnel and into the brilliant glare of the building's lights. Jackrabbit watched them go, and a tear trickled down into his grizzled beard.

The two men trotted their horses around the arena, taking the first turn alone, waving their hats and smiling as the crowd erupted in acclamation. This was the pinnacle of their lives, and they were sharing the moment together.

Wes Ballard moved the stagecoach up to the entrance to the arena. The coach would lead the rest of the procession out, once Corrigan and Travers had completed their circuit and taken their places in the spotlight at the center of the arena. This would be the Texan's last time at the reins of the coach. Ballard spotted Jackrabbit standing next to the wall and motioned for the old-timer to join him on the box.

"Something wrong?" Ballard asked him as Jackrabbit climbed onto the coach.

Jackrabbit shook his head, his eyes fixed on his two old friends as they cantered slowly to the center of the arena. "Not a thing," he replied. "Not a damn thing."

Corrigan and Travers came to a stop as the spotlight pinned them to the floor of the arena, and their outfits shone and sparkled in the brilliant illumination. Both men doffed their hats again, holding them high over their heads as they pulled back on the reins, making their mounts rear dramatically.

Without warning, two shots rang out, and the slugs kicked up dust from the arena floor, first on one side of the two men, then the other, with only a fraction of a second between the shots.

Ballard heard the two cracks and leaned forward anxiously. Somewhere in the grandstand, someone screamed in fear, and somebody else shouted, "Up there!"

Corrigan and Travers stayed where they were. The way the shots had bracketed them, there was a good chance they would be gunned down if they broke for cover in either direction. Ballard and Jackrabbit flung themselves off the stagecoach and ran out a few steps into the arena, craning their necks as they peered up toward the ceiling. Brian raced out of the tunnel to join them.

Jackrabbit grasped the Texan's arm and pointed. "Look!"

Ballard's startled gaze followed Jackrabbit's finger, and he saw a man crouched in the rafters high above the floor of the arena. He held a rifle in his hands, and it was pointed at Corrigan and Travers. Over the din of the frightened crowd, the man shouted down, "Everybody out! Everybody but Corrigan and Travers!"

Police were already hustling the fearful spectators toward the exits, and they now speeded up their efforts. Ballard, Jackrabbit, and Brian stayed where they were, watching the gunman, while in the center of the arena Corrigan and Travers sat their horses calmly. This was not the first time they had been under the gun; keeping a cool head in a situation like this was the best way to stay alive.

"It's that son of a bitch Decker!" Brian exclaimed.

"He must've followed us here to Denver," Ballard muttered. "What in blazes is he trying to gain by pulling a stunt like this?"

Decker waited until the arena had been cleared, keeping the rifle trained on the showmen the whole time. When he was good and ready, he finally called down, "You two old bastards cost me my whole gang! I reckon you owe me for that!"

Corrigan looked up at him coolly. "You had my daughter," he said.

"And the man who hired you is already in jail, Decker," Travers added. "You might as well put that gun down and give up whatever crazy idea you've got in your head."

"No, sir," Decker shouted back. "I got to be paid for losing all my men, so I want all the money this place has taken in." Using his foot, he pushed something off the rafter beside him. As the object fell, Ballard saw that it was a wicker basket with a rope tied to its handle. The rope brought the basket up short about four feet off the ground. Decker continued, "Put all the receipts in that basket."

Someone behind Ballard was saying, "Oh, my God. Oh, my God," over and over. The Texan looked back and recognized the manager of the arena.

Stepping back beside the man, Ballard caught his arm and asked sharply, "How'd Decker get up there?"

The manager shook himself out of his shocked stupor and managed to reply after a moment, "There are catwalks and trapdoors leading up there, so we can work on the rafters and the roof if need be."

"That means once Decker gets that money, he can probably slip out the same way he got in?"

The man nodded wordlessly.

"Isn't there some way to douse all those lights so Decker can't get a bead on Cactus and Travers?" Ballard asked.

The manager shook his head. "I'm afraid that wouldn't work. You see, all those lights are on different circuits.

We have to have people all around the arena throwing switches at exactly the same moment—and it's unlikely we could do that."

"Then get the money together," Ballard said grimly. "We're going to have to cooperate with that madman. I'd rather take a chance on the police catching him when he tries to get away than have him shoot down Cactus and the Kid." Ballard glanced at Brian and Jackrabbit, who nodded their agreement.

While the manager hurried toward the ticket office to see to the gathering of the gate receipts, Ballard stepped into the arena again and called, "Decker! We're getting the money, Decker!"

"You do that, cowboy," the gunman replied. The muzzle of his Winchester never wavered.

In the center of the arena, Travers glanced over at his friend and grinned. "Well, we seem to be in trouble again, Cactus," he said lightly. "I thought those days were supposed to be over."

Nodding, Corrigan remarked, "There'll always be owlhoots, Kid." The pain had eased a little now, but it was not going away—not entirely. He realized that it never would.

"Even if he gets the money, Decker's going to try to kill us anyway."

Corrigan nodded again. "I know."

"When he starts shooting, you go one way and I'll go the other. Maybe he won't get us both. And I have a hunch he won't be coming down from there alive, not if our friends have anything to say about it."

Corrigan said nothing, letting Travers take his silence for agreement.

In the tunnel, Brian had pulled his Winchester from the saddle boot and emptied the blank cartridges from it. He was thumbing live rounds into the chamber as the manager hurried back past him, in his arms a burlap bag stuffed full of bills.

Ballard took the money from the manager and said, "I'll carry it out there." Turning to Jackrabbit, he went on, "Dig out that Henry of yours."

The old-timer nodded. "It'll be ready for you, Wes."

Slowly Ballard walked toward the center of the arena and the dangling basket. He was confident that Decker would not shoot him—not until the loot was in the basket, anyway. When he reached the wicker container, he placed the money bag in it carefully, then backed away.

Decker laughed and shouted down, "I can fire this rifle one-handed, so don't anybody get any dumb ideas." Holding the weapon in his right hand and keeping it pointed toward Corrigan and Travers, he used his left to start hauling the basket up again.

Ballard kept backing away slowly. Now that the money had been delivered, Decker paid no attention to him. It took several minutes for the outlaw to pull the basket up to the broad rafter where he was perched, but the time seemed even longer than that.

Jackrabbit was holding the old Henry when Ballard reached the tunnel again. The Texan took the rifle and nodded to Brian, who stood waiting with his Winchester. "If Decker keeps his word, we'll let the police deal with him," Ballard said. "But if he starts shooting . . ."

Brian nodded. There was no need to say anything else.

Finally Decker had the basket on the rafter next to him, and he put both hands on the rifle again. Laughing, he said, "Thanks for the loot. But before I go, I reckon I'll just kill you two fancy show-offs anyway." His voice rose insanely. "You're first, Travers!"

Corrigan moved before anyone else, throwing himself out of the saddle and driving his shoulder into Travers. The Kid spilled off his horse as Decker's rifle cracked, and Corrigan felt the outlaw's lead tear into his body.

At the same instant, Ballard and Brian sprang into the arena. The Winchester and Jackrabbit's old Henry spoke together as both young men blazed away at Decker, firing as fast as they could lever the weapons. Slugs slammed into the outlaw, straightening him up from his crouch. His rifle slipped out of his fingers as he did a macabre dance on the rafter, his body jerking in time to the lead crashing into it. One foot hit the basket and knocked it off, and money tumbled out of the burlap bag, showering down on the arena.

Ballard and Brian stopped firing as Decker's riddled body fell, plummeting down to land with an ugly thud.

Jackrabbit, Lucy, and Morgan raced toward the center of the arena, where Travers was kneeling beside the sprawled form of his old friend. Corrigan's fancy buckskin jacket had a large bloodstain on it, and he was coughing softly as Travers held up his head. Lucy went down on one knee next to him and, sobbing, caught his hand.

"He took the bullet meant for me," the Yakima Kid said solemnly. "We were supposed to go in opposite directions, each man for himself. But he didn't listen, the old rascal." Travers's voice was choked with emotion.

"The . . . hell . . . I didn't," Corrigan managed to say, eyeing Travers. "I figured . . . you were so slow . . . in your old age . . . you'd never get out of the way . . . in time. Wanted to . . . give you a hand . . . Just an accident . . . Decker got me. . . ."

"Sure, Cactus," Travers whispered.

Jackrabbit leaned over and said urgently, "You hang on, Cactus. Help's on the way."

"Too late . . . for that. What about . . . Decker?"

"He won't ever hurt anybody again," Ballard told him.

"Good. Jackrabbit, you remember . . . what you promised me. . . ."

"Don't worry, Cactus," the old-timer said.

"Lucy . . ."

"I-I'm right here, Father," she said, sniffing.

"You're a fine woman, gal. You and Brian . . . you have plenty of children, you hear? And tell 'em . . . about their old granddaddy every now and then. . . ."

"I'll tell them," Lucy whispered.

Corrigan lifted a hand and clasped Travers's. "Blaze of glory," he muttered. "So long, Kid. . . ."

A moment later Travers gently closed Corrigan's unseeing eyes.

"There won't never be another one like him," Jackrabbit Dawkins said into the silence of the arena.

An hour later Wes Ballard stood with Jackrabbit Dawkins and John Travers, looking out at the now-darkened arena. The evening's show had been canceled. "How long had he known about his sickness?" Ballard asked Jackrabbit.

"A pretty good while, I reckon," the driver answered quietly. "Cactus was a stubborn ol' cuss. I figure he went out the way he would've wanted."

"I'm glad you decided to tell Lucy," Travers said. "I think it made things a little easier for her. I'm sure knowing how he really felt will help her in the future, too."

"Is she going along with your suggestion, Kid?" Ballard asked.

Travers managed to grin. "You mean for the combined Cactus Corrigan-Yakima Kid Wild West show? I think so. Once she's over the worst of her grief, she'll see that it makes sense. Life in a Wild West show is the only life Lucy has ever known, and if we put the troupes together, we'll have an outfit to rival Cody's!"

"For a whole passel o' years, Cactus wouldn't have liked that idea," Jackrabbit remarked. "But I reckon he changed his way of thinkin' lately. He would've been happy to be your partner again, Kid."

"I hope Lucy knows that."

"I'll make sure she does." He hesitated, then asked, "How 'bout me, Kid? I still got a job?"

The silver-haired showman threw back his head and laughed. "How could I run a Wild West show without you, Jackrabbit?"

"You been managin' all right," the old-timer pointed out.

"Yes, but I always knew what I was missing. Shoot, I'll need you to drive my stagecoach." Travers glanced at Ballard. "Unless Wes here . . ."

Ballard quickly shook his head. He looked back down the tunnel and saw the raven-haired figure waiting there for him. "I've been away from Texas too long already," he said. "I've got a ranch to tend to."

"And some other business to tend to as well, I reckon," Jackrabbit chortled. Ballard just grinned.

The three men turned to walk slowly out of the arena. "Are you going to take the train back to Texas?" Travers asked Ballard.

"I expect so. I know one thing. I've seen enough of stagecoaches to last me the rest of my life."

And as their footsteps echoed and died away in the tunnel, they seemed to blend with the sound of hoofbeats in the arena. Ghostly hoofbeats, and the cheers of a phantom crowd reliving the glorious days of the Old West. . . .

STAGECOACH STATION 52:
THE LAST FRONTIER
by Hank Mitchum

The year is 1919, and the stagecoach bouncing over the dusty road, racing from bandits, is no longer a common feature on the landscape; but then the outlaws chasing it are merely movie stuntmen—or are they?

On location at a ranch near Hollywood to film his script *The Last Frontier*, screenwriter Oliver McBride suddenly becomes embroiled in a real-life adventure. He and Tom Farnsworth, an old jehu hired to drive a stagecoach in the film, are caught in the middle of a cattle-rustling ring and gangland rivalry—which by a strange twist of fate might reveal the killer of Farnsworth's partner, who died some forty years before.

Although McBride is reluctant at first to put himself in danger, his secret longing—to live out the kind of adventurous fantasy he writes about—prompts him to help Farnsworth. An added incentive is that, like the undaunted heroes of his scripts, he might end up winning the heart of the beautiful but unapproachable young heroine, trick rider and stuntwoman Betty Raymond. But in the process his newly learned cowboy skills and innate ingenuity are severely tested—and this is one story for which McBride doesn't know the ending.

Read THE LAST FRONTIER, on sale March 1991 wherever Bantam paperbacks are sold.

★ WAGONS WEST ★

This continuing, magnificent saga recounts the adventures of a brave
band of settlers, all of different backgrounds, all sharing one dream—
to find a new and better life.

☐	26822	**INDEPENDENCE! #1**	$4.50
☐	26162	**NEBRASKA! #2**	$4.50
☐	26242	**WYOMING! #3**	$4.50
☐	26072	**OREGON! #4**	$4.50
☐	26070	**TEXAS! #5**	$4.50
☐	26377	**CALIFORNIA! #6**	$4.50
☐	26546	**COLORADO! #7**	$4.95
☐	26069	**NEVADA! #8**	$4.50
☐	26163	**WASHINGTON! #9**	$4.50
☐	26073	**MONTANA! #10**	$4.50
☐	26184	**DAKOTA! #11**	$4.50
☐	26521	**UTAH! #12**	$4.50
☐	26071	**IDAHO! #13**	$4.50
☐	26367	**MISSOURI! #14**	$4.50
☐	27141	**MISSISSIPPI! #15**	$4.50
☐	25247	**LOUISIANA! #16**	$4.50
☐	25622	**TENNESSEE! #17**	$4.50
☐	26022	**ILLINOIS! #18**	$4.50
☐	26533	**WISCONSIN! #19**	$4.50
☐	26849	**KENTUCKY! #20**	$4.50
☐	27065	**ARIZONA! #21**	$4.50
☐	27458	**NEW MEXICO! #22**	$4.95
☐	27703	**OKLAHOMA! #23**	$4.50
☐	28180	**CELEBRATION! #24**	$4.50